Perhaps the ~~~ might
add to the "it"   own

T

naked

Knitting

Club

love Louise x   Dec 18

*Cate's life is about to change when her New Year's
resolution sets in motion a year of transformation,
new friendships, adventure and romance.*

JANET GROOM

This edition is published by That Guys House in 2018

www.ThatGuysHouse.com

Copyright © 2018 Janet Groom

First Edition

The author asserts the moral rights under the Copyright, Designs
and Patents Act 1988 to be identified as the author of this work.

A catalogue record of this book is available from the British Library

ISBN: 978-1-912779-37-6

This novel is entirely a work of fiction.
The names, characters, incidents portrayed in it
are the work of the author's imagination.
Any resemblance to actual persons, living or dead,
events or localities is entirely coincidental.

All right reserved.
No part of this publication may be reproduced, stored in a retrieval
system, or transmitted, in any form or by any means, electronic,
mechanical, photocopying, recording or otherwise, without the
prior consent of the author, nor be otherwise circulated in any form
of binding or cover other than that which it is published and without
a similar condition being imposed on the subsequent purchaser.

hey,

Welcome to this wonderful book brought to you by That Guy's House Publishing.

At That Guy's House we believe in real and raw wellness books that inspire the reader from a place of authenticity and honesty.

This book has been carefully crafted by both the author and publisher with the intention that it will bring you a glimmer of hope, a rush of inspiration and sensation of inner peace.

It is our hope that you thoroughly enjoy this book and pass it onto friends who may also be in need of a glimpse into their own magnificence.

Have a wonderful day.

Love,

Sean Patrick

That Guy.

DEDICATED TO

To my dearest sister, Lorna,
and all the amazingly talented women
who continue to inspire me.

xxx

"Believe in yourself. Trust Your Dreams. Follow Your Heart. Allow your Brilliance to Shine Bright and Illuminate the World."

Janet Groom

Chapter 1
New Year's Eve

What the hell?

Cate stood staring down at the gold-embossed invitation card in her hand that had just fallen out of the formal gold and cream Christmas card.

She had returned from a long day at work, and for a few seconds her interest was aroused to see the neatly typed envelope amongst the deluge of junk mail, but she should have known better.

Just who does she think she is?

Cate read the text aloud: "Mr and Mrs Peter Hamilton request the pleasure of Mr and Mrs Michael Taylor's company to dinner on 31 December at 8pm to herald in the New Year."

Heavens above, she has circled the R.S.V.P. in case I forget to let her know — unbelievable! Honestly, who does she think she is? We've always had New Year's Eve together for years — I didn't think we needed to start sending formal invitations. She really thinks she is someone special since she moved to Mayfair. Wait 'til Mike sees this; he'll piss himself.

Mike and Pete had been best friends since they were at University. When Pete was offered a position at a high-profile accountancy firm in London, he had managed to wangle a job in the Marketing Department for his best mate too. Over the years, Pete had steadily worked his way up to become a senior partner, while Mike took a much more lackadaisical approach to his career. He only achieved manager status because Pete made it happen. For the past seventeen years, without fail, the two couples spent the evening together welcoming in the New Year.

A few years ago, Pete and Gill had moved to a luxury penthouse apartment in Mayfair — Cate loathed going there. With its crystal chandeliers, cream carpets and expensive artworks, the place looked like many of the celebrity show homes featured in glossy magazines — somewhere, in Cate's opinion, too perfect and pristine to relax and feel at home.

***

As instructed, Pete had switched on the flat screen TV just before midnight. Until then it had been imitating a log fire, throwing out a warming and welcoming glow. Together they watched Big Ben strike midnight, along with bursts of fireworks illuminating the skies high above the River Thames. Its deep toll was only just audible above the raucous cries of 'Happy New Year', followed by drunken renditions of *Auld Lang Syne* by party revellers — and another year rolled in.

"Happy New Year!" shouted Mike, squeezing Cate in a hug. As he did, her thoughts turned to what the New Year would bring.

I wonder what will happen this year… my life is so bloody boring. I need something to change. I want some excitement. I want adventure. Perhaps I need to learn to say 'yes' to more things and get past my fears. After all, I'm almost forty — I still have time to change. Oh, could I be brave enough to try more things? Who am I kidding — my life never changes.

Gill was in full flight, as usual, being a fantastic hostess: part domestic goddess and part military commander. She swanned around in her element, while Pete was on a mission to ensure that their guests' champagne glasses were never empty, resulting in everyone, apart from Gill, feeling drunk.

There was no denying it; Gill had gone to town, preparing an excellent gourmet meal, good enough to rival any top-class restaurant. The entire place was decorated to perfection with a white and gold theme, making Cate imagine the 'Ice Queen from Narnia' sweeping through leaving everything in her path a frozen white. This grated on Cate's nerves — back at home in their apartment, she had put up their old artificial tree and decorated it with baubles they had had since before they were first married. It had seen better days. It was now a little lopsided since Mike collapsed into it one Christmas Eve after partying too much with his rugby pals.

Cate, take note — you'd better go out in the sales and buy a new Christmas tree and trimmings for next year.

As far as Cate could remember, there had been only one occasion when Gill had let her hair down. It had been back when Pete had first introduced his new girlfriend to Mike and Cate, who themselves had only been going out for a few months. That first night, poor Gill had accidentally drunk an entire jug of Long Island Ice Tea. Unfortunately for her, she had thought it was regular iced tea and not, as she later learned, a potent cocktail laced with generous measures of five spirits finished with a squeeze of lime and a mere splash of Coke Cola.

It had been a hilarious first meeting, at least from Cate's point of view. Gill was so drunk that she ended up dancing on the bar top, receiving a standing ovation, and an invitation from the owner to become a regular act. It was an image that Cate would never forget. It had never happened again and nor was it likely to, since Gill was always in control.

In spite of her tipsy state, Cate's thoughts turned to her habit of making New Year's resolutions, and she pondered what this New Year would have in store for her. This time she was adamant that she would be sticking to whatever resolutions she set herself, unlike in previous years. January always started full of good intentions, but after the initial excitement waned, she reverted to her usual routines and bad habits in no time at all.

Perhaps I need to just do it — choose to be open to any new things that come my way. Just say 'yes' and do it! Oh no, that's not me though — but could it be? What's that mantra I read recently, 'I can and I will'? I guess I could try — couldn't I?

Gill joined Cate on the sofa, a luxurious cream leather that matched the pristine carpet. Spending time in Gill's immaculate designer home always made Cate feel anxious — terrified that she, or Mike, would spill or damage something. Mike had now been forbidden to drink red wine when they visited, in an effort to alleviate everyone's stress levels. On one occasion, at their modest home, Mike was mid-flow telling Pete a tale with great gusto, when he managed to fling his glass from his hand, smashing it against the magnolia wall. Cate thought Gill was going to have kittens watching in horror the red wine trickle down the wall. Even now there was a slight stain, but Cate barely noticed it.

Gill clinked glasses with Cate's, as she light-heartedly enquired, "Well, Happy New Year, darling. Go on tell me, what are your resolutions for this coming year?"

Before Cate could answer, Mike, on overhearing their conversation, piped up. "Excuse me, folks! Your attention please, it's time for another tradition, the sharing of our New Year's resolutions. Wait for it — wait for it. This year, I'm going to do the same as I've done every year — not making any!"

Everyone laughed.

"However, I'd be interested to know what yours are. Let's start with Cate," Mike teased, as he winked at Pete.

Cate blushed. Mike always treated her New Year's resolutions as a joke, and Pete — who was trying without success to knock a decoration off the mantelpiece with his party blower — was in on the joke too.

Gill stood up to join her husband and, with a playful slap on his bottom, she guided him away from the fireplace. Disaster averted.

"Now darlings, Cate is perfectly entitled to make her New Year's resolutions if she wants to. I think it's quite a sweet tradition. Some people can't help it if they have an on-going battle with their weight, and maybe this year she'll do it. Good for you, Cate."

Cate could have screamed. Her so-called best friend was telling her that she did think she had a weight problem. Funny, whenever they had gone shopping in the past, Gill had always been so supportive about Cate's utter frustration over finding fashionable clothes to fit her curvaceous frame.

Gill was petite and always immaculately groomed, with her coiffured blonde bob and her signature scarlet red nails manicured to perfection. Everything about Gill was elegant and perfect: perfect hostess, perfect businesswoman, and, no doubt, perfect wife.

Come to think of it, even though they had been good friends for over a decade, Cate was yet to see Gill without makeup, or even a hair out of place. She often wondered how Gill did it. At times, Cate's rather vivid imagination ran wild and imagined that her friend was a robot or an alien in disguise.

In contrast, Cate was curvy with a voluptuous bosom, which she cursed. Her most striking feature was her mass of auburn-red hair, which she usually wore pulled back in a ponytail. Mike often said that it was Cate's red hair and bright blue eyes that stole his heart the first night they'd met. At best, Cate felt like a clumsy giant next to her diminutive friend.

Unlike Gill's fitted designer suits, Cate's wardrobe was geared more for comfort, with the ultimate aim of trying to conceal her enormous boobs. Most items in her wardrobe were loose fitting tops or sweaters in black, with matching stretchy trousers. Cate had little interest or time for makeup — a quick lick of lip-gloss and a sweep of mascara was enough in her book.

Oh, what I wouldn't give to be at home right now — in comfy PJs curled up on the sofa with a glass of prosecco and a slice of pizza, watching a movie.

Tonight, though, she had made a concerted effort and purchased a new little black dress; thanks to the guidance of the helpful shop assistant in a trendy boutique near her office. She had also been encouraged to buy an elegant pair of stilettos and a matching clutch bag, as the perfect accessories for her new dress.

Right now, though, she regretted wearing the shoes, as they were crippling her feet. She wanted to kick them off and wiggle her toes; forcing some feeling back to them and preventing any permanent damage. But she dared not — she knew that Gill wouldn't be impressed. She also knew that once off, she would never get her feet squeezed back into them again.

As a Christmas present, Mike had treated her to a makeover at a trendy hair and beauty salon near their home. To her surprise, she had enjoyed being pampered by a team of three glam young things, under the watchful supervision of the proprietor, Monsieur Olivier. They had worked a miracle. Even the stern Monsieur Olivier gave a congratulatory clap of the hands in approval of their efforts.

She had left the salon floating on air, with her nails shimmering and her hair elegantly tied up with a few curls tumbling down. Her makeup was way over the top by Cate's standards, but she quite liked the overall effect. She had barely recognised her reflection in the mirror. She looked glamorous.

When they had arrived for the evening's festivities, Gill had given her a cursory once-over, and to her astonishment, her new look had won a nod of approval. Mike, too, seemed to be impressed, as he was a lot more attentive tonight than he had been for a very long time. At one point in the evening, she was sure that even Pete had pinched her bottom.

Gill's hurtful comment was still ringing in her ears, which tingled as the blood rushed to her face. Fuelled by alcohol, she was about to let her have it — when the doorbell rang, announcing the arrival of their taxi ride home.

Saved by the bell.

Pete awkwardly helped Cate on with her coat, as they bade their hosts farewell.

***

Back home at the front door of their apartment, Cate struggled to find her key, while Mike wrapped his arms tightly around her from behind. She could feel his hot breath on the back of her neck and, between nuzzles, he whispered in her ear, "I still love you Kitty Cat. You might be a bit cuddlier these days, but you are my favourite teddy bear wifey."

Chapter 2
The Naked Truth

The following morning, Cate was lying in bed cocooned in the duvet. Although her head was throbbing, she smiled to herself because she could hear Mike whistling along to a song on the radio. He was in the kitchen, making their traditional New Year's Day breakfast.

My head hurts… Mike hurry up, I'd kill for a strong coffee right now! Cate, come on, you know just how damn lucky you are — Mike is a great husband. Yes, but I need coffee!

***

Like any married couple, they had their fair share of ups and downs, with the hardest blow not being able to have the children they both dearly wanted. After two failed attempts at IVF, they had decided to call it a day.

Each failure was emotionally draining and brought Cate closer to the brink of total despair. Since the last failed attempt a few years earlier, neither one had mentioned their desire for parenthood again. It was like an unspoken agreement between them; it was time to close that particular door.

Cate had tried to broach the subject of adoption, but it had been met with a very forcible 'no'. Mike was just not prepared to take on 'someone else's kid — they could be damaged goods'. No matter what Cate did to try and coax him along to an information evening to find out more about the adoption process, and perhaps even meet a few of the kids; he point blank refused.

They had only been married a few years when the warning bells began to sound. In spite of their determined efforts to make a baby, there had been no signs of the pitter-patter of tiny feet on the horizon at all. After five years of trying, their lovely GP had persuaded them to have 'things checked out'.

This led to a long drawn out period of prodding and testing by various specialists across London. In the end, they were informed, in a rather cold and brusque way, that the fault lay firmly with Cate.

As far as the consultant could gather, Cate had suffered 'Primary Ovarian Failure'; and against the odds, it must have happened in her teens. In other words, Cate had gone through puberty followed by menopause. This news had left them reeling in shock. Cate's heart shattered into a million pieces — she would never have the babies she longed for, and never be the mother she dreamed of becoming.

Apparently, according to several fertility specialists, and a very expensive Harley Street consultant, their only chance of parenthood was through IVF with a donor egg, and this had not happened for them. The only other option left was to use a surrogate, and this was a non-starter for both Mike and Cate — it just didn't feel right.

Cate had learnt at an early age to soldier on, put on a brave face and get on with it. To the outside world, nothing had changed, but on the inside, it was an entirely different story. This pretence just led her down a slippery slope into depression — a deep, dark, and scary place that Cate never wished to revisit.

In the midst of her darkest hours, Mike had been her rock. He would hold her tight on those long nights, as she cried her heart out. He had been the strong one, even though he, too, was devastated. Witnessing Cate's despair was breaking his heart, and he was also disappointed that they would not have the children they had both wanted.

At times, Cate often wondered how things would have been if they had had a family. She would imagine tucking their children — a daughter and a son — into bed at night after reading them a bedtime story. She could easily see herself waving from the window as Mike took their son to the football on Saturday. At times when she saw parents playing and laughing with their children, she would walk on by smiling sweetly at the family, while inside her head a voice would be screaming and berating herself for her inability to do something that was so natural and easy for most women.

Over time she was learning to accept her fate. Life could be cruel, and she knew deep down that compared to many people in this often unkind and harsh world, she was fortunate on so many levels. In her efforts to cope, she focussed her attention on her job and housework. Thank goodness for washing and ironing, cooking and cleaning. It was hard to believe that tedious household chores were her saving grace when the darkness tried to creep back in. Her emotions on the topic of motherhood were shut down and a wall of protection erected around her grieving heart.

Likewise, Mike threw himself into his job, working long hours at the office. More often than not, he came home late, opting to get involved with more and more demanding marketing projects. He had also chosen to focus on his love of sports. At work, he was extremely good at what he did, and his confident, cheeky demeanour made him a hit with the clients. He spent his free time playing or watching sports — golf with Pete and a few of his old university friends; playing rugby; working out at the gym; or glued to a sporting program on the television — leaving less and less time for Cate.

***

Cate closed her eyes and bit her lip, forcing the painful memories to evaporate, allowing her thoughts to focus instead on ways she could learn to accept herself. Images drifted across her mind — one of her bungee jumping appeared; only to be replaced by another of her sitting cross-legged, meditating at a spiritual retreat; and then one of her gliding around an ice-skating rink.

Will I ever be happy again? I want to be free from this never-ending pain. I want to laugh and have fun again. I want to be me — the happy and carefree me, the person I used to be.

Mike wandered into the bedroom carrying a tray laden with their breakfast, shattering her daydream. He set it down on the bed next to her.

"Here, a little something for my sleeping beauty." He handed her a glass of Bucks Fizz, a welcome 'hair of the dog' that she hoped would cure her niggling hangover.

Mike slipped off his robe; she caught a glimpse of his naked body, and for a fleeting moment, a shiver ran through hers. To her, he was still attractive. He was her tall, dark, handsome rugby player. At 6'1", he made

Cate feel small, and his muscular arms made her feel safe and protected.

Cate remembered clearly the night they met. He was standing at the bar; he had won her over easily with his cheeky grin, boyish charm and mop of unruly black hair. Now his hair was peppered with grey making him, if anything, even more attractive.

Between mouthfuls of pancakes, Cate shared her thoughts with him about her New Year's resolutions.

"Hun, the only way you will learn to accept your body is to run around buck naked. You could become a nudist — and that would be the day pigs learn to fly," joked Mike, as he slid under the covers and pulled her towards him. Before long, they were in the throes of familiar and comfortable lovemaking.

***

Mike cleared away the breakfast tray and disappeared off to have a shower. Today was his annual Old Boys' match at his rugby club, a tradition that, thankfully, Cate was no longer expected to attend. She had done her time standing on the sidelines freezing her butt off.

Snuggling up with the duvet again, Cate allowed her mind to wander off. Perhaps Mike was onto something. There was only one way that she could see herself accepting her body — she would have to become a *naturist*.

She giggled to herself at the sheer foolhardiness of the idea of her swanning around on a beach in the buff. She was the type of person who wouldn't even undress in the communal changing rooms at the gym, so the idea of stripping off and walking around in front of other people was total lunacy.

She shuddered as an image unfolded in her mind. It was a memory of the trauma of gym classes at school and the obligatory cold communal showers after freezing on a hockey pitch in the icy rain. It had been a form of torture at her all-girls' school back in her native Northern Ireland. Cate still firmly believed her gym teacher had enjoyed watching the pubescent girls squirm with embarrassment. To this day, the experience had instilled a deep-seated hatred of undressing in public, as well as feelings of self-loathing and awkwardness about her body.

***

Later that afternoon, Cate called Gill to thank her for the previous evening and to inform her that indeed she had made a New Year's resolution, and one she was planning to keep.

After Cate calmly explained her idea about becoming a naturist, Gill's response was to burst into hysterical laughter and, if Cate wasn't mistaken, she was sure she heard Gill snort.

"I'm so sorry darling, but you are just hilarious at times. You're …" Cate could detect muffled sniggering. "You're not serious, are you? You know we all love you just the way you are. I really couldn't see you strutting around a campsite totally in the nude. Remember, you're the person who won't change in front of other people, even me, in the changing rooms at the gym! Anyway, I must go. I hear Pete shuffling around in the kitchen. I think he might be starting to wash up my crystal glasses; I'd better go and check, I don't want any breakages. See you soon; we can talk more about it then. Goodbye, darling, love to Mike."

With her friend's laughter still ringing in her ears — it was as if someone had flicked a switch within her, a desire to prove to everyone that she could damn well do it.

I'll show them. I will do it this year. I know I can bloody do this. I can and I will.

***

Soon the holidays were over, and Cate was back at work sitting in front of her computer. Luckily, it was a quiet day, as many of her colleagues were still absent. With no one immediately around her, she found herself searching the internet for information about naturism.

Cate was genuinely surprised; there were more naturist clubs and activities in the London area than she could have imagined in her wildest dreams. Who would have thought that bare-ballroom dancing, nude fly-fishing, or even naked painting classes (where the artists were naked, not the models) were possibilities? The most impressive, in Cate's opinion, and the one that conjured a string of frightening images in her mind, was 'The Naked Acrobats and Fire-Eaters Club of Lower Hampstead'.

Hell's bells, just who are all these crazy people?

Had she missed the memo about a 'get naked' trend? When she passed by people on the street, were they secret naturists who were hurrying home to strip off or rushing off to some strange pastime or hobby, *au naturel*? It was really all quite bizarre, and at some level quite disturbing.

Cate was transfixed and, as she trawled through the vast array of offerings, she noticed a small advert about a knitting club in London near Notting Hill.

That's it! That's the one — a knitting club. It's bound to be just women, and it would be cool to learn to knit. Yes — a new hobby. Perfect.

She clicked on the link and quickly jotted down the number on a scrap of paper and stuffed it into her handbag.

Just as she was leaning under her desk at her bag, her colleague Chris — also known by many of the female employees as Creepy Chris — walked in and spied her screen.

"My, my… since when has naturism got anything to do with HR? Don't tell me you are thinking of offering a naturist training course in the office? As much as it might appeal to you, I don't think our employees would go for it. However, if we had some scantily clad young women delivering the courses, I think we would have a captive market with our male members of staff," and just in case Cate has missed his double entendre, he re-stressed the word 'members' and accompanied it with some lewd hand gestures. "I suggest you close that website before all the guys in IT get to hear about it. You do know that they can check what websites you view," and with that, he turned around and walked out of the room sniggering like a snotty-nosed schoolboy.

Cate blushed. It would take a long time to live it down, especially if the guys in the IT Department got wind of it. They would make her life a living hell for as long as they could, until the next victim was found.

Chapter 3
Coffee and Memories

A few days later, Cate received a text message from Gill, who had sent the details for their annual January sales outing to Oxford Street. Cate rolled her eyes and sighed. Based on her experiences in previous years, the outing usually involved Cate being dragged around to all the designer shops Gill wanted to visit. To crown it all, last year Gill had bought so much that Cate spent the entire day as her personal bag carrier.

"Not this year," she proclaimed, as she responded to the text with a 'thumbs up' emoji.

***

Cate stepped in through the door and pulled off her woolly hat. The heat inside the welcoming café added a rosy glow to her cheeks. The aroma of roasted coffee filled her nostrils, and she felt her body relax. Looking around, Cate spotted a small table towards the back of the shop. She settled herself into a seat with a panoramic view and hung her long down-filled coat, which was starting to shed a few feathers here and there, over the back of her chair. She looked up to see a rather stout waiter leave his station behind the polished mahogany bar and march over to her.

"*Ma chérie* Catherine, it has been far too long! You look frozen! Give your Papa Jean a big hug."

Cate smiled as the man pulled her tight into a bear hug. His embrace was warm, welcoming and safe.

"It's been way too long. You never change, Jean, and thankfully, neither does this place."

"And what can I get for you today, *ma petite*?"

"Oh, I'd love your wonderful *café au lait* with a pinch of cinnamon. Do you have any of your famous *pain au chocolat* left?"

"*Bien sûr, ma petite*. The one with no calories," he winked.

It had been months since Cate had last visited and, sitting here right now, she wondered why she did not come more often. It was a little out of the way, but when she got there, it was worth it.

Jean Marcel, or Papa Jean as many of the regulars called him, had left France as a child during the Second World War. His parents had been in the French Resistance and had fled for their lives. Although he had lived most of his life in London, he was a true Frenchman in his heart. He was her very special French *oncle* — a big cuddly bear of a man, with a real soft heart under all the French pride. Cate had heard rumours over the years that Jean had a reputation for having a fierce temper, in particular towards anyone who crossed him on his two passions: first, his beloved home country, France, and all things French (especially his football team *Paris St. Germain*); and his second, food. Cate could well believe he had a temper, but thankfully had never witnessed it for herself.

Every time she stepped into the café, hidden at the back of the courtyard at St. Christopher's place, the smell of the ground coffee and freshly baked French pastries would, without fail, whisk her away to a time long ago in her past. She had taken a gap year between leaving school and heading to University, working as an *au pair* in France — life before Mike, before marriage, and before the pain of infertility.

As Cate sat back and breathed in the comforting smell, her mind wandered back to her summer of love in the beautiful French Alps. During her year as an *au pair*, Cate had worked for an English family living in Paris. The father of the family had been in the diplomatic service, working at the prestigious British Embassy on the *Faubourg St. Honoré*, and Cate had been hired to look after the family's four young children. She had landed on her feet as the family were lovely, and she adored the children.

The mother was a fragile woman who often suffered from bouts of ill health. She reminded Cate of a character from a Jane Austen novel. In spite of her illness, Eleanor Taylor-Grant loved her children very much. Cate witnessed how deeply saddened she would become when fatigue and pain would set in, meaning she could barely interact with her offspring.

The children, on the other hand, were a hale and hearty bunch. The eldest, Christopher, aged eight, had a mop of untamed dark hair, which was often seen poking out the top of an adventure book. Next was Natalie who, at age six, was quite a little diva. She was a bossy girl, forever giving orders to her siblings. Then came Sarah, who had a great sense of curiosity at only four years old. She was always on a quest with her pink backpack, a dog-eared map of Paris, and her favourite travelling companion,

Patsy Panda, tucked under her arm. Last, but not least, was eighteen-month-old baby Madeleine, who was a happy easy-going child.

The three older children were bilingual and quite happily used both languages in their day-to-day endeavours. At times, it made Cate feel stupid with her broad Northern Irish accent, particularly when the children poked fun at how she pronounced certain words. The kids, though, had been a delight for Cate, and she was amazed at their impeccable manners, thirst for knowledge, and drive for adventure.

Cate's temporary place in the midst of this upper-class English family starkly contrasted with her own family upbringing.

Cate had been born the middle child of three, to parents who believed that children should be instructed to learn through fear, which was reinforced with a quick slap around the head or the back of the legs. Growing up in Northern Ireland at the end of 'The Troubles' had been a challenging time.

Cate had instilled in her — both from school and through her attendance at the local chapel — a massive dose of 'Catholic guilt'; along with a negative outlook, low self-esteem, and a deep-seated fear of going to hell. Even though she tried to be a 'good girl', she always found that by the time her next confession was due, she had accumulated a long list of misdemeanours.

Cate had an older brother, Michael, who had emigrated from Ireland to America, as soon as he left school. She had only seen him three times since his departure. The last time he was 'home', he brought with him his two sons, Bradley and Cooper. They were two great big lads, standing at over six feet tall and were the epitome of the stereotypical American teens and full of self-confidence. Michael had grown into a confident businessman, running his own printing company with his brother-in-law. By all accounts, he had done well for himself when he married his wife and had been welcomed into his new family with open arms. He also had two daughters who were keen athletes. Cate had only ever seen photos of them on Michael's Facebook page. They were good-looking girls, more like their mother in looks, with broad smiles and wavy curls. They were not only picture-perfect, but were also high achievers, both on and off the sports field.

Cate's younger sister, Tara, had gone off to Australia on a yearlong work visa at the age of eighteen and had never come back. Within the first six months of her stay, she had met and married a plumber named Jim who lived in Brisbane. From what Cate could glean from the sporadic correspondence over the ensuing years, Tara had three girls. In the last letter, received two years ago, it transpired that Tara had divorced Jim and was now living 'in sin' — much to the chagrin of Cate's parents — with a successful property developer in Sydney. The letter contained a photo showing Tara arm-in-arm with her new beau, standing outside a large modern colonial-style mansion, complete with a sports car and pool evident in the background. Tara certainly looked happy. Cate had often thought about making a trip to the USA and then to Australia to see her siblings, but somehow there was never enough time or money.

Mike had no siblings and rarely made an effort to visit his ageing parents. On the other hand, Cate travelled back at least twice a year to see her parents and friends. During Cate's annual Christmas visit 'home', there was always a family gathering — hosted now by two of her cousins — which was an excellent occasion for catching up with all the family in one fell swoop.

In all their years of marriage, Mike had been back to Northern Ireland with her on only a handful of visits. The first time for a wedding party thrown for them by her parents so the extended family could meet him; and then a few Christmases; and more recently, for the funeral of her uncle, John. Mike and John had hit it off sharing a love of sports, and their mutual respect for one another had been cemented when John had taken Mike along to watch the local Gaelic football team play.

Cate's family genuinely seemed to adore Mike. When he was there, he would be engaging, sociable and could drink with the best of them, but back home in England, he never asked about them, except for the occasional question about John or the football team.

**

Cate had befriended some of the other *au pairs*, and from the tales she heard, she had been fortunate with her family. She'd heard horror stories from other girls who were treated like live-in slaves. Several girls relayed incidents where the fathers had expected more than just childminding from the young ladies, too. Cate was lucky; she loved playing with the children and even taking the baby out in the buggy to the nearby *Jardin du Luxembourg* in the warm spring months.

Her French had improved leaps and bounds, and she had loved spending the summer months at a rented chalet

— complete with live-in housekeeper, Madam Hubert — in the French Alps near Chamonix. It was a relief from the heat and humidity of the city, which had felt oppressive to her sensitive and pale Irish skin. In the mountains, she felt she could breathe again. Every morning when she drew back her curtains, she had to pinch herself at the view of the snow-capped mountains. These were real mountains, nothing like the so-called 'mountains' back home.

In her first week there, she had been given an afternoon off. Eleanor's health had taken a turn for the better in the mountains, and she had been eager to take the children, on her own, to the lake for swimming and a picnic. Madame Hubert invited herself to go along as the custodian of the picnic, although Cate suspected that the housekeeper felt it was her unwritten responsibility to take care of the family at all times during their stay.

Cate had been thrilled to get out and explore and, after a stroll around the small village, she had decided to climb up the mountain slope behind the church to obtain a better view of the surrounding area. It had been a steeper climb than she imagined, but all the effort was well worth it when she saw the valley laid out before her. Cate sat for ages drinking in the beauty of the world around her, mesmerised by the sheer scale of the mountain range. She had seen photos of the Alps in geography books, but nothing had prepared her for their imposing vastness and unparalleled beauty.

Time had flown, and before long, it was time to head back for supper. Cate commenced her descent and, if she had thought it was tough climbing up, it was surprisingly more difficult walking down. At one point, her foot slipped on the grass. She let out a high-pitched squeal as a pain shot through her ankle and up her leg. When she righted herself and tried to put weight on her foot to walk, the pain was too great. Trying to hop down a steep slope made the experience even more challenging. She had managed to go another few hundred metres when she had to stop and rest. She looked down toward the village, which was still a long way to go. The wind was picking up, and a mass of threatening dark clouds rolled in. Cate knew she had to get going; before long, it would be raining. She gathered herself up and started her slow descent once more. It was frustrating and painful. Her heart beat faster in her chest. She focussed on getting down, willing each step, while forcing the tears back.

Out of nowhere, she heard someone whistle. She looked around to see where the sound had come from, and in the distance she could just about make out the figure of a man. He was waving at her and indicating for her to stay where she was. Given that she was tired and about to burst into tears, Cate sat down and waited. A few moments later, the man bounded down towards her. She could see in the failing light that he was young; perhaps only a few years older than she was. As he drew nearer, she could hear him speaking away to her. She understood enough to make out that he was telling her off for being so stupid. Cate tried to explain in her broken French what had happened.

"Ah, you are the girl with the red hair," he said, and as he studied her, his face lit up into a broad smile. He could speak a little English, which he'd learned at school. Between their limited language skills, they managed to converse. He explained that he was a nephew of Madame Hubert. His name was Louis Hubert, and he was a mountain guide. But right now, they needed to find a safe place to wait out the storm, and he knew where to find such a shelter.

As the sky continued to darken, the claps of thunder were growing louder. Cate leant on Louis and managed to limp along. It was slow progress, and ten minutes into their journey the heavens had opened and, along with the thunder, there was lightning. Their clothes were soaked through by the time they arrived at a small, run-down, wooden cabin. Louis led Cate inside to safety. It smelt of old straw, and in one corner of the dwelling, the rain dripped through. Cate was relieved to be inside; she had never seen such bolts of lightning striking down through the sky. It was like a storm scene in a movie.

Louis set about making Cate as comfortable as he could. He had been able to make a fire. Luckily, there had been lots of scrap wood lying around and he had a lighter. The fire he built warmed them both and helped to dry them off. She remembered Louis taking off his shirt and holding it up by the fire to dry, the image forever etched in her mind. He stood naked to the waist; his body was lean with toned muscles.

At that moment, a switch was flipped in her body. In the flickering light, she yearned for him to take her and hold her tight in his strong arms. The strange stirrings in her body grew stronger. It was like an awakening of a deep primal urge. Driven by her body's desire, she longed to taste his lips against hers; to run her hands over his body; to feel his muscular body against hers and become one.

When his shirt was dry, Louis proceeded to rip it up into long strips. He then found a piece of wood and broke it into several pieces. Cate sat in silence, watching what he was doing and studying him.

The next thing Cate knew, he was kneeling at her feet, setting to work to wrap up her twisted ankle. She was too overwhelmed by her feelings to cry out in pain, as she looked down at the top of his head. She had to fight the temptation to reach out and run her fingers through his dark wavy hair. When he had finished administering first aid, she was shivering with cold, fear and exhaustion. Louis felt her shiver and saw the fear in her eyes. He sat down beside her and wrapped his strong arms around her shoulders, drawing her into his warmth. She felt protected and safe in his arms, but more than that, she felt like her body wanted to break free and entwine itself with his.

The fire flickered, and the storm raged on. Cate could not call the family to let them know she was safe; it was the era before mobile phones. She remembered how Louis had held her, and as the darkness drew in for the night, he had started to sing songs she could barely understand. The soothing melodies eventually lulled her into sleep. When Cate opened her eyes, sunlight was streaming through the dust-covered windows. She sat up and looked around. There was no sign of Louis, apart from the ashes in the fireplace and the shredded shirt wound around her ankle. At least she was dry, had slept a little, and her ankle felt much better. She found a piece of discarded plank that was just about the right height for her to use as a crutch.

"Typical. The man runs away and I'm left to fend for myself," she growled to herself. Armed with her crutch, she pushed open the cabin door. She hobbled out and looked around to get her bearings. The reality was, she had no clue where she was and no idea of what direction she needed to walk to head to the village. Last night's journey to the cabin had been a blur. Trying to figure out what she should do, she sat down on a rock and allowed her face to gaze up and enjoy the warmth of the sun on her skin.

It was then Cate heard voices in the woods to the left of the cabin. Slowly the voices came nearer, and she thought she recognised Louis' voice. Three men appeared into the clearing. Louis was looking tired. He smiled at her, and her heart fluttered. It turned out that the storm had finally eased in the early morning and Louis had made Cate as comfortable as he could before heading down to the village for help. The two other men, Louis' father and brother, had returned with him to rescue the red-haired damsel in distress.

The men each took turns helping Cate down the mountain, and they returned to a hero's welcome back in the village. Eleanor, the children, and even Madame Hubert had rallied around her with hugs, relieved to see her safely returned to them. From then on, everyone in the village knew who Cate was and made an extra special effort to speak to her.

Her relationship with Louis developed quickly and deeply.

That had been Cate's summer of love. She had fallen for her handsome rescuer. It had been her first real encounter with *l'amour*, and it had indeed left its mark forever etched on her heart. Louis had taken her for hikes through the green mountain meadows filled with alpine flowers. He taught her about passion — even now, her heart skipped a beat when she remembered the feel of his warm breath on the back of her neck and the sweet kisses over her body as they had made love. It had been her first time; he has been gentle, considerate, and sensitive enough to make it an experience she would remember forever, in all the right ways.

The summer had evaporated into September all too quickly, and she returned to Paris with the family. It was a bittersweet parting. The two had tried to stay in touch through letters and the occasional telephone call, but their limited language skills made it difficult for them to express their feelings. By the time she returned home ready to start university, their communications had petered out completely, leaving Cate free to start the next chapter of her life as a carefree student.

Cate would always have Louis Hubert, and that summer in the French Alps, imprinted on her heart. Even now, when she heard someone speaking French, *la langue de l'amour*, her heart would dance.

Chapter 4
January Sales

Cate glanced at her watch, realising that she needed to get a move on to meet Gill. She finished off her coffee and donned her coat. She bid Papa Jean farewell with another big hug and braced herself ready to do battle with the winter chill and the hordes of sale shoppers. In no time at all, she went from the safety and warmth of the café and was swept along into the flow of shoppers on Oxford Street.

Cate pushed and shoved her way to the edge of the mob, in an effort to break free from the crowd. She managed to cross the road, dodging buses and black cabs, and ducked down New Bond Street, zigzagging her way through to Regent Street where she was due to meet Gill outside the entrance to Liberty. Their annual shopping trip always began with, as Gill put it, a 'light lunch at Libby's'.

Cate was inherently punctual for appointments, thanks to the influence of Sister Mary Magdalene, who was incredibly lethal with her birch cane, as was well known by anyone who was ever late for one of her classes. Such was the lashing received, the poor unfortunate soul could barely sit down for a week. Cate had been on the receiving end once; never again was she late for class — or any appointment.

Cate did not have to wait long until Gill appeared.

Gill's small frame, wrapped in a pale beige cashmere coat, stepped out of a London black cab. She waved across to Cate while returning her purse to its matching Prada handbag. To complete the ensemble, she wore a pair of Gucci suede boots in soft caramel, and around her neck, tied in an elegant bow, was a large silk Hermès scarf. Gill was like a poster-girl for 'designers-r-us'. Cate squirmed as she gazed down at her well-worn winter attire.

At least I'm warm and comfortable. I don't know how she walks in those heels all day. I'd be crippled. I'm more and more convinced she must be a robot — she really mustn't feel any pain.

"Darling, have you been here long?" crooned Gill, as she air-kissed Cate and proceeded to link arms with her, guiding her in through the entrance door.

Inside it was heaving with shoppers. Gill navigated the crowds with ease, and before long, they were greeted and seated at a small table near the window in the restaurant. They placed their orders with the waitress, and Gill proceeded to describe her horrendous ordeal to get across town. Cate zoned out while she droned on, having no interest in the trials and tribulations of getting a taxi in London. She was well versed with this scenario, and provided the slight smile and appropriate nod to give the illusion that she was listening intently, when she was actually enjoying watching the other diners.

Their respective lunch requests arrived promptly. Gill had opted for scrambled eggs with smoked salmon and a glass of champagne, while Cate had gone for the veggie burger and a side of fries, washed down with a glass of pinot noir. Cate munched away, as Gill continued her tales of some business mishap or other, pushing her food around the plate while she spoke. By the time the waitress returned to clear their plates, all that was left on Cate's plate was a piece of gherkin, which she despised. Gill's plate was barely touched, apart from a couple of small bites. It was as if she had to force each mouthful down with a gulp of champagne.

"Ladies, would you like to see the dessert menu?" enquired the young waitress, balancing the plates precariously in her hands.

Cate ordered a slice of homemade brownie and a latte, while Gill opted for another glass of champagne. As Cate tucked into the gooey chocolate slice, she caught Gill giving her one of her looks. It was the look of disbelief wrapped up with embarrassment. Cate had witnessed this look many times over the years, mostly addressed at Pete, but lately she had spotted the same look being thrown, more and more, in her direction. Cate chose to ignore it, and turned her attention to enjoying the last morsel of the best brownie she had ever eaten. Gill paid the bill.

"I would like to pop over to New Bond Street. Is that OK with you, darling?" said Gill. Before Cate had time to respond, Gill had flagged down a black cab and climbed in. Cate clambered in after her.

It was a good fifteen-minute stop-start ride, which covered more or less the distance that Cate had walked earlier in ten minutes. The black cab halted right outside the entrance to the Chanel store.

As they walked towards the door, it was opened for them. Gill stepped in, and a sales lady — who looked as if she could have been a former model — glided across and welcomed her with air-kisses. She blanked Cate, who waddled into the store in Gill's wake. Cate only frequented such upmarket designer shops with Gill, and she had the feeling it was apparent to everyone who glanced in her direction. She felt as if they were judging her and found her lacking on many levels, from the top of her red head to her scuffed winter boots. As for her faithful old black handbag, she could have sworn that one haughty male assistant took one look and shook his head in disgust.

She felt physically uncomfortable in such places and feared she would trip and bring tumbling down a display cabinet filled with unbelievably expensive items, causing mass hysteria. She had visions of appearing in the evening news for causing the death of several wealthy and fragile-looking heiresses.

By the time Cate caught up with Gill, she was seated at the back of the store trying on a pair of black stilettos. To Cate's untrained eye, the shoes looked exactly like several pairs languishing in Gill's specially designed walk-in wardrobe. Cate stood in silence as she watched the interaction between Gill and the expressionless sales assistant. Cate suspected that the assistant had succumbed to Botox treatment in an attempt to claw back her long-gone youth. The scene continued for a further ten minutes until Gill announced that she would take the first pair, much to Cate's relief. Then ensued the pantomime of paying, wrapping up the shoes, and finally leaving the shop with more air-kisses.

"Where shall we go next?" asked Gill, more to herself than to Cate, as she glanced up and down the street while passing the Chanel carrier bag to Cate. "Oh, I know. Come along darling, I need to pop into Fenwick and pick up some new makeup," announced Gill, as she strode off in the direction of the upmarket department store. Cate was impressed by how quickly Gill could walk in high heels.

Gill breezed in and headed straight to her favourite makeup counter. Within a fraction of second, she had been attended to by not one, but two young women who had, in Cate's opinion, overdone the products they were selling. As she moved closer to the cosmetic counter, the strong smell of the commingled fragrances and perfumes assaulted her nasal passages, causing her to sneeze loudly.

"Oh darling, I'm just going to have a makeup session. I'll only be ten minutes or so," stated Gill, as she gracefully slid into the reclining pink chair. The girl with the incredibly full red lips mouthed to Cate that it would more likely be at least thirty. Cate nodded and motioned in response that she would go for a walk and return later.

Cate was quite glad to get away and enjoy her own company. She stepped onto the escalator and rode all the way to the top, taking her time wandering through each section. She was amazed at the range of colours, fabrics and designs on display.

Who in their right mind would wear these clothes? Honestly, you'd think that the Mad Hatter and a two-year-old had a crazy design session together and created the wackiest ideas imaginable.

In spite of signage indicating that some selected items were reduced, Cate reckoned you would still need the bank balance of a small nation to afford the scandalous price tags.

Eventually, Cate found her way to the food section on the lower ground floor. Her interest was piqued, and as she explored, she couldn't help herself from drooling over the array of foods on offer. Her senses ignited, and although it hadn't been long since lunch, she gave in and purchased a slice of lemon tart.

Glancing at her watch, she guessed she had only another ten minutes before meeting Gill. Armed with her treat, she exited onto the street and proceeded to gobble it down. She was enjoying every forbidden mouthful when Gill materialised, looking like a clone of the sales assistants — with her bright shiny red lips — and toting a small blue bag. She stared in bewilderment at Cate, who shoved the last bite of pie into her mouth before wiping it with the back of her hand. With a disapproving sigh, Gill handed over her latest acquisition and stepped out to the edge of the pavement, flagging down a cab.

Next stop was Harrods. Gill needed to stop off and pick up a new cashmere sweater for Pete. Gill, like a military trained sniper, wove through the men's section with her eyes sharpened to spot her target. It didn't take long before the sweater was procured and the carrier bag was, yet again, thrust upon Cate. Gill made a beeline for the ladies' department, in case there was something she 'had to have'.

As they were sauntering through, Cate spotted a stunning black cocktail dress. It was a simple black design, knee-length, with an elegant lace overlay. Cate sidled over, and to her surprise; the dress was in her size. She held the dress up to look at it, wondering if she dared try it on. Gill appeared at her shoulder and suggested, that she should at least try it on. Before she had time to argue, Cate was in the salubrious fitting room armed with the black dress.

"No harm in trying it on," thought Cate, as she undressed.

Standing in her well-worn black underwear, she unzipped the dress and slipped it on over her head. It was a bit of a squeeze, but she just about managed to get the zipper halfway up. The dress clung to her every curve. Her mother would have said it was a snug fit. In reality, the fabric was under duress. If she had been a size smaller, the dress would have fitted quite nicely. Cate reached around to find the zipper so she could liberate her squashed flesh. As she did, she heard a sound that made her wish for the earth to open up and swallow her whole. Reaching her arm round had been the final straw for the stretched fabric, and it ripped down the seam.

Oh, holy crap! What on earth am I going to do? You stupid fat bitch, what have you done? Come on, Cate; quick think — what are you going to do now? Oh crap!

Cate swore to herself as she removed the offensive item from her body. She quickly dressed and picked up the ruined garment to study the damage in more detail. It was as she suspected — the seam had split and there was now a huge gaping hole. Cate realised she had two choices open to her: she could hang up the dress and discreetly place it back without anyone noticing, or she could buy it. The first choice might have been the more appealing option, but her moral compass would not permit her to do so. She took a deep breath to muster up the courage to look at the price tag. The dress has been £500 full price, but thankfully it was on sale at half price. Still, it was £250 for a dress she would probably never wear. Perhaps she could have it mended and then sell it on eBay, allowing her to recoup some of her losses. That sounded like a plan, or at least an option she could live with.

Cate left the fitting room. Gill was patiently waiting for her with a look of anticipation on her face.

"Yes, it's perfect — I have to have it," said Cate; working hard to hide her shame.

At the cashier's desk, Cate handed it over, and the young woman rang up the charge. To her surprise, the girl held up the dress in preparation to package it. Cate instinctively lunged across the counter grabbing for the dress; managing to knock a display of accessories, perched at the edge of the desk, to the floor. All eyes turned to see what was going on.

Before Cate could manage to retrieve the torn dress and hide it in the bag, the young woman spotted the damage.

"Give it here," shouted Cate, as she tugged at the tail of the dress. Shoppers were both horrified and enthralled by the drama unfolding in front of them.

"I can't sell you this. Did you rip it?" enquired the shop assistant, eyeing Cate with suspicion. Cate's face glowed bright red. She felt everyone in the vicinity staring at her. From somewhere behind, Cate could make out Gill's distinctive voice.

"This is ridiculous. Please call over your senior manager; I want to have a word about this situation." Her voice was calm, relaxed and commanding. It was a tone Cate had only ever heard from Gill a couple of times before. Judging by the look of fear on the young woman's face, Gill was already making her point.

The senior manager arrived promptly. Gill proceeded to launch into a lecture that left both the young sales assistant and the senior manager looking sheepish. She put such a spin on the unfortunate events; complaining that the dress was faulty and the garment malfunction had caused her friend much distress. The senior manager was apologetic and agreed to reduce the cost of the dress further, as well as offering to have the garment repaired at no additional charge.

Anyone listening would have been in awe of what Gill had achieved. It was like watching a talented artist in full creative flow. Cate would not have been surprised to hear a round of applause.

Cate handed over her credit card, gave her contact details, and concluded the transaction. Unfortunately for Cate, it would mean a return visit to collect the dress once it was repaired, but that would be a matter for another day. Right now, she just wanted to escape.

After the debacle, Gill wished her friend a fond farewell with the customary air-kisses, took her designer shopping bags, and vanished into yet another cab. With mixed feelings, Cate trudged back to the heaving Tube and headed home.

Just as she was walking back to their apartment block, she saw she had missed a call from Mike — she listened to the message:

"Hi love, how was your day with Gill? I'm sure you two girls had fun. Just wanted to let you know I've had to head up to Birmingham tonight for an exhibition; I need to catch up with a few contacts. Sorry. I'll be back home Wednesday night. Bye."

Cate had hoped that an evening of pizza and a movie with Mike would help expel the traumas of her day. Instead, she would have to make do with a chilled bottle of prosecco to drown her misfortunes alone.

Chapter 5
First Contact

Recovered from her shopping ordeal and back into her usual work routine, Cate mustered up the courage, a few days later, to call the number for the knitting club. This time, she made sure she was well away from the office, in a quiet meeting room where she wouldn't be overheard. She dialled the number on her mobile phone and heard it ring several times. Her nerves got the better of her, and she hung up — convincing herself there was no one home.

Back at her desk, her phone rang. It made her jump, and her immediate reaction was to answer it, expecting it to be Gill with some trivial bit of news, or Mike to say he was going to be home late. She was quite taken aback to hear a woman's voice she didn't recognise.

"Hello, hello… Get down Soot. Get off the chair, you naughty boy! Hello?"

"Hello?" answered Cate, confused by the strange voice.

"Oh hello, dearie. I just missed your call. Did you call a few seconds ago? I was just in the kitchen, and it rang off by the time I got to it… I said down Soot. Get out, shoo! Sorry, that's my cat, Soot. He's a lovely cat, but a bit of a naughty boy. He'll try and get up on the chair to the fish tank when he thinks I'm not looking… Sorry, hold on a tick, I'll put him out."

In the ensuing silence, Cate panicked as she suddenly realised with whom she was speaking — it was the woman from the naked knitting club. Just as she was contemplating hanging up, the woman returned. "Sorry, dearie. Now, is it about the knitting club, or do you need a little help in the love department?"

To Cate, the next few seconds seemed like an eternity as she frantically decided what to say.

"Look, I'm sorry. I did dial your number, but changed my mind about the knitting club — I'm sorry for wasting your time." It would have been rude not to explain at the very least, as the woman at the other end of the phone came across as friendly.

"Oh, I'm sorry to hear that, as we always have room for one more — the more, the merrier and all that. I know what, why don't we meet up and I can tell you all about it. I guess it will be your first time — am I right?"

Before Cate could answer, the woman continued, "Do you know the Evergreen Café, right beside Notting Hill Tube Station? You can't miss it. It has a sign with a huge green leaf on it. Let's say we meet about 3pm this coming Saturday afternoon — we can chat about it then. I'm much happier talking face-to-face. Yes, let's meet Saturday, and I've got your phone number if plans change. See you there. They have great vegan chai lattes, and the carrot cake is to die for. Yes — Saturday at 3pm works for me. See you then. Bye, dearie."

Before Cate could contest the arrangements, the phone went dead, and the woman's voice disappeared into the ether.

Cate looked at her mobile phone in disbelief.

What just happened? Oh no, what the hell have I done? I can't do it. Oh, crap!

***

For the next few days, Cate was in a quandary — should she go or not?

She had no idea what the woman looked like or even what her name was, and what did she mean about 'help in the love department'? The more Cate reflected on their conversation; the more intrigued she became.

***

Saturday arrived quicker than Cate had anticipated.

She had had a hectic week at work. All the partners of the law firm were back in force ready to start the New Year, and business was booming between divorce cases, property development projects, and a few white-collar criminal cases thrown in for good measure.

For Cate there was the on-boarding and training of new employees, helping them settle into their new roles and life within a small city law firm. It was a role that Cate enjoyed immensely — apart from working with Creepy Chris.

Cate wasn't sure how Chris had been with the firm for so long. It seemed everyone turned a blind eye to his behaviour.

In fact, a few years back, just before Cate had started to work for the firm, Chris' name had been linked to a sexual harassment case involving a rather attractive young blonde secretary in the Family Law Department. Strangely, the whole incident had blown over very quickly, with the young secretary leaving the firm. There had been rumours of a handsome settlement to the girl in question; said to have been paid out by Chris' father who was an influential figure in a major financial firm in the city.

Either way, Cate kept her distance from Chris as much as she possibly could. He thought he was a ladies man, a real 'Jack the Lad', and his overinflated ego allowed him to think that everyone loved him. It was hard to believe that he was a married man with two adorable daughters. Cate had met the family a few times when they would pop into the office during a day out in the city, and his wife, to Cate's total amazement, was a charming and gentle soul.

Cate was still in a flap about whether or not to make an appearance at the café.

In the end, her good manners, along with a healthy dose of curiosity, took over. Saturday afternoon arrived, and she was on her way to Notting Hill Tube Station for her scheduled meeting at the Evergreen Café.

Mike had already left for an afternoon of golf, so she had slipped out without having to provide a reason for her absence, planning to be back home long before his return.

Interestingly, she had opted not to say anything to Gill about it either. It was her little secret. She would go along, be polite, make her excuses and leave — and that would be the end of that. No one would know, so no harm would be done.

Cate exited the Tube station and was studying the map on her phone, trying to get her bearings, just as a large group of students jostled past her. One rather large brute almost knocked her off her feet as he swung his massive rucksack onto his back. Luckily, she managed to catch hold of the handrail behind her, narrowly avoiding falling back down the steps.

She stood clutching the handrail in one hand and her phone in the other, trying to steady and compose herself. Once she caught her breath, she was so infuriated that she yelled, "Idiot!" after the descending group. They probably didn't even hear her, although an elderly woman slowly climbing the steps behind her shot her a look of disdain, as if the insult had been directed at her.

Cate had forgotten what this part of London was like, full of visitors and day-trippers, unlike the newly re-urbanised area of the old Docklands where she and Mike lived. Although it was busy during the week with business people and office workers filing into the growing number of large shiny high-rise offices, at weekends it was surprisingly tranquil with very few tourists.

Once recovered, she walked to the end of the street. When she glanced up, she spotted the rather large luminous green sign for the Evergreen Café. It was hard to miss.

It was almost ten to three. Cate's heart pounded as she crossed the street towards the café. Her legs felt like lead weights. She hadn't felt this nervous since she had her first official date with Mike, some seventeen years ago after they had met in a bar and she had fallen for him.

At the door of the café, she hesitated and peered in, spying a young couple holding hands and staring lovingly into each other's eyes. Near the window, a group of trendy young students were immersed in a heated discussion. The vibe was 'hippy-meets-veggie', and one that, if Cate was honest with herself, did little to make her feel any more comfortable.

"Maybe she'll not come," muttered Cate hopefully, as she pushed open the door and took a seat at the closest available table to the window. From her vantage point, she could watch the droves of pedestrians pass by and see any new customers enter the café.

As she picked up the menu, she had another furtive glance around, but as far as she could make out, no one appeared to match the voice on the telephone. She thought that she felt like a spy, like she was about to have an illicit meeting, when the waitress came over to take her order.

"Hi, I'm Jules. Welcome to the Evergreen Café, the best organic vegan café in London — what do you want?"

Jules, the server, was a bizarrely dressed young woman with a large green badge emblazoned with her name. Behind her gothic-punk makeup and shocking-blue dreadlocks, she wore the typical 'I can't be bothered' look of many young adults.

Cate tried not to stare, but she was mesmerised by her vast range of intricate tattoos and piercings that appeared to be on every inch of visible flesh. It was a fashion trend that Cate could never fathom, why anyone would want to pierce their tongue and other parts of their anatomy was beyond her comprehension.

"I'll have a coffee, please," replied Cate, trying hard not to look at the massive spike in Jules' lip, as it was making her stomach heave.

"OK. Do you want the dandelion or burdock — and would that be with soy, almond or rice milk?" mumbled

Jules, avoiding direct eye contact with Cate at all costs, which suited her just fine.

Somewhat taken aback by the strange list of options, Cate sheepishly responded, "Don't you have ordinary coffee with ordinary cow's milk?"

"Nope. That's not in line with our vegan and organic policies being a fair trade business with ecological and environmental responsibilities. We do not serve any non-natural or animal products. We do not condone the use of pesticides or any environmentally harmful chemicals. We believe that natural is best," Jules responded, as she disinterestedly chewed the top of her pen. Cate was secretly impressed that she had actually remembered the spiel and delivered it quite eloquently.

"OK, I'll have the burdock coffee, no milk, thanks," ordered Cate.

"OK, one burdock coffee without," confirmed Jules as she swung around and headed back to the counter.

Cate rolled her eyes and muttered to herself; "What am I doing?"

Then she heard the jingle of the wind chimes as the door opened, and turned in time to see a rather small and rotund woman enter. The woman was wearing a purple kaftan with a bright green coat and purple floral wellington boots. In her grey frizzy hair, she wore a matching purple and green sequined clip.

The woman paused for a millisecond and looked around, and then to Cate's dismay, strode across the café to her table.

There was something very 'earth mother' about her, and she looked very much at home in the bohemian decor of the Evergreen Café, whereas Cate would have been more comfortable sipping on a tall low-fat latte with a shot of caramel at Starbucks.

"Hello, dearie. Sorry, I'm late. I had to deal with Soot, and then Trouble needed a little attention and, by the time I got myself organised I was late, but I'm here now. Anyway, let me introduce myself — I'm Luna, like the moon," as she plonked herself down in the seat opposite Cate and continued talking, organising her huge carpetbag in the seat next to her.

"You know, I don't even know your name. No, let me guess — I'm normally quite good at this, yes." Luna closed her eyes and rocked her head from side to side as she grabbed hold of Cate's hand. Her hands were warm and soft.

"Yes, I can see the letter K. Is that right, dearie? Is it something like Kitty — no hold on — no, go on, tell me."

"Well, it's Cate – Cate Taylor. Look, I'm sorry, but I think I've changed my mind. I'm so sorry…" but before Cate could finish, Luna interrupted.

"There, I knew it. I thought Kitty — wow, Cate, which is very like cat. Boy, I am good. Look, I can tell the others will love you; I feel it in my bones. Come along to our next meeting; we meet once a month at my place. It's usually the last Wednesday of the month, seven 'til nine, although sometimes the dates change, you know, to suit everyone's plans. You really must come, as we have such good fun. Half the time there is more gossip and chat than knitting. I think people call it 'Stitch and Bitch' now, but I'm not fond of that myself, I prefer 'Knit and Natter' — more friendly, don't you think? Don't worry if you can't knit; I can teach you. Can you knit? The group is great, and we meet at my place, which is not far from here — cosy and convenient.

Hope you don't mind cats. They mostly stay out of the way, but Soot is a real tinker, and he often sneaks in and finds a spot to watch for an opportunity to play with a ball of wool. It's in their nature you know. They love wool, and Soot loves to play and loves attention."

Cate stared at Luna, like a deer caught in headlights, unable to flee.

Luna continued in full flow without, it seemed to Cate, taking a breath. "You could start with something simple — start with a square, and then work up to something like a scarf or a shawl. Don't worry, I can take you to my friend's shop where you'll find everything you need. I haven't been for ages, and it is time I called in. I'll probably get myself some bits and pieces. Now that we've got that sorted, shall we have a cuppa? Oh, I see you have one already."

With the barrage from Luna, Cate hadn't even noticed that Jules had placed her mug of burdock coffee on the table in front of her. Taking a glance at it, Cate was reminded of the muddy cups of water she produced as a little girl for her dolls' tea parties, primarily made with soil and water. It certainly didn't look appetising, let alone drinkable.

"Jules, dearie, my usual — the decaf chai latte and a small slice of organic, vegan, gluten-free carrot cake. Would you like to try some, Cate?"

"No thanks, I'm good," spluttered Cate, as she had unintentionally taken a drink of the coffee. As soon as she had done so, she wished she hadn't, and now she wanted to spit the vile-tasting liquid out of her mouth but instead had to swallow it politely.

Between mouthfuls of carrot cake and slurps of her chai latte, Luna waffled on about the joys of knitting and how therapeutic it was, and about her cats. She explained how knitting had been making a revival as several young pop stars and some Hollywood actresses had been photographed knitting while hanging around on-set.

Cate literally could not get a word in edgeways.

After what Cate considered a polite amount of time, she made her apologises to leave and explained that she had to get back home as she had plans that evening. Not a complete lie, but Cate felt the need to escape from Luna's incessant talking.

"So that's a date. Let's meet here next Saturday at the same time, and we'll take a wander over to the yarn shop. It's not far from here. See you next week," Luna shouted after Cate as she made her escape.

Cate was almost out the door when Luna came rushing behind her. "Here, you almost forgot this; it's my address for the meetings and my telephone number, although you should have that already. See you next Saturday. I'm so excited. I know you'll love it — just you wait and see. Namaste."

Luna returned to her table and continued to strike up a conversation with a rather forlorn-looking student with heavy-rimmed glasses who was wearing a green and pink crocheted beanie that reminded Cate of her grandmother's tea cosy. The young woman looked to have a good dose of social issues, but as Luna prattled on, the girl genuinely seemed quite pleased to have someone to talk to.

Cate walked down the street back towards the Tube station. She felt a little excited, and yet at the same time, petrified. Again, her mind was in turmoil about whether to go to the next meeting or to forget the whole thing.

As Cate rode the Tube home, she kept wondering:

What if I look odd in the nude? What if they don't like me? What if I can't knit to save my life? What if I like it? What if the others are good fun? Luna certainly is a little eccentric, but she seems friendly — well, very chatty and a little cat-lady crazy, but not in a creepy weird serial-killer way. Oh crap!

***

By the time Cate got back home, Mike was lounging on the sofa glued to the latest football results. He barely noticed Cate walking in and taking off her coat. He certainly didn't see the look on her face.

In silence, she ditched her handbag onto the closest chair and headed down the hall towards the bathroom. What she needed right now was a long pampering soak — time to relax and mull things over.

As the bath filled up, she stood in front of the full-length mirror and stared at the voluptuous woman looking back. If she had been forced to describe herself, she would say that she had curves in all the right places — with extra padding. When she and Mike had first met, she had a reasonably neat figure. Mike always said she was built for comfort rather than speed.

Slowly, she started to undress. First, off came the boots and socks, then the jeans, finally the 'good-old faithful black, hide-anything' sweater. Dressed only in her underwear she stared at her reflection.

Well, it could be worse. OK, I'm a little bit cuddly, but then lots of women are. I'm just like one of those women in the famous paintings, and lots of people think they are beautiful. I'm lucky that Mike loves me just the way I am.

As she slipped off her bra and pants and was about to step into the bath, Mike appeared in the doorway. He slid his hands around her waist and pulled her close, looking over her shoulder into their reflection in the mirror.

"I do love you, you know, and I love the way you look and the way you feel. You're just you, Cate, and I wish you'd forget those silly diets. All they do is make you irritable when they're not going well. By the way, did you know that you were talking to yourself out loud?" He planted a kiss on her neck, sending a shiver down her spine.

Mike didn't often say much to her, but it was at times like this when she felt loved.

"You remember at New Year we ended up talking about making resolutions? Well, I was thinking I'm going to do something about it. Actually, I've already decided what I'm going to do... I'm going to join a knitting club."

"Great," replied Mike, as he squeezed her plump bottom. "It's about time you took up a new hobby, and you might even make some new friends. It would be good for you to get out more."

Before Cate could add that it was a nudist club, Mike left and resumed his usual Saturday evening position sprawled across the sofa in front of their massive plasma screen, shouting and ranting at some football or rugby match.

Cate went to bed later than usual; she had a lot on her mind. She turned off her bedside lamp and slipped under the duvet next to her snoring husband.

She couldn't help but think about what she was getting herself involved in. It was no surprise her dreams were filled with odd people in various states of undress, knitting an intricate web in a myriad of colours with the biggest knitting needles she had ever seen, along with several large cats playing with giant balls of green and purple wool.

Chapter 6
The Wool Emporium

Fast forward one week, and Cate was back at the Evergreen Café.

She placed her order at the counter and took up residence by the window, waiting for Jules to bring it over. This time, she opted for peppermint tea in the hope that it would be less offensive than the burdock coffee.

As she waited, her focus shifted to the large drops of rain trickling down the windowpane. She sat entranced by the patterns they were creating; some merged while others ran free.

"Penny for your thoughts," interrupted Luna, as she settled into the seat opposite.

"Oh, sorry, I was just daydreaming and didn't see you come in," responded Cate, as she sat cradling her tea.

"I'll just have a quick one, and then we should head on as the shop closes at 6pm." Cate looked at the clock above the shop counter, which showed the time as 3.15pm.

"Why, is it far from here?" asked Cate.

"Oh no, just around the corner really. It's just that once you get in, you need time; there is so much to choose from."

At precisely 3.40pm, they walked down a side street — the sort that Cate didn't choose to walk down on her own. There on the corner was a small shop with an old-fashioned hanging sign — *Yarns of Yarns*. Luna bustled past and pushed open the worn wooden door.

Inside, a bell rang to announce their arrival. As Cate stepped into the dimly lit shop, a Japanese gentleman popped up from behind the counter and proceeded to launch into greeting Luna as if they were long-lost friends, giving Cate a few moments to study the curious little man in more detail.

He was small in stature, a good few inches shorter than Cate. He wore a long plain black kimono, with his grey hair scraped back into a topknot. The wrinkles on his face told of a life of hardships, challenges and sadness, whereas his eyes reflected a youthful glow of hope, calmness, and wisdom. His hands were small, with long delicate fingers and neatly cut nails; the hands of an artist — a skilled craftsman.

As the man chatted with Luna, his smile was both warm and attentive. There was something about this shopkeeper that made Cate feel safe and protected. In spite of his diminutive stature, Cate imagined him, in a previous life, to have been a Japanese Samurai warrior, wielding a sword to protect the poor and unfortunate. He had a noble and honourable air about him.

Cate looked around the shop. It would have looked at home on the set of the 'Harry Potter' movies, along with its unusual owner.

Luna and the man were now in deep conversation, leaving her free to explore. Perhaps she could find what she needed without their assistance.

As her eyes adjusted to the lighting, she stood in awe of the fantastic range of colours and textures on display. Every nook and cranny invited her to delve deeper. It was like a great Aladdin's cave for crafters. There were large knobbly bundles of chunky yarns; there were beautiful colourful silks; there were yarns for knitting socks to cream-coloured yarn for Aran sweaters; and many more choices in-between.

In another section, she stumbled across a massive assortment of decorative trimmings and baubles, buttons and bows in every possible hue — some with feathers, others with sparkling crystals, and her favourite, the beautiful fur trims. She wondered if they were real or fake fur, as she stroked her cheek with a gorgeous pink fluffy pom-pom.

As she explored a little further, she spotted an armoury of crafting tools in a dark mahogany wooden display. It was an unbelievable array of sharp implements. Some looked quite dangerous, like weapons, and a few others looked as if they would be quite at home in a torture chamber.

There were of needles of all descriptions: some in pairs for knitting; some sets with points at both ends; circular ones; some made out of plastics, metals or woods. They appeared to come in a range of sizes, from thin to thick. Some were so large that Cate wondered how you could hold them, let alone knit with them.

In a nearby cabinet, there were sewing needles, darning needles, and a range of what she found out later were crochet hooks, again in an assortment of colours and sizes.

Cate headed further towards the back of the shop.

She couldn't resist the temptation to reach out and touch some of the wools, as their textures varied from fluffy to velvety. Never in her wildest dreams did she think that there were so many different types of yarns, wools and threads. She felt like a child in a sweet shop.

As she rounded the next corner towards the rear of the shop, her gaze fell upon the most amazingly detailed garment she had ever seen.

It was a magnificent kimono, decorated with the most beautiful oriental gardens, right down to a lifelike butterfly sitting on a bonsai. Tentatively, Cate reached out to touch it. It was as soft and smooth as silk. To her amazement, she realised that it was knitted. She tenderly held a corner up to study it in more detail. She could just about make out the tiniest stitches.

Even with her limited knitting knowledge, she recognised the sheer mastery in creating something so intricate and detailed. It must have taken hours of patient work to produce. Not only was it beautiful; it was perfection — a work of art — a masterpiece.

In all her years of trawling around art galleries and museums, she had never seen anything like it. This piece of art felt like it touched her soul in a way that words could not express. A tear trickled down her cheek. She would have loved to try it on and feel the cool softness of the silk yarn against her bare flesh.

"It is mesmerising, isn't it?" said a soft voice behind her, bursting her bubble.

"Sorry," apologised Cate, as she released the fabric from her grasp.

"I see that you appreciate its beauty. It was a labour of love. I created it in memory of the person I loved most in this world. Her name was Hiroko — which means 'abundant child' in Japanese — and to me, she was precisely that.

She was abundant in love, beauty and wisdom. She was a shining star. She filled my heart with joy. But, alas, her time upon this earth was brief. She was my childhood sweetheart and were we betrothed. To this day, I do not feel whole without her. She was the light in my world, and my heart still mourns the day she was taken from me. She fell ill, and her poor body faded, ravaged by pain. She never complained. She was only sixteen. So many years ago now, a past life for me, like a dream.

"Oh, I'm so sorry to hear that."

"Thank you. Not long after I was sent to this country to live with relatives, I spent many nights alone in this foreign land. At that time, I started working on this as a tribute to her memory. It took me twenty-five years to finish, and with each stitch, I felt the spirit of my beloved beside me. The thought of her being close by helped me to cope, and eventually, I settled into life here. Even now, when I feel alone and afraid, my love is here in my heart. In my dreams, she is in a place such as this garden, where she is waiting for me to join her — one day — a place of beauty, love, and peace."

Cate could see the tears well up in his eyes as he told his story, and it pulled at her heartstrings. The depth of emotion was raw and pure.

"My apologies. Allow me to introduce myself. My name is Kiyoshi Yamamoto, and I am delighted to make your acquaintance. You, my dear new friend, are most honourably welcome to my humble shop. Please call me Kiyo; all my friends do, and I know that you are a special one indeed."

Cate introduced herself and Kiyo bowed his head in greeting.

Then, very gently, he ushered Cate in the direction of the knitting patterns; the place, he explained, where her knitting journey would begin.

"Now, my dear friend, let's find you a suitable pattern. No doubt Luna will help you with the basics so you can create something — not too complicated, but enough to keep you interested," said Kiyo, as he rummaged in a large mahogany cupboard.

"You will wish to have something beautiful at the end. Something to bring you much joy, as you will have crafted it with love."

He had almost disappeared into the cupboard, and just as Cate was going to ask if he needed help, he re-appeared with an arm full of knitting patterns.

"Please, have a look at these," as he spread a range of patterns out on the counter for Cate and Luna to study.

"How about a lovely shawl? I think this one is perfect. Very simple and elegant, and with the right wool, it will look beautiful," piped up Luna, as she enthusiastically waved a pattern under Cate's nose. Cate wasn't quite sure, as it looked complicated. The symbols and hieroglyphics on the inside were daunting. However, the idea of a lovely shawl she had made herself appealed to her.

"Good," nodded Kiyo in quiet agreement.

"Now we need to find the perfect needles. Please step this way," he kindly waved in the direction he wished her to go.

Cate ended up following the fleet-footed Kiyo down a maze of shelving jam-packed with a variety of assorted objects, half of which left Cate wondering what they were and curious as to what they could possibly be for.

"Ah, here we are."

They were back at yet another large mahogany display, part of the armoury that Cate had spotted earlier.

As Kiyo handed different knitting needles over for Cate to hold, he elaborated on the importance of selecting the right pair; not only the right size for the pattern, but also, in his professional opinion, the right feel for the knitter.

"It is essential for any crafter to feel comfortable when handling and working with their creative tools, and after all, that is what needles are — tools," he explained. After what seemed like aeons of having endless pairs of knitting needles handed to her, Kiyo gave Cate a pair of size ten needles in beechwood.

"How do they feel?" enquired Kiyo, eyeing how Cate was handling the needles. To her utter amazement, the needles felt just right. They felt comfortable — light and balanced in her hands, completely different to the metal ones.

"Excellent, now we need to find you the perfect wool," said Luna, getting excited about Cate's first project.

Cate wanted a chunky yarn in the most fantastic shades of the rainbow. Instead, Luna guided her towards a lighter-weight yarn, which was a better choice for her shawl. Cate chose a beautiful wool/cotton mix, which reminded her of swimming in the Aegean Sea when she and Mike honeymooned in the Greek Islands. It felt summery and happy.

All too soon, Cate was heading out the door clutching her purchases, which were now safely ensconced in an old-fashioned brown paper bag.

Kiyo bowed politely, as Cate bid them farewell.

As she stepped out into the darkness of the street, Luna's voice carried on the wind, reminding Cate that she would call to arrange a date for her trial evening, when she would help her to get started on her knitting journey.

There was a damp chill in the air, but Cate didn't feel it; she felt a rush of excitement deep inside her with the prospect of the beautiful shawl she was going to make.

Chapter 7
Casting On

Cate stood across the street from the address written on the note Luna had pushed into her hand a few weeks earlier. She gazed at the red brick end-of-terrace house; the typical two-up two-down style recognisable in most towns and cities across the UK.

A welcoming glow radiated, particularly from the house on the end of the terrace. There was something special about No.32 Cherrytree Road. It stood apart from the other houses on the street, but Cate couldn't quite put her finger on what it was that made it look more inviting than the other homes in the street.

Most of the houses in the street had overgrown gardens littered with rubbish; telltale signs, Cate surmised, that renters probably occupied them. It made Cate a little sad to see unkempt houses. Her mother had been fiercely house-proud — not on par with Gill's obsessiveness — her childhood home had been clean and tidy, always ready to welcome guests. In Cate's opinion, there was a considerable difference between a house and a home. Many of the houses were missing the little extras that would have made them homely. Nowadays, people moved so much more — merely passing through and living in a rented place before life whisked them off somewhere new.

No.32 appeared to be a place where roots had firmly been planted and life was being played out in the long-term. It reflected Luna's warm and eccentric personality, with subtle nods to her 'woo-woo' ways: the wind chimes strung up at the entrance to the porch, a black cat decal on the window, and the purple curtains with golden swirls.

Cate sighed, pulled her coat collar tighter around her neck and walked across the street. Even if Cate had not known the exact house number, she would have guessed which one was Luna's.

When they had last met at the café, Luna had mentioned that her favourite colour was purple. Cate picked up that it was something to do with your 'crown chakra', whatever that was. To be honest, most of what Luna had said had gone entirely over her head. She still had no clue what a 'chakra' was and was not brave enough to ask, in case Luna launched into another one of her passionate and rather lengthy explanations.

Am I really going to do this? I must be barking mad... Go on, you can do this. I can and I will. It won't hurt to give it a try. Oh, my good heavens, what am I doing? Ok, here goes nothing!

Cate stood at the door and looked around for the doorbell. She couldn't see one. Her hand was poised to use the knocker on the letterbox when the door flung open.

"There you are, dearie, very punctual. Come on in." Luna grasped Cate by the arm and practically yanked her in, causing Cate to stumble over the doorstep into the entrance hall. Once she found her feet, she was relieved that the feeling was returning to her cold extremities.

She looked around and noted that in spite of the rather gaudy decor, Luna's home was neat and tidy. It was cosy, and now that she was inside, it felt like Luna — warm and comfortable.

"Here, I'll take your coat, and you can leave your shoes here. When you're ready, just come through to the sitting room and we'll get you sorted."

Cate did as she was told and made her way through into the sitting room.

Before she even stepped in through the open door, a strong and slightly overpowering aroma assaulted her nasal passages. She stifled a sneeze. Cate was, like her Mum, very sensitive to smells. In fact, she would often walk well out of her way to avoid bath and beauty shops, as the pungent perfumes caused her to break into a manic sneezing fit — she did not do ladylike sneezes.

This smell was not unpleasant, and in her mind, it conjured up the image of drinking hot cocoa sprinkled with cinnamon while wearing an eye mask filled with lavender — a very comforting and heart-warming image on a cold wintry night.

Cate stood in the centre of the room. It was compact — furnished with a floral sofa, and matching armchair. Against one wall sat a small dining table, the type that the sides fold down, and a couple of chairs. From the looks of it, it was not used often for its original purpose, and on top sat a small fish tank and an old-fashioned dial telephone set.

Cate hadn't seen a telephone set like that since she was a teenager, when she would sneakily call her boyfriends without her parents knowing. She had been able to stretch the cable to the nearby bathroom, and with some effort she could even shut the door, ensuring that her parents couldn't hear her romantic ramblings.

In the corner of the room, Cate spotted a small shelving unit overflowing with books. As a lapsed reader, Cate took a step forward to read some of the titles. She had always felt that you could learn a lot about people by the books they read. On this occasion, she was impressed that trashy romances stood side-by-side with books on philosophy, inter-mingled with books on Wicca and herbal healing remedies. Certainly, the books about Wicca piqued Cate's curiosity, but she was not surprised to see it here in Luna's room. In fact, it was starting to make a lot of sense — there was something 'witchy' about Luna, not in the Halloween horror way, but more your motherly white witch.

The focal point of the room was the fireplace with an electric fire. It was on and the real-effect flickering flame added to the cosy atmosphere. It was certainly toasty, a bit too hot for Cate, as a bead of sweat rolled down her forehead, making her start to regret her choice of attire. That morning she had spent ages debating what to wear. In the end, she had opted for a chunky jumper, scarf, and black elasticated trousers — items that made dressing and undressing easier. It wasn't her usual work gear, and a few people in the office had commented. Indeed, Creepy Chris had made a few off-hand remarks: "Is there a blizzard on the way?" and "Are we expecting the pitter-patter of tiny feet?"

Cate could usually switch off to his endless annoying comments, but the one suggesting that she was pregnant hit a raw nerve. It was all she could do to restrain herself from reaching out and punching him in his big fat mouth.

"Be with you in a tick, dearie!" shouted Luna from the next room.

Cate walked towards the direction of the voice and stopped short in the open doorway. She tentatively peered around the corner into Luna's kitchen.

Everywhere she looked in the cramped kitchen there were cookbooks, or at least that was what she guessed they were. There were bundles of herbs hanging above the cooker, and the shelves were packed with glass jars containing a range of strange looking ingredients. The word 'apothecary' popped into her mind.

Just as she was about to step into the room, a ginger cat pounced at her feet and almost caused her to tumble. In her scramble to keep her balance, Cate grabbed the nearest thing to hand, which happened to be a jar filled with large seeds. It crashed to the floor and smashed into a thousand glass shards — the seeds scattered across the tiled floor.

"Oh no!" exclaimed Cate, as she hurriedly bent down to clear up the mess.

"Oh don't worry, dearie. I saw what that naughty boy did. That's Trouble; he's not so good with people he doesn't know. Don't fuss. I'll grab a dustpan and brush, and we'll soon have it as right as rain," chirped Luna.

Cate did the best she could to clear up. She tended to be accident-prone, particularly when she got nervous.

Way back when she had first started dating Mike, there had been a similar incident as they were heading out to a concert by bus. The two lovebirds had been standing engrossed in conversation, and she had not noticed a man sitting down next to them holding an aluminium pole. Coincidentally, it resembled the metal poles at the back of the seats used by standing passengers to hold on to.

At one point in the journey, the bus raced onto a roundabout at full speed, throwing Cate off-balance. She had reached out to grab the pole for safety. Unfortunately, she grabbed hold of the wrong pole, and Cate was flung across to the other side of the bus, where she landed face first in the lap of a startled businessman. It had been embarrassing. Mike had been no help, as he was doubled over in laughter with tears rolling down his cheeks. As for the man with the aluminium pole, he just shot her an angry glance. The accosted man was trying to push her off his crotch like she was a piece of dog filth on his shoe. In the end, a very kind Asian lady had been the one to come to her rescue.

It ranked as one of her most embarrassing moments in public, but was by no means the only one. It had taken almost the entire evening for her flushed face to go back to normal, and even now, every time she thought about the experience she could feel her face start to burn bright red.

"There, all cleaned up. Come on. Let's get you settled and then we can get started on some knitting. I would suggest, if you feel up to it, it might be a good idea to get naked too. I get the feeling you are new to this, and there's only you and me here. You know we all have the same bits, dearie, don't we?"

Cate nodded and timidly followed Luna back into the sitting room, like a chick following the mother hen.

"Why don't you sit here," said Luna, as she pointed to the floral armchair in the corner. "It's a little darker, and the armchair will make you feel more comfortable. It's my favourite spot in the room and where I do my best work, and it's very comfy for a quick forty-winks," smiled Luna.

"Did I ask you to bring along a towel or something to sit on?"

Cate stood and shook her head. It was all getting a bit too real now.

"Not to worry. Here, have this," said Luna, as she handed Cate a woollen blanket made up of lots of knitted squares in shades of purple.

Cate draped the blanket across the expanse of the seat, desperately trying not to think that it was the cats' blanket that her bare backside would be seated upon.

"When you take off your bits and pieces, you can put them here," said Luna, pointing to a tiny space on the floor beside the chair.

"I'll give you a few minutes to sort yourself out while I pop upstairs."

Luna left the room.

Cate faced the reality that she was going to get naked in a virtual stranger's house. At some level it beggared belief. Just what did she think she was doing? No one had a clue where she was, unless Mike thought to check her whereabouts on the 'Find-a-Friend' app on his phone. That was highly unlikely as he was due to be away at a conference in Edinburgh for the next two days. She might be murdered, eaten, and her bones buried in the back garden, and no one would have a clue.

Come on, Cate, it's OK. You can do this. Luna might be a little crazy, but she doesn't come across as a serial killer.

She took a couple of deep breaths to generate the courage she needed, and started to undress.

First, she stripped off her socks, feeling her toes dig into the soft shag pile carpet; next off came her scarf and her 'one-size-fits-all' sweater, which she folded neatly and placed on the armchair; then her stretchy trousers; and finally her vest top.

She paused to take a cursory look around the room, and it felt that the menagerie of animals in the various pictures and paintings adorning the walls were staring at her in anticipation. She fought hard to push down the fear in the pit of her stomach.

It was the same feeling she used to have before gym classes at school. She was transported back to a room full of pubescent girls scrambling to shower and get dressed without anyone witnessing their nudity and varying stages of physical maturity.

Cate had always had the feeling that the gym teacher did not like her, and that she had gone out of her way to embarrass her. On one occasion, Miss McKee had made a remark about her flat chest, exclaiming that no one was interested in seeing 'Catherine's wee boobies'.

It had been a draconian experience, with a book — known as the shower register— which Miss McKee was like a zealot at marking. Most girls went into the communal shower room clutching their towels tight to their bare frames. Inside the white tiled area, there were four showerheads placed around the space, and most of the girls would sheepishly splash a little water around their shoulders to make it look as if they had indeed taken a shower. Miss McKee would check each girl as they exited the shower area, and a few water droplets were usually enough to keep her satisfied.

There was only one acceptable excuse to miss the shower experience, and that was when you had your 'Aunt Flo'. It was an excuse that Cate had tried to use all too often. One day Miss McKee had asked her to prove it. It had been mortifying with all the other girls sniggering at her.

Of course, there were always one or two girls who were not so self-conscious, and they delighted in flaunting their perfect athletic bodies with tan lines, much to the annoyance and awe of the other scrawny misfits.

This weekly ritual, Cate seriously believed, had scarred her for life. She shivered with the memory of it all — like an icy chill running through her very core.

Naturally, she now understood the importance of cleanliness, but still, the ordeal had been intolerable. In Cate's mind, better explanations about personal hygiene, along with separate shower cubicles, would have made all the difference.

Cate shook her head to dislodge the harrowingly vivid image from her mind, as she bent over to retrieve her knitting gear from her newly purchased knitting bag. It was a lovely floral bag she had bought as a little treat to herself for taking this huge step, and seeing it now made her smile. The colours and pattern were bright and cheery, helping to dispel the images in her head of her school-day horrors.

She took a deep breath and unhooked her black bra. She had been shocked to learn that her bust was now a generous 34GG cup when she last availed herself of a bra-fitting service. It was no laughing matter, as her boobs were a pain — literally. Her narrow shoulders struggled to accommodate her massive breasts. When Mike had discovered she now wore a double G, he started to refer to her bosoms as his 'Gorgeous Girls'.

Finally, off came her 'big girl knickers'.

In her effort to choose the right outfit for tonight's proceedings, she had not once considered her underwear. Now it struck her that perhaps she ought to invest in a new set for the real first night — something a little more feminine.

Cate set the folded clothes on top of her battered handbag, as she didn't entirely trust the cleanliness of the floor. She cautiously sat down onto the purple throw and felt the chair cocoon her flesh. She waited patiently for Luna to re-appear, clutching her knitting needles and wool close to her body, as if they could miraculously make her invisible, or in some way provide coverage for her nudity.

Luna breezed back into the room clad in a rather garish gold and purple floral kimono. Her grey wavy hair had been pulled back and held in place with a clip adorned with a floral display of vivid pinks and yellows. Cate couldn't quite decide if they complemented or clashed with the print on the kimono.

"Let's get started," announced Luna, as she excitedly clapped her hands like a child about to be dished up a bowl of ice cream. She proceeded to slip off her robe and plonked her sturdy frame onto the end of the sofa nearest to Cate.

"I adore starting a new project; it has so much energy of anticipation. I just know you'll love it. I think we will start you with a simple square until you get the hang of the basics, don't you think?" said Luna.

Cate was, at this point, frantically trying to look anywhere apart from Luna's rather large and somewhat sagging physique. No matter how hard she tried to look elsewhere, her eyes kept finding their way back, as if there was some hypnotic force at work. Luna was, thankfully, oblivious to Cate's predicament and prattled on.

"Well, you probably don't, but you will soon. Now, have you ever knit before? I think you said you had, quite a while ago, I believe," as she gazed up to the skies as if looking for the answer.

"No matter, dearie, you'll soon get the hang of it again."

Luna smiled at Cate as she stretched across the settee, flashing a rather ample backside in Cate's direction, trying to locate a spare pair of needles and a ball of wool in her knitting box.

"Got it," cried Luna, as she shuffled her large frame back into place.

Cate, still clinging to her needles and a ball of wool as if her life depended on it, was speechless. What she had seen could never be unseen — it was not a pretty sight by any stretch of the imagination, and the image would now be forever embedded in her mind.

As traumatic as it was to witness Luna's backside in all its glory; at some unconscious level it made Cate feel more confident about her own body. It might not be perfect, but in comparison to Luna's body, it was quite acceptable. Cate might not be as slim, or as toned, as she once was — however, she was at least fastidious about her personal grooming. She made every effort to ensure her lady bits were neat and kept trim and tidy. The one thing she did regularly was wax. Luna was someone who opted for the natural look.

Cate chuckled when she thought what Gill would have said to see the pair of them in their birthday suits, with everything on display. She would have had a fit for sure. For one thing, she would have had an issue just being in Luna's room, let alone getting undressed and sitting on the furniture. An image of a naked Gill exploding as her tiny perfect ass came into contact with the purple knitted blanket popped in her mind.

"OK, dearie, let's get started. I'm going to start with casting on forty stitches. If you watch what I'm doing first of all, then I'll help you."

Cate watched as Luna used her needles to cast on forty stitches. Then it was her turn.

She followed Luna's directions, and in her head she followed the steps, while Luna sang a rhyme to help her:

"In through the window,

Run around back.

Out through the window,

Off jumps Jack."

Slowly, the needles worked together, and under the watchful gaze of Luna, Cate soon had forty stitches cast on her needle. She held the needle up to look at her handiwork and had to admit that she felt quite proud. She had vague recollections of her Nanny Eileen teaching her to knit on a wet Sunday afternoon many, many years ago when she was a little girl.

Next came the first knitted row. Cate followed Luna's example, and slowly she worked the needles and the yarn together, slipping each knit stitch onto the other needle. The needles and yarn felt alien and cumbersome in her hands. She repeated the process for the next row, and soon she was midway through her third row.

Luna kindly guided her, while offering some helpful tips on holding the needles and yarn to make it more comfortable.

Cate was hooked, and in no time at all, she had knit ten rows. Once she got the hang of the routine, it was relatively simple, and at the same time quite therapeutic. As she concentrated on knitting each stitch, the cares and worries of the world fell away — it was a form of meditation with her mind firmly focussed on the task at hand.

Cate began to understand the appeal. She had read that knitting was hailed as a great way to combat stress and had made a comeback in the last number of years. Not only was there a mindfulness side to it, but it also encouraged the creative side of the brain — a major plus point for Cate, as she had no real creative outlets in her life.

"Time for a cuppa?" asked Luna.

Cate nodded in agreement; she realised that she was ready for one. The last hour had flown by and not once did she even think about being naked. The knitting commanded her complete attention. She had noticed that Luna didn't look at her needles or yarn as she worked away on her project, a complicated looking mix of five short-double ended needles, a large safety-pin and a giant ball of very fine colourful wool.

"Erm... Luna, what are you knitting? It looks complicated," asked Cate.

"A pair of socks. There is just something about knitting socks I adore, and they make great presents," winked Luna, as she placed her knitting to one side and left for the kitchen.

Seeing the half-knit sock reminded Cate, again, of her grandmother. She could see Nanny Eileen perched on the edge of her favourite chair by the fire, knitting a pair of thick cream woollen socks. Everyone in the family had received a pair each Christmas. It had been a running joke in the family for years.

When Cate had been about thirteen, she had badgered Nanny Eileen into knitting her a set of rainbow-coloured legwarmers. Nanny Eileen had been a little put out by her request, as she said the fun part of knitting socks for her was turning the heel. Cate had no idea what that meant, but she had adored her bright colourful legwarmers, and had been the envy of her friends.

It was only now Cate realised the hours of work and love that had gone into the making of each pair — reminding her how much she missed her granny. She secretly hoped that Nanny Eileen was looking down from her perch in heaven, having a giggle at the scene below and, perhaps, at the same time proud that Cate had once again picked up a pair of knitting needles.

Luna appeared back with two mugs and handed one to Cate. She set her knitting aside and cradled her drink. She took a quick sniff of the steaming beverage; it smelt delicious. She took a tentative sip, and although she could not quite recognise the concoction, it was very drinkable.

Cate ended up staying for a further hour, enjoying the ease and peace of the atmosphere. Luna appeared to have entered a semi-meditative state, with the silence in the room punctuated only by the clicking of their knitting needles and the ticking of the clock on the mantelpiece. Even Soot had curled up on her feet, keeping them warm, and the rhythmic rise and fall of his body as he breathed made Cate feel relaxed. It was the most peaceful and content she had felt for years. If someone had told her how she would feel in such a bizarre scenario, she would not have believed it possible.

As Cate packed away her knitting, dressed, and hugged Luna goodnight, she knew in her heart that things were shifting. Change was afoot and that was a good thing.

Chapter 8
The Real First Night

A week later, Cate was making her way back to Luna's. Since her last visit, she had been very upbeat about the experience and had even managed to knit most of the rest of the square on her own. She had also bought a lovely set of lacy red underwear embroidered with pink flowers, and a new pink hand towel to sit on, embellished in the season's romantic theme with red hearts. She was pleased with her purchases, and the towel would be much softer for her backside than the purple knitted blanket.

As she drew nearer to Luna's, her nerves were kicking in, like a swarm of butterflies fluttering in her stomach. She was thinking how it wouldn't be an issue now getting naked with Luna, but this time, there would be others; strangers who would judge her pasty pale body and big boobs. What if they didn't like her?

Cate was desperately trying to quell her unease:

Should I just turn around and go home? No, stop thinking like that; it'll be fine. I'm sure no one is interested in my body, and they're probably used to it. Thank goodness it's only women. Just imagine going to a nudist beach with men, too, now that would be horrendous. Come on, Cate; you can do this. I can and I will.

Too late — Luna was already at the door, regaled in her purple and gold floral kimono, and this time, in her hair she wore an even more elaborate gold-coloured floral and feather decoration. Luna embraced her in a warm and welcoming hug.

Cate had hoped to be the first one there, so she could undress in privacy and use the armchair to hide some of her modesty. However, this was not to be the case, because as Luna ushered Cate into the sitting room, she called out to an unseen presence.

"Lady, we have a new girl joining us tonight. You'll adore her. This is Cate," said Luna, as she presented her to a rather tall, slim lady with white-cropped hair and piercing steel-blue eyes. The woman was in a state of half-undress and did not bat an eyelid as she extended her hand to welcome Cate.

"Charmed, I'm sure. My name is Prudence Hampton-Bond, but everyone calls me Lady. Just don't call me Prudence, reminds me of my old nanny, a ghastly battle-axe of a woman. She used to scream my name at me all the time. Welcome on-board." She released Cate's hand and proceeded to undress.

"Pleased to meet you," mumbled Cate, as she looked around to find somewhere she could disrobe unnoticed — a feat that only the Great Houdini himself could have managed in such a tight space.

Lady and Luna disappeared into the kitchen to prepare some drinks and nibbles, thankfully leaving Cate a few moments alone to start the process of undressing. Quickly, she removed each layer of clothing, screwed them into a ball, placed her towel onto the cushion of the armchair and sat down. She was busy trying to arrange her knitting in such a way to afford as much coverage as possible — pretty hard as she was knitting a small square. The ladies returned, just as the door from the hallway opened, and in stepped a woman who would make anyone sit up and take notice. To Cate, this goddess was the incarnation of an Amazonian Princess in the flesh. She was at least six-foot tall, with a shaved head, athletic build, and the most beautiful shiny ebony skin.

"Hello, darling, you must be the new girl. Welcome to our merry tribe. I'm Jo." Her accent belied a soft Southern drawl. Cate was mesmerised by Jo, so much so that she could hardly stammer out her own name. Jo greeted both Luna and Lady with big hugs before undressing and settling herself on a yoga cushion placed on the floor with her long legs outstretched.

Next, a figure wrapped up against the winter chill bustled into the room already apologising for being late. According to Lady, this was Alice. Alice peeled off each layer of clothing, bunching them together as she did so. She then placed the pile on the end of the sofa nearest to Cate and proceeded to sit down on top of them. After a few moments of wriggling around to make herself comfortable, she noticed Cate.

"Oh, hello there, I'm Alice," as she extended a hand in greeting. "Oh, I see you are knitting a square. Are you new to knitting? If you need any help, ask me, I'm happy to help." Her voice was soft and held a very nurturing tone. If Cate had to guess, she had the feeling that Alice probably worked with children.

Knitting projects started to appear, and needles were clicking away as conversations started. Luna squeezed onto the settee between Lady and Alice.

Surprisingly, Cate did not feel strange at all, and soon passed the initial shock of seeing the others completely naked. Her companions were all lovely, and she started to feel at ease. They also did not bombard her with lots of personal questions, meaning the focus was not drawn directly onto her. After a while, there was something about being together in this space that felt comfortable to her; almost familiar and safe, like home.

As Cate slowly worked her needles, she would sneak glances at the other ladies; each one different and all seemed to be very comfortable in their own unique bodies. Cate was, in particular, drawn to Jo. She was fascinated by this 'Grace Jones-esque' woman, and her curiosity was aroused by the elaborate snake tattoo that coiled its way up from Jo's left ankle, around her thigh and worked its way up her back. The hissing face of the snake appeared to be nestling into her neck, like a lover planting a kiss.

"I see you like my snake," said Jo, breaking Cate's trance.

"Oh, I'm so sorry. I didn't mean to stare; it's just that I have never seen anything like it — it looks so real," explained an embarrassed Cate.

"Well, there's a story behind it. When I was a baby growing up in Louisiana, my mama found me playing with a snake in our backyard one day. It was a diamondback water snake. My mama went crazy as she thought it was a rattler, and she nearly passed out when I came toddling up with the thing coiled around me. So, I got the nickname 'Snake', and it stuck. I adore snakes and even use one in my act."

"Oh, what do you do?"

"I'm a stripper and pole dancer at a gentleman's club in Soho, and my snake, Charlie, is my partner. It works well as it keeps the gropers away and it means I don't have to leave Charlie at home alone. He loves it."

Cate was speechless. For one thing, she was not fond of snakes, albeit she had never been closer to one than on the other side of a reinforced window at the zoo. She was blown away by the fact that here she was — almost forty years of age — sitting in a relative stranger's room, in the nude, with a stripper. Her mother would have had a fit.

Cate returned to her knitting and soon realised her first square was almost complete. Alice was chatting with Luna about natural remedies to soothe teething tots; Cate waited patiently until they had finished, as she needed Alice's assistance to show her how to cast-off.

While Alice was helping Cate, Luna disappeared off into the kitchen, and to Cate's surprise the door opened and in strode a guy. Her heart nearly stopped, and to crown it all; he was a handsome young man in his early thirties. The man walked around the room and kissed each of the women on the cheek. He stopped in his tracks when he came to Cate.

"Oh, hello sweetie, and who might you be?" as he gave her the once-over. Cate noted the hint of a foreign accent, as she looked into his deep brown eyes. She felt her face erupt into a bright shade of red, exaggerating both the red in her hair and the paleness of her skin.

In response, she just about managed to mumble her name. He reached down, gently lifted her hand and kissed it lightly. He was one smooth operator. Not only was this guy handsome, he was also immaculately groomed and smelt incredible. Cate suspected he was clad head to toe, in expensive designer gear. She had spotted a few well-known brand logos on his apparel when he walked in — brands that she had only heard of through Gill's expensive shopping habits.

Luna appeared from the kitchen balancing a tray on one arm and carrying a teapot in the other.

"Oh Carlos, dearie, would you help me, please? Just set it on the table for me. Have you met Cate? It's her first night, so please be nice to her. We want her to come back."

"Yes, Luna, my best behaviour. I promise," he smiled, flashing his perfect white teeth, as he relieved Luna of the heavy tray, doing as he was told.

Luna served out the hot tea and then offered around a plate of homemade tray bakes. The tea was the same as Cate had enjoyed on her last visit, and the vegan oatmeal fruit slice was delicious.

By the time everyone had a drink in hand, Carlos had undressed and taken up a spot next to Jo on the floor, where they were now chatting away.

After the mugs were cleared away, Alice offered to keep a watchful eye over Cate as she casted on a new square. She was extremely chuffed with herself that she had remembered how to cast on, and soon had one needle filled with stitches ready to start again. She was a like proud child waving her needle under Alice's nose.

"Would you like to learn to do a purl stitch this time?" asked Alice kindly.

"Yes, please," replied Cate, aware that she sounded like an excited child.

Alice, who Cate guessed was her mid-thirties, had a body that bore the hallmarks of motherhood. She showed Cate patiently how to do the new stitch.

Cate started working away, one row knit stitch and the next one purl stitch. Alice explained that this was called stocking stitch and the overall look would be different to the one she had just completed in garter stitch.

As Alice and Cate knitted, they chatted, and Cate learned that Alice was married to Ned. They had four young children, and she had given up being a nursery school teacher to raise her family. She loved babies and children, and if she could have her way, she would have four more. Coming to the knitting club was her night out when Ned would stay in to look after the children with the help of his mother, who lived across the street from them. Cate explained that she did not have any children, but shared anecdotes of her time in France as an *au pair*. She had Alice in stitches relaying tales about some of the antics of the older children.

Soon the night drew to a close, and everyone retrieved their clothes and dressed ready to face the cold February night.

Luna reminded everyone of the date of the next meeting and gave everyone a small glass bottle as they left.

When it was Cate's turn to leave, Luna pressed a bottle into her hand.

"A little gift from me to make your Valentine's extra special," she winked. "I call it 'The Elixir of Love'. Just sprinkle three or four drops on your lover's pillow, or pour a few drops into their drink to boost passion."

***

On the Tube journey home, Cate's head was full of the evening's events and all her newfound naked knitting buddies. She noticed in her reflection in the window opposite that she was smiling to herself as she clutched 'The Elixir of Love' protectively in her hand.

On reflection, the evening had gone quite well. Meeting the other knitters had not been as scary as she had expected, although it was a little disconcerting having a man there too, especially when he was so damn cute.

Chapter 9
Valentine's Night

14th February – Valentine's Day — was also Cate and Mike's wedding anniversary.

This year, they would be celebrating their thirteenth wedding anniversary, and Cate was planning something special. She felt that with Mike having been away a lot with work, it would be lovely to have a romantic evening together. Over the past few years, their anniversary celebrations had been a little lacklustre. Last year, they had been so busy they had both forgotten and ended up with a take-out pizza washed down with a cheap bottle of fizz. The year before that had not been much better. It had been a night out at the cinema, which might have been OK except Mike had chosen the film — an action movie with lots of car chases and gratuitous violence — not Cate's type of movie at all.

This year was going to be different — she was determined to pull out all the stops and give them an anniversary to remember. With that in mind, she had booked a table at a fabulous new restaurant in the West End; one that had received rave reviews. Cate had checked the online menu and made sure it would appeal to Mike, and with steak being one of their specialities; it was bound to be a winner.

Cate had also picked up the dress from Harrods and was pleased that she managed to do so without any further embarrassing scenes. In fact, the manager had been, once again, very apologetic and had even given Cate a voucher to use at their hair and beauty spa. Cate was so impressed that she booked an appointment on Valentine's morning to get her nails, makeup, and hair done. She was going all out and felt sure that the money would be a worthwhile investment.

When she got home, she was even more thrilled to discover that when the dress had been faultlessly repaired, they had somehow made it slightly more forgiving, and it now fitted perfectly.

To add a little spice to the whole experience, and to surprise Mike with her makeover, she had left his Valentine/Anniversary card in the kitchen when she had slipped out early that morning. The card included an invitation to join her for dinner with the details of the restaurant and the time. She had also booked a room at a nearby hotel for, what she hoped, would be a night of passion. Additionally, it provided her with space to get ready without being disturbed — she wanted to walk in and make an impression, reminding Mike of why he had married her.

***

At 7.30pm on the dot, a glamorous redhead stepped through the door of the restaurant; her hair piled high with a few loose curls floating down the side of her face, contrasting with her milky white skin. She slipped off her faux-fur coat and handed it to the hostess, as she confirmed the details of her reservation.

Clutching her little evening bag, Cate was feeling slightly uncomfortable in her snug-fitting dress and high heels, as she sauntered behind the hostess to their reserved table. She was aware of people looking at her, making her feel incredibly self-conscious and, to some degree, quite vulnerable. If only Cate could have read the minds of many of the onlookers, she would have learned that they were in fact in awe of her radiance and beauty. In their eyes, this tall, curvaceous, red-haired woman was a total stunner.

When she was seated, she was handed a menu and offered a pre-dinner drink. Cate opted for a glass of champagne; after all, she was on a mission to make this a night to remember, and a glass would help calm her nerves.

How funny? Why do I feel so nervous about meeting my own husband?

While she waited, she glanced around the restaurant and was surprised to see that the majority of her fellow diners were middle-aged men in business suits, interspersed with a few romantic couples, and in the very far corner, a man was dining alone.

The champagne arrived, and Cate mulled over the menu. Some of the items were very pretentious and, in Cate's personal opinion, sounded quite dreadful. In the end, she decided that the Goat's cheese *soufflé* with truffle cream would be a safe choice for starter; followed by the filet of steak served with a mushroom and shallot *jus* for main; and for dessert, the *Fondant au Chocolate avec Coulis Framboise* would be perfect. Looking through the menu, Cate being Cate, she always started with the dessert selection first and worked her way back.

Twenty minutes later, her champagne glass was empty, and there was still no sign of her husband. Retrieving her bag from under the chair, Cate discreetly pulled out her mobile phone to see if Mike had called. There were no missed calls, no voicemail messages and no texts.

The waiter appeared and asked, "Madame, would you like to order now or wait a little longer?"

Cate, now feeling a little more self-conscious, confirmed she would wait a bit longer and ordered another glass of champagne.

In her head, she was running through all the reasons why Mike was late: perhaps he had to work last minute; maybe he had not seen the envelope and read the card; or worst of all, something terrible had happened to him on his way there. She was sure there must be a good excuse, because although Mike was a little easy-going regarding punctuality, in their time together, he had always shown up for a date.

In her state of heightening worry and embarrassment, she had managed to down the second glass of champagne like lemonade — not a wise thing to do in her famished state. She had forgone lunch early in the day due to her busy schedule at the hair and beauty spa, and the alcohol on an empty stomach was starting to go to her head, making her a little tipsy.

It was now almost an hour since her arrival. Cate saw the *Maître d'* talking with the hostess and looking over in her direction. It was apparent they wanted her to order or go. Cate had pulled quite a few strings at work to persuade the senior partner's secretary to call and make the reservation for her, and she was not about to give it up without a fight.

Sensing that she needed to do something, she decided that perhaps a visit to the ladies' room would give her time and an opportunity to track down her missing husband. As she stood up, she had not realised how intoxicated she was. The sudden motion of standing up made her feel extremely dizzy and she stumbled, tripping over the leg of her chair. She reached out to steady herself and found herself clasped in a sturdy pair of arms. The rescuing arms belonged to a handsome stranger, who had been returning from the restrooms and just happened to be in the right place at the right time. Anyone watching would have said it was like a scene from a movie — perfectly staged.

Cate righted herself and thanked the man profusely.

"Please, I'm just glad I could help," he said, with a twinkle in his brown eyes and a soft confident American accent. "I see you are dining alone. I am too. Would you care to join me?"

Cate, by this stage, was so annoyed with Mike that she agreed to join the handsome brown-eyed businessman. After all, he seemed like a decent guy; and if Mike did show up, it would perhaps make him a little jealous to see Cate in the company of another man.

The American waved across to the waiter, and in moments a second place had been set at the man's table, and a fresh glass of champagne was placed before her. As the gentleman had already finished his starter, Cate opted to order just the main course, allowing them to dine together.

It didn't take long for Warren to introduce himself and explain that he was often in London for business; it was a drag to spend so much time in meetings, in hotel rooms and dining alone in restaurants. He looked genuinely pleased to have Cate's company.

Warren, originally from Massachusetts, now lived in Connecticut with his daughter. He had been married, once, but his wife had died almost six years before of breast cancer when their daughter was only ten years old. He had never married again, as he had never met a woman who could match up to his late wife. He told Cate about his love for outdoor sports: skiing, hiking, fishing, and more recently, paragliding. He talked about his business trips all over the world, but admitted that he never got to see much of the cities or countries he visited. He shared his dream to retire one day and make a trip around the world, one that would be better to share with someone he loved.

Cate was captivated by Warren's warmth and charm, his ageing good looks, his accent, and his talk of adventures. If she had not been so happily married, she would have said he was the type of man who could easily sweep her off her feet.

Cate told Warren about her own life and how her husband had not shown up for their anniversary dinner. She confided in him, cradling a large glass of an exceptionally smooth red wine, that she was feeling a little lonely in her marriage right now and how she felt that Mike didn't fancy her any more.

Warren reached over and took her hand in his, looked her straight in the eyes and declared, "Your husband really is a fool. You are a beautiful — no — an exquisite woman. If you were mine, I would tell you I loved you every moment of every day without fail."

Cate blushed but had to admit she was, on some level, falling for this handsome charmer.

Dessert came and went, and Warren paid the bill, saying it was the least he could do for her agreeing to spend time with 'a lonely old Yank'.

The hostess brought over their coats, and they stepped out into a heavy rainstorm. Cate tried to seek refuge under her tiny evening bag, but to no avail. The rain was coming down sideways— even if she had had an umbrella, the wind would have rendered it useless. Warren, a true gentleman, removed his raincoat and held it over her head while flagging down a cab.

As they clambered in like two drowned rats, the cab driver asked them where they were heading. Without thinking, Cate replied with the name of the hotel she was staying in, and moments later the cab did a U-turn and drove off towards her hotel.

In the back, Warren reached across and moved an escaped piece of wet hair from Cate's face. As he did so, she shifted around to face him and the next thing she knew, they were engaged in a full-on kiss. Cate's first reaction was to relax into it, as it was not unpleasant. She could taste the wine on his lips, and his aroma was quite light and manly. He was an excellent kisser for sure. She had not been kissed in such a passionate way in years. Mike was, nowadays, more likely to give her a peck on the cheek or a light brief kiss on the lips, more endearing than passionate. It seemed that passion had faded from their marriage, replaced instead with familiarity and routine. Since Mike's job had become more demanding with more frequent absences on business trips, their sex life was virtually non-existent.

Cate was lost in the moment, her heart was pumping, and she could feel the blood rushing to her lady parts, making them feel on fire and ready for action. Somewhere in the midst of all the hormones, a voice in Cate's head reminded her that she was married and this was no way to behave.

She pulled herself free from Warren's embrace, and turned away from him, mumbling excuses, "Sorry, I shouldn't have done that. It was all the champagne. Sorry, I'm a married woman."

"No, please excuse me. I'm so sorry — it was my mistake. Please accept my humble apologies," begged Warren, looking deep into her eyes. "I know it's no excuse, but it has been such a long time since I have enjoyed the company of such an interesting and beautiful young woman. Please, what can I do to earn your forgiveness?"

There was a tone of sincerity to his voice, which made Cate reach out her hand and place it on his knee. Instead of being angry with him for overstepping the mark, she excused his actions, "We've both had too much to drink tonight. So I forgive you. I have had a lovely time. Thank you."

The cab pulled up at the front of her hotel. Warren helped Cate out, and in true gentleman-style, escorted her inside the revolving door into the lobby. There he kissed her gently on the cheek and thanked her again for her companionship. With a smile, he disappeared into the rainy night.

Cate made her way up to her hotel room, and as she undressed, dried off, and slipped into the fresh cotton sheets, her head was replaying over and over the kiss with

Warren. Even just thinking about him was making her body crave his touch. She fell asleep to images of them together, lips kissing and bodies entwined.

***

The following morning, Cate woke with a start.

At first, she wasn't sure where she was, and then she remembered she had stayed at the hotel. She grappled for her bag and looked at her phone to see if Mike had called her, wondering where she was and worried that she had not come home. There were no missed calls, no messages, and no worried voicemails.

Her head ached from too much champagne and red wine the prior evening. A warm bubble bath was needed — after a long, cold glass of water and a much-needed headache tablet.

As she stripped off and was ready to jump in the bath, there was a knock at the door. It was room service with the special Valentine's breakfast for two, complete with two glasses of champagne and a red rose.

Cate grabbed a bath towel and opened the door. She directed for the tray to be set on the bed and sent the young bellboy away with a handsome tip and a story that her husband was in the bathroom. She didn't know why she had to justify that the breakfast was for two, but she felt she ought to, probably more for her own sake than for the bellboy. Gone were her plans for a romantic breakfast in bed for her and her husband, so instead, she grabbed a quick coffee and croissant. She also downed both glasses of champagne; in part not wanting to waste them, and partly as a cure for her hangover.

The spa bath with jacuzzi jets worked wonders, and very soon she was refreshed, dressed and ready to head home. She was curious about Mike, and sincerely hoped that nothing bad had happened to him. With the events of the previous evening, she realised she had not tried to contact him at all. She checked-out, thanking the man on reception for a wonderful stay and again making up a story to explain the absence of her missing husband, before making her way to the nearest Tube station.

On arriving home, she was surprised to see there was no sign of Mike; their bed had not been slept in, and the envelope was still sitting, unopened, on the kitchen bench.

Panic started to rise in her chest, and she began to feel guilty that something awful indeed had befallen her wayward husband. She called his mobile. It went straight to voicemail. She called again and left a short message asking him to call her back as soon as possible. She also sent a quick text message too, just in case.

Leaving it for a few minutes, Cate boiled the kettle and made herself a cup of tea. She sat down on the sofa and stared at the phone in her hand, willing it to ring.

Nothing happened — only silence.

After, what seemed like an eternity, Cate decided to call Pete and find out if he knew of Mike's whereabouts. She called Gill's number on her mobile.

"Hi, darling, happy anniversary for yesterday. Hard to believe it's been thirteen years since you two walked down the aisle. It was a lovely day, and you were such beautiful bride," answered Gill.

"Look, can I talk with Pete?"

"What's wrong? Is everything all right?"

"Can I just talk with Pete a moment, please?" Gill could detect the urgency in Cate's voice.

"Yes, of course. Pete darling, Cate wants a quick word with you," as she handed the phone over.

"Hi, Cate. Congratulations. Hope Mike bought you something spectacular to celebrate," Pete said brightly.

"Look, there must have been a mix-up, but did Mike have to go away at short notice for work? I booked a restaurant last night, and he didn't show up," whispered Cate, as tears started to trickle down her face.

There was a moment of silence before Pete responded. "Look, I'm sure that's exactly what's happened. You know how it's been. He's involved in a major project for a big client, pretty important for the company. I am sure he'll call when he has time. Don't worry, I'm sure all is well."

Was it Cate being anxious, or could she detect a slight pitch to Pete's voice that made her not quite believe what he was saying? The thought passed swiftly, as she agreed with him that Mike would call when he could.

She hung up and sat staring at the phone. In her head, she continued to admonish herself for her selfish behaviour the previous evening.

It wasn't until 7pm that evening when Mike called. He apologised for missing Valentine's. He did not mention their anniversary, and what's more, he was none the wiser about her night away. He did, however — between apologies — promise to make it up to her when he would come home mid-week.

Cate was relieved to hear from Mike, but angry at his casual attitude about the whole thing. She unpacked her bag, hung up her dress, and when she found the small bottle — the 'Elixir of Love' from Luna — she threw it in the bin.

Chapter 10
Flowers & Promises

On Monday, Cate was back at work. Back to her daily routine filled with dull and mundane tasks. The events of the previous Friday evening seemed like a distant memory — fading away like a soon forgotten dream.

The only exciting thing Cate had in her schedule was a lunch date with Gill, who had called, out of the blue, that morning asking if she was free. Gill claimed she felt awful about the mix-up with Mike and thought that a girlie lunch would help to cheer her up.

Mid-morning came and her concentration was broken when Kourtney, the 'Kardashian-wannabe' receptionist, burst into her office carrying the largest bouquet of flowers Cate had ever seen.

"These were just delivered for you. I thought it was for one of the partners, but no, they're for you. Aren't they beautiful?" squealed Kourtney in delight, as she pushed the bouquet under Cate's nose. "Who are they from?"

"My husband, I'd guess — he forgot our anniversary last week," smiled Cate, as she took the bouquet from a curious Kourtney. "Great, they're already in the water. Thanks, Kourtney."

Cate waited until Kourtney had bounced out of the office before opening the card attached to the top of the bouquet. She was secretly impressed that Mike had gone to town with his apology, as this bunch of flowers must have cost a pretty penny.

She read the message inside the card and gasped.

They were not from Mike, but Warren.

Cate stared at the exquisite flowers.

What? How did he know where I worked? Should I be flattered, or is that just creepy? Is he a stalker? What's he playing at? He knows I'm married.

Cate vaguely remembered having mentioned she worked at a law firm, but she was sure she had not said which one. Staring at the flowers, her head immediately replayed the mini-movie of them kissing in the cab. Her heart beat faster, as she imagined the smell of his aftershave and the taste of his lips on hers.

She tried to push the image from her mind, setting the bouquet on the top of a filing cabinet, out of her line of sight. She made a mental note to give the flowers to Kourtney on her way out to lunch.

***

Cate was already seated in a wooden booth in the pub bistro, mulling over the menu, waiting for Gill. The pub was a firm favourite of Cate's. She loved all the old English pub charm with wooden beams and polished dark wood. In the last year, it had been transformed from a typical drinking pub to a gastro-pub, which now focussed on offering gourmet dining.

Gill breezed in, immaculate as usual, and spotted Cate. They greeted each other with the usual air-kisses and Gill slid into the booth opposite Cate. She took a moment to look around, and Cate could see that it was not quite up to her exacting standards, as the muscle on the right side of her mouth was twitching. A little 'tell' that Cate recognised all too well when Gill was displeased or unimpressed. But today it didn't matter.

"Cate, darling, I am so sorry about Mike. He is such a fool to forget your anniversary, but I guess he has so much going on at the moment at work with this big project, you know. Pete was telling me about it, and it is such an important client. Still, not a good excuse I know," said Gill, as she read through the menu options.

Cate expressed how hurt she had been, and after ordering, she recounted her Valentine 's Day fiasco; choosing to omit the part about dining with a handsome stranger and the kiss. She wasn't quite sure why she didn't tell Gill about Warren, but something made her hold back.

Gill made all the right noises, shaking and nodding her head at the appropriate moments as Cate told her story. Gill seemed to be impressed that Cate had made such an effort with her hair, makeup, and dress for the occasion and agreed that it was inexcusable of Mike not even to have called her and have her worried out of her mind.

"I will make sure that Pete will have a word with him and tell him off for being such an idiot. I will tell him to make sure that Mike does make it up to you. How does an expensive piece of jewellery sound? Would that help to smooth things over?" asked Gill.

Cate half-heartedly nodded, but she was not interested in jewellery or an expensive token to 'smooth things over'. She just wanted to know that her husband cared enough to at least have called and explained his absence.

That was a conversation they would have to have on his return.

***

Cate was strolling back to the office, having seen Gill off in a cab, enjoying the warmth of the winter sun on her face, when she spotted something that made her stop in her tracks and her heart almost leap out of her chest. A few feet in front of her, she saw a man getting into a limo — perhaps it was a trick of her mind, but she could have sworn it was Warren.

The limo drove off, and after taking a few moments to gather her thoughts; she convinced herself that it was her mind playing tricks on her.

Cate returned to the sanctuary of her office, and for once she was quite glad to have an afternoon filled with tedious routine tasks. It was a great way to distract her mind from both Mike and Warren.

***

Wednesday evening, Cate was in the kitchen preparing dinner. Mike had called earlier promising to be home by 8pm, in time to eat together. He had been a little abrupt on the call, but Cate put this down to stress and being a bit distracted as he was still at work. She had heard a woman's voice in the background.

True to his word, Mike walked in just before 8pm. He looked particularly hassled and walked through to the bedroom to drop off his bags, before reappearing in the kitchen with his hands behind his back.

"Look, Cate, I'm sorry about missing our wedding anniversary, but work has been a real drag lately. I was so stressed out I completely forgot. Am I forgiven?" He reached around from behind his back and presented Cate with a bunch of flowers, which were a little battered and looked as if he had bought them as an afterthought at a corner shop, along with a small gift bag.

Cate took the flowers and set them to the side.

"I realise that work has been full on with this big project, but Mike, it is unforgivable that you didn't even call me to let me know. I was worried sick when I didn't hear anything. I thought something awful had happened to you."

Mike looked sheepishly at the floor. Cate was angry, but at the same time, he seemed so wretched that she reached out and pulled him close and hugged him.

"Just don't do it again. Promise me."

"I won't, I promise," whispered Mike as he gave her a full-on kiss on the lips. It was hard and uncomfortable; worlds apart from the kiss she had shared with Warren.

Inside the gift bag was a bottle of perfume, but one that Cate disliked. She didn't say anything.

"Let's eat, I'm starving," said Cate, as she finished off serving up their dinner of chicken wrapped in Parma ham on a bed of fresh fettuccine with a creamy tomato sauce and lashings of parmesan cheese. She knew that it was one of Mike's favourite dishes. As she sat down at the table, Mike poured her out a glass of Italian Chianti, again his favourite.

Conversation at the table was stilted. Cate ended up making up stories about work. It filled the silence, as she knew that Mike was not listening. He seemed miles away.

Cate cleared up, and Mike went to have a shower. By the time the kitchen was tidy, and Cate finished off her wine, Mike was already tucked up in bed. Cate turned off the lights, undressed in the dark and slipped in next to him.

There was strange atmosphere. She could sense it — a strong feeling of foreboding that something between them had shifted. It felt like an invisible wall was forming.

Chapter 11
A Broken Heart

"Hello, is that Cate?" asked a vaguely familiar voice on the other end of the phone.

"Yes, it's me, Cate. Who's that?"

"Oh, sorry for disturbing you, dearie. It's me, Luna — Luna from the knitting club."

"Oh, hi Luna. What's up?"

"Look, there has been a terrible incident. Poor Carlos is in a bad way, and I wondered if you might be able to help. I've phoned the other ladies, and we are each taking turns to visit him."

"Oh my heavens, what's happened?" enquired Cate, as an image of the dashing young man popped into her head.

"Well, it's a bit of long story, but the short of it is his boyfriend dumped him at Valentine's and he's heartbroken, really upset — he even attempted suicide. Anyway, poor soul, he has no family here. We're his family, and I thought, if you didn't mind, perhaps you could spend time with him this coming Saturday, if you're available?"

"That's awful! Yes, I'm free. What can I do?" gasped Cate, as she now felt bad about moping around about her Valentine's disaster when poor Carlos had had a much worse time.

"Oh, I'm so glad. Would you mind bringing him some breakfast? He loves gooey French pastries, I think it would cheer him up; and perhaps you could also persuade him to go out for a walk. It would do him good to get up, dressed and get some fresh air. But the main thing is that he is not on his own. I'd really appreciate it."

"Yes, it really isn't a problem. What's the address?"

Luna relayed an address located in Chelsea, and just before she hung up, she asked whether Cate could stay the night too, if it was not too much to ask. Luna had visited a couple of nights, with Lady and Jo covering the rest of this week, but they all had commitments this coming Saturday night. Luna said she would feel much happier knowing that he was not left on his own.

What could Cate say, but yes?

Mike would be away again, so she would be on her own anyway. It did seem a little weird to be spending a full day and night with a guy she had only met once, but then nothing — or not much — in her life right now really seemed to be normal.

As she tried to refocus on her work, she was a little surprised that she had not realised that Carlos was gay. In some ways, it was a relief, because it would not be an issue stripping off in front of him next time at the naked knitting club.

All the same, the situation was a real shame for Carlos, who seemed like a lovely guy. He must have been hurting to attempt suicide. This was something Cate knew a little about from her past. When she had learnt that they would never have the family she so desired, she had spiralled down into a deep depression, and life down there had been dark, lonely and pretty damn scary.

***

On Saturday morning, Cate was up bright and breezy. She was both nervous and excited about the day ahead with Carlos. She felt uneasy about spending the day with someone in such a delicate emotional state, and a little anxious, because she had never really spent any time in the company of anyone gay. It was not that she had anything against homosexual people, although her staunch Catholic upbringing might have led to a different opinion. Cate's personal opinion about other people's sexuality was – 'it's none of my business'. Over the top forms of affection in public, by any couple, was just not acceptable in her book. There is a time and a place for everything.

A few years ago, she had been on the Tube when one couple got very amorous after a night out on the town, and they were all but having sex there in the busy carriage. Typically, everyone tried to look the other way, but it was getting slightly obscene. Cate had been tempted to get up move to another carriage, too embarrassed to say anything. But just in the nick of time, an elderly lady stood up, walked over to the pair, and slapped them both with her umbrella. Her bravado raised a loud round of applause from onlookers, and it certainly knocked sense into the couple — so much so that they both sat quietly with their heads hung low, while the carriage of commuters glared at them with contempt until they got off.

Cate stopped off at Papa Jean's café to grab breakfast to take to Carlos'. Papa Jean was delighted to see her as always, and after a big hug and an exchange of pleasantries, she was on her way laden with coffees and a bag filled to the brim with freshly baked French pastries. The smell was too enticing, and Cate had nibbled her way through a *pain au raisin* by the time she got off the bus.

She had a rough idea where she needed to go using the map app on her phone. She wove her way through a few streets of four-storey tall white terrace houses. It was undoubtedly an affluent area for sure, given that every other car parked on the road was a Mercedes, Audi, or Range Rover. There were a few people on the move, but not many. Cate wondered who lived in such elegant homes and what they did to afford them, as she surmised each one must cost several million pounds at least, maybe even more.

She rounded the next corner into the street where Carlos' flat was. Counting down the numbers on the houses, she soon arrived at No.11. It was a tall, elegant terrace house, which at some point in the not too distant past had been converted into apartments.

Cate climbed the steps to the front door and looked through names on the panel to find Carlos Santos. She juggled the items in her hands and pushed the buzzer. It took a few moments before there came a muffled response.

"Hi."

"Oh, hi Carlos. It's Cate here. Erm… we met at the knitting club. Luna asked me to call around."

There followed a moment of silence before Carlos replied. "I'm on the third floor. Come on up; the door should be open."

Cate heard the door click, and she pushed it open. She stepped into a massive entrance hallway, complete with a magnificent sweeping staircase. She glanced around, but there didn't appear to be a lift; grumbling, she started to climb the stairs.

By the time she reached the third floor, she honestly felt like her heart was going to burst out of her chest from the exertion. She was unfit, that was for sure. As she tried to catch her breath, she saw that the door at the end of the hallway was open, and assumed that it must be Carlos' place.

If the entrance hall had been impressive, the inside of Carlos' flat rivalled any luxury apartment from the pages of the upmarket house and home magazines. It was decorated with subtle accents in beige and gold, which Gill would have loved.

"Hello," called out Cate, not wishing to intrude.

"I'm in here, in the drawing room. Come on through."

"Honestly, who says 'drawing room' these days," Cate muttered, as she followed the direction of the voice to the room at the end of a short corridor. She pushed open the door and walked in.

There, lying on a *chaise longue* with a beautiful turquoise cashmere throw draped over him; was Carlos.

The room boasted high vaulted ceilings, large windows, an ornate fireplace, and a chandelier fit for any palace. Cate had to bite back her words; indeed, this was a drawing room and would have looked quite at home in a Jane Austen inspired novel, as would Carlos lying morosely on his *chaise longue*.

"I have coffee and French pastries," said Cate, waving the bag for Carlos to see.

"Fine, the kitchen is through there," replied a disinterested Carlos, gesturing towards a door behind him. Cate took her cue.

Behind the door, there was a small and rather unimpressive kitchen area. It was tiny, more like an excuse for a kitchen designed for someone who detested cooking. It was a small galley layout with a window at one end. Cate felt that if she stood in the centre, she could touch all four walls without moving. The apartment might be stunning, but the kitchen, in Cate's opinion, left a lot to be desired.

On a plus note, it didn't take her long to find everything she needed, and soon she had managed to re-heat the coffee and warm the pastries. Before too long, she was on her way back to Carlos carrying a tray.

The delicious aroma was enough to get Carlos sitting up, and without much prompting, he was soon tucking into a gigantic *pain au chocolat*. Cate watched with delight, as she firmly believed in the healing power of food, a trait inherited from her mother and grandmother. Certainly, in Ireland, food was used to cure all sorts of ailments, and her mother stuck firmly to the notion that even if you were vomiting your guts up, you still needed to eat.

Cate, realising she was still wearing her winter coat, took it off and sat down on an expansive chintz sofa. She tucked into a *croissant aux amandes* between sips of her coffee. She was in heaven between the luxurious surroundings, the aroma of the coffee, and the taste of the croissant. If Carlos hadn't spoken, she would have forgotten where she was.

"I think I needed that. It was delicious. Where did you get it from?" asked a perkier Carlos.

Cate explained about Papa Jean's café and shared that it was the best coffee and French pastries in the whole of London, if not the entire United Kingdom. Cate promised to take Carlos to the café, one day, to meet Papa Jean.

Carlos found the TV remote and turned on the TV, a large plasma screen above the fireplace, which had been displaying a piece of art before coming to life. He flicked disinterestedly through a few of the channels, before turning to Cate and asking her if there was something she wanted to watch.

"Well, I'm not fussy, but I don't mind anything about cookery, travel, or the occasional quiz show."

Carlos kept flicking through the endless channels until he stopped at a cookery show, one that Cate did like to watch and had set to record at home. This one, in particular, she loved, as it was a group of amateur cooks who would battle against each other in several cook-off heats to win a chance to open a high-end restaurant of their own. Every time she watched it, she secretly imagined herself going in for the show and winning. She was an excellent cook, and perhaps if life had been different, she would have followed a culinary career.

Cate sat back and allowed herself to be swallowed up by the comfortable sofa, enjoying the show. She had gotten quite comfortable when, out of nowhere, a fluffy white cat jumped up on her knee. Cate let out a high-pitched scream. The cat just looked at her very haughtily and proceeded to make itself comfortable on her lap.

Carlos burst out laughing. "Oh, that's Miss Dior. She's a bit of a diva, but she likes you. She never normally goes to strangers; I hope you don't mind."

Cate looked down at the cat purring contently on her lap and shook her head. She was not a cat lover, but if Miss Dior was happy there, then she was content enough to let her be.

At the end of the program, Carlos announced he was going to have a shower, and invited Cate to make herself at home. He wouldn't be too long.

Cate relaxed back into the sofa. The warmth of the sun streaming in through the windows, the contented purr of the cat and the soothing voice of the TV presenter were relaxing. So much so that Cate closed her eyes and drifted off to sleep. She was exhausted. She hadn't slept very well since the incident with Warren. She put it down to guilt, and it reminded her of something her mother used to say: 'only those without sin get a good night's sleep'. It had been on her mind, and she was torn whether or not to tell Mike the truth; but either he was away on business, or when he was at home, he was too tired to talk.

She awoke to find the TV show had changed and now showed a couple wishing to find a new home overseas in the sun. Miss Dior had wandered off, and Carlos was sitting, clean-shaven and dressed in dark jeans, with a soft dove-grey cashmere crew neck and loafers. He was staring at her.

"Oh, my redheaded sleeping beauty awakes. Did you know that you breathe quite deeply in a rhythm like the purr of a cat? It is quite cute, and your nose twitches like a bunny rabbit."

Cate sat up, stretched, and quickly wiped her mouth with the back of her hand, just in case she had been dribbling as she dozed.

"How long have I been asleep?"

"About an hour. You looked like you needed it."

"Oh, sorry. I've been feeling tired lately, and it was just so comfortable here."

"So, spill the beans. What's going on with you? Why are you so tired that you would fall asleep on my sofa?"

Cate wasn't quite sure how to answer the question. She didn't know if she wanted to tell anyone about Mike and Warren, and she was not sure that it was appropriate to tell Carlos, as he had his own issues.

"Come on, you can tell me. I know when something is up. It is my superpower, and I'm famous in the salon for my trouble radar. Shame it didn't work for me, but hey, it might help to share, as they say. Let me come over there, and you can tell your very own 'Agony Uncle' all about it."

Carlos walked across the room and sat down next to Cate, and as soon as he did so, the floodgates opened. She told him about her big plans for their anniversary; she told him about making a real effort to dress up; she told him about the restaurant, and without hesitation, she even told him all about dining with Warren and the forbidden kiss. Tears were streaming down her face as she explained how distant Mike was and how she hated herself for this terrible secret and the heavy burden of guilt she was carrying around.

Carlos reached out and pulled her into his arms. There was something warm, caring, and protective about being cradled in his arms that made Cate cry like a baby.

"Oh my goodness. I'm so sorry, rabbiting on about my woes when you have your own," sniffled Cate, as she sat back.

Carlos then proceeded to tell Cate about his disastrous Valentine's night. His boyfriend, Sergei, was due to come over and Carlos had planned a romantic candle-lit dinner for two, all ordered in from their favourite restaurant. He had the champagne on ice. He had dressed in a new tailored suit, which made his buns look hot. Sergei had arrived late, but that was normal, and as Carlos was popping open the champers, he delivered the fatal blow.

"You see Sergei is Russian, and a successful businessman. Did you know that being gay is illegal in Russia? So poor Sergei ended up getting married. I still can't believe he is married — with two kids, no less — I often wondered if they were actually his. Anyway, his awful wife Olga put up with his dalliances, as long as it was never found out and she could have whatever she wanted. It was a scenario that worked well for us all. Well, it did until Olga decided that she wanted to move back to Mother Russia and insisted that Sergei needed to give up his deviant ways. Olga is a real tyrant when it comes to getting what she wants. I understand that she is the only child, and heir, of an influential Russian family. I think her father is an oligarch or at least someone extremely wealthy and powerful. She threatened to destroy Sergei, and he couldn't take that risk. So, I'm out on my ear. I'm furious that Sergei didn't fight for us. I loved being with him. You wouldn't believe it, but he was worried that she would take a 'hit' out on me, if we continued to see each other. How scary is that? Crazy — right? Anyway, it was a real shock, and my heart feels like an evil Babushka has crushed it."

Cate could see his pain as he relayed his saga. She also noted his dramatic flair for storytelling, which included an array of facial expressions and hand movements.

"So, what did I do? I drank the champagne, and decided that if I couldn't have Sergei, my life wasn't worth living. I took a handful of painkillers and washed them down with Sergei's gold-leaf vodka. Not my wisest move — I thought it would serve him right to find me gone, and hoped that it would hurt him as much as he had hurt me. Luckily for me it didn't work, and I just woke up with one stinking hangover and a crippling headache. That's when I called Luna. She is a true angel. She is like a mother to me. You know, my family is still in Brazil, and since I came out as gay, they don't want to know me. I disgust them, and my father called me a 'disease'. My mother did try to talk him around, but he is just stuck in his ways. So, I knew I had to go. Move to somewhere I would be accepted and not persecuted."

"Heavens above, Carlos, that is awful. I guess it is still the same in Northern Ireland, my home country — many people do not tolerate homosexuality."

"You know, I met Luna at a yoga and meditation retreat, and she persuaded me to join the knitting group. She looks out for me, and the rest of the girls are like my sisters, particularly Jo. I realise now how incredibly lucky I really am, and now I have a new sister." He grabbed and squeezed Cate's hand, and smiled.

"Enough sad talk — how do you fancy getting a takeaway pizza and watching a movie? I feel like I need some carbs to dull the pain. What do you think? Are you up for some pizza, a side order of garlic bread and chips? Do you like champagne? I think I have a bottle in the fridge."

It sounded like a plan to Cate.

Oh no, I must look a mess. I feel drained and my eyes are stinging. Pizza, champagne, and a movie — sounds perfect, just what I need!

Carlos went off to call the pizzeria, while Cate went in search of a bathroom.

The bathroom, as expected, was decorated like a wellness spa with lots of wood and stone features. There was a large walk-in shower with a huge rainforest showerhead, a jacuzzi bath big enough for two people, and a large sink with a mirror surrounded by light bulbs — the sort you see actors using — as well as a toilet and bidet. Cate could never see the point of a bidet, except once on a holiday in the South of France, she had used it to bathe her hot feet.

Cate did the best she could to make her face less scary. She washed her hands and dried them off. The towel was so fluffy and soft as she dried her hands, she couldn't resist stroking it against her cheek. It had a fresh smell that somehow reminded her of Warren.

On her return, Carlos handed her a glass of champagne, as he lit the faux log fire and closed the blinds on the windows, all by the touch of a button.

"Here's to life, love, and failed romances!"

They clinked glasses.

While they waited for the food delivery, Carlos confided that if he was honest with himself, he had seen his relationship with Sergei coming to an end. Sergei had been spending more time away on business trips, and, more often than not, when he was here in town he would have other commitments. In fact, over the last few months, they had only seen each other a handful of times. Still, it was hard to let go. They had enjoyed almost five wonderful years together.

For one, he would miss the lifestyle that being with Sergei had provided, like access to red carpet events, celebrity parties and, best of all, his own Platinum American Express Card, as well as an account at Harrods and at a few designer shops across London.

Now he would have to see what would happen, and how would he cope living on his meagre pay from the hair salon in Knightsbridge. He earned good tips from his VIP clients, but not enough to buy the high-end designer clothes and all the finer things in life he now accepted as the norm.

Saved by the bell.

Carlos was about to descend into a melancholy spiral again when the door buzzer rang announcing the delivery of their feast.

Cate dashed into the kitchen and set out some plates for their meal, having the distinct feeling that it was not the type of place you ate the pizza from the delivery box. Together they danced around each other in the confines of the kitchen, and soon everything was plated and ready to enjoy.

Carlos settled himself back on his *chaise longue* while Cate perched on the edge of the sofa balancing her full plate and her glass. All in all, it was what she needed right now.

Carlos took control of the remote, and he proposed two movie options — *Sex in the City* or *Confessions of a Shopaholic*. Cate was happy with either choice; she had not seen either of them and was quite glad to have the chance to watch something other than *Star Wars* or the terrible *Hangover* movies, which Mike insisted on watching time and time again.

Carlos opted for *Sex in the City*, his favourite — a choice that had them laughing about the exploits of the group of ladies in New York City. Cate loved it.

By the end of the scrolling credits, Cate had to admit that the movie lifted her mood, along with two large glasses of champagne and her belly full of too much pizza. The two talked about the movie, life, love, and relationships well into the early hours.

"I think it's time for bed," said Carlos as he cleared away the dishes. "Do you mind sleeping in with me? I don't want to be on my own."

"No problem," replied Cate, as she did not wish to be alone either.

Carlos' bedroom had all the luxury of a 5-star hotel. Wooden panels behind the bed created an impressive backdrop, and the bed itself was enormous with the duvet and pillows bedecked in 1000 thread count Egyptian cotton bedding, in soft shades of creams, beiges, and greys.

Cate had been to the bathroom and was in her PJs; she slipped into the bed next to Carlos. The sheets were fresh and crisp, smooth and luxurious to the touch.

Carlos wore a pair of cotton lounge pants but no top. As she made herself comfortable, Carlos rolled over and spooned up to her. Cate could feel his firm chest and body next to her, and the warmth reassuring. There was nothing sexual about their embrace, nothing untoward. It was just two people comforting each other. Sometimes all we need is the touch of another human filled with love and compassion to help us heal.

They both slept deeply and soundly.

***

The following morning, Cate awoke to find Miss Dior curled up where Carlos had been. She got up and went off in search of her friend.

She found him in the kitchen. He had tidied up from the night before, and to Cate's amazement was making pancakes. Music was playing, and Carlos was singing along. He was a completely different person from the forlorn soul who greeted her the previous day.

They sat, ate, and chatted at the small round table in the corner of the drawing room. The sunlight streamed in, and all was well. Cate knew, deep within her heart, that she had a bond with Carlos that would last forever. It was as if her soul had connected with his, making them both whole. It was something she had once shared with Mike, but lately that connection was fading. This connection with Carlos transcended comprehension. It was as if he was the missing part of her.

They were still sitting, laughing, and chatting when the buzzer rang. Carlos disappeared to answer it. Cate had no clue what time of day it was, and she was still in her PJs.

Carlos reappeared, with Luna hot on his heels. She looked at Cate, and there was almost a nod of approval and understanding as if she knew that these two unique souls needed to come together, like a matchmaker seeing that her work was done.

"Good morning, dearies. Glad to see that you are both up and about. Did I miss breakfast?"

"No, there's plenty here," said Carlos, pulling out a chair so that Luna could join them.

Luna sat down and dug out a thermos of her homemade dandelion coffee, and within moments, Miss Dior was happily purring away on her lap. The three chatted away, until Cate finally excused herself to use the bathroom and get dressed.

It was not that she needed to hurry home, but she felt it was time to go and for once enjoy some contemplation time on her own. She felt that Carlos might need some space to chat with Luna, who might be able to work her special magic to help heal his broken heart a little more.

Chapter 12
Homeless

"Come on, get your stuff. You're coming with me, no excuses!" shouted Cate into the door entry intercom. "I know you are there. Come on. I don't want to go on my own, and you know it will do you good."

Silence.

"Get your sorry ass down here right now, Carlos Santos!"

"OK, OK. Stop getting your big girl knickers in a twist. Come on up."

Cate pushed the door open and made her way back up the winding stairs to Carlos' apartment. The door was ajar, so she let herself in and took a seat back in the drawing room. She could hear the shower running in the bathroom.

Miss Dior sauntered in, giving Cate a haughty look. She leapt up on the sofa and curled up next to Cate, but just far enough away to be clear that she was the one permitting Cate to sit there, and not the other way around.

A few minutes later, a freshly showered and dressed Carlos walked in. He quickened his step upon seeing Cate. He bent down and hugged her.

"Right, Miss Bossy Boots, I'm ready. Just need to grab my bag."

As they left the building and headed to the nearest bus stop, Cate was conscious that Carlos was a little distracted. He was quiet, and his shoulders were a little hunched over. He had the look of a man who had lost hope.

Before Cate could start making some gentle probing as to what was wrong, the bus arrived, and Carlos clambered aboard and took a seat. Cate slid into the place next to him.

The bus trundled along. Cate glanced at Carlos. He was staring out through the steamed-up window, as life on the London streets rattled past. He looked lost in his thoughts.

Just as Cate plucked up the courage to ask what was wrong, they pulled up to their stop, and Carlos ushered her off the bus. He linked his arm into hers, and they made their way, silently, through the streets until they were safely ensconced in Luna's living room.

The others were already there and jumped up to greet Carlos with warm, caring hugs and kisses.

Cate stripped, folded her clothes, and settled down on the sofa next to Lady. Alice was seated on the armchair, with Jo on a cushion on the floor with her long, limber legs curled up. Carlos sorted himself out, pulling out the half-knitted sleeve of the sweater he was working on, and joined Jo on the floor. Cate noticed that Jo kept gently touching Carlos' arm as they chatted.

There was an atmosphere in the room. Cate could feel it, and she was sure everyone else was aware of it too. The conversation was a little stilted as if everyone was avoiding talking about the elephant in the room.

Eventually, Luna stood up and left.

Cate assumed it was time for refreshments, but when Luna returned, she was waving a large pink crystal in one hand and in the other she clutched a small set of cymbals. She stood in the centre of the group, closed her eyes, and started to chant. She waved the crystal around and every so often there would be a *ting* from the cymbals.

Cate had never witnessed anything like it. It was, to Cate, peculiar; yet everyone else looked entirely at home with the proceedings.

They all sat quietly and watched. Cate was intrigued.

After a few minutes, Cate was aware that the energy in the room was becoming lighter. It was as if a heavy weight had been lifted. Cate felt inclined to close her eyes, and in her mind's eye, she saw a scene where the mist was clearing to reveal a beautiful garden bathed in a radiant golden light. Cate imagined herself standing in the garden, as a wave of peace descended; she felt a deep-seated sense of calm, and a feeling of being loved unconditionally. There was a sensation of having no worries, no cares, and of being at one with the world.

When Cate finally prised her eyes open — finding it hard to tear herself away from such a magical place — she noticed that the energy in the room had changed. It was now calmer and lighter.

Luna had disappeared into the kitchen, and the remainder of the group were chatting away. Even Carlos looked like a weight had been lifted off his shoulders and hope had been restored.

Luna returned with drinks and cakes. As she served, Carlos finally announced to the group, "I'm going to be homeless! I have until the end of the week to find a new place to live. I love that apartment. What am I going to do? I don't have enough to rent anything decent. It's a nightmare!"

Everyone stared at Carlos following his outburst.

Before Cate put her brain in gear, she blurted out, "Come and stay with me until you find a new place."

Carlos looked at her in disbelief, and after a moment of processing, his mouth broke into a broad smile.

"Oh Cate, you are a true lifesaver. That would be unbelievable. Miss Dior would have to come too, would that be a problem?"

"No, of course she can come too," lied Cate, as her brain flashed up images of Miss Dior sitting in Mike's favourite seat on the sofa; then one of Miss Dior clinging to Mike's face with her claws, and blood trickling down, with Mike screaming and trying to free himself from her grasp.

Oh crap, what have I done? I hope Mike will be OK with it... Well, he will just have to put up with it. It's only for a short time, and anyway, he is hardly ever at home these days. He probably won't even notice.

When Luna cleared away the snacks and drinks, she stopped for a second, smiled down at Cate and mouthed 'thank you'.

As they wound up the evening and knitting projects were put away, Cate knew that she was doing the right thing. She felt that her connection with Carlos was much more than a fleeting acquaintance. It was hard for her to explain — or indeed, it could not be rationalised. The truth was crazy. It was as if there was an invisible cord linking them together, and it felt like they were now, and always would be, inextricably tethered for eternity.

It made no sense in Cate's head. But then again, since the beginning of the year, her life had taken a shift in direction and was making less and less sense. However, at a fundamental level, she felt she had to accept things for what they were and go with the flow. She had a strong feeling that all would become clear in time.

Chapter 13
House Guests

When Cate arrived at Carlos' apartment, the door was already ajar. She shouted hello and wandered on through.

There was no immediate sign of Carlos, although she was greeted in the long hallway by an array of half-packed boxes. It was a bit of a minefield to negotiate, but she managed to work her way through. She found Carlos sitting on the end of his bed, with his head bent over in his hands. She could hear his heart-rending sobs. With every sob, his body shook. Her immediate response was to hold him. Without thinking she reached out and put her arms around him and held him tight.

Finally, the sobbing ceased, and Carlos turned around to face her. His eyes were puffy and bloodshot from crying. Words weren't needed — Cate knew instinctively — she could feel his pain.

She retrieved a tissue from her battered bag and dabbed his face. It was precisely the sort of thing her mother used to do when she was a child — like when she was distraught after a fight with one of her siblings, or when she had not been chosen to be in the school version of *Grease* with the boys' school. It wasn't that she wanted to be Sandy, but she had had her heart set on being one of the Pink Ladies. Instead, it had been a resounding 'no' from the drama teacher. Of course, a pre-requisite had been the ability to sing, and this was one talent she lacked. Everyone in her family had been gifted a great singing voice, but somehow it had skipped over her, with Cate being the only one unable to hold a tune. It had been a pain point for such a long time, and the fiasco with her audition for the show had been a traumatic experience for her. Again, she felt she was not good enough. At least her drama teacher was a kind soul, who upon seeing how hurt she had been had thrown her a lifeline. She offered her a position assisting backstage with wardrobe and makeup. It had been a hard blow, but in the end, being part of the backstage crew had been fun, and looking back, she had enjoyed it.

If someone had said to her a few weeks earlier that she would have been consoling Carlos like a mother with her child, she would have laughed at how ridiculous that sounded. But here she was, and her heart was bleeding for him. She just wanted to make everything OK, to see him smile, and somehow shift him back to his self-assured adorable self. Right now, that seemed like a tall order.

"It's OK, Carlos. Let it all out, and you will feel much better."

Carlos dug his head in her shoulder and blubbered a bit more.

"That's it," she said as she stroked his back. "A good cry helps to clear the head and the heart."

Hearing herself say the words out loud, she nearly laughed as she realised that she sounded just like her Nanny Eileen.

After what seemed like an eternity of hugs and more tears, Carlos finally sat up, straightened his shoulders back and announced, "Come on, sweetie, let's do it."

He jumped up, turned around, and pulled her by the hand up off the bed.

"Time to move on. Bigger and better, bigger and better," he said as he spun Cate round like a couple dancing the tango.

Cate smiled at his positivity as he swung into gear.

In no time at all, the boxes in the hallway were filled and taped shut. Armed with a marker pen, Carlos wrote a short description of the contents on each box. Most of the boxes were to go to a small storage room at the salon, and a couple of smaller boxes, along with two rather large suitcases, were coming to Cate's place.

Looking around her, Cate was glad she had spent the last couple of evenings clearing space for their new lodger. The spare room had become a dumping ground for the previous few years. Many of the items should have been thrown away years ago. Carlos' imminent arrival was the catalyst she needed to finally clear it out.

There were now three big bags of clothes, along with a box of books and unwanted bric-a-brac to go to the local charity shop. She had lugged them down to their small storage area near the underground parking, with the intention of dropping them off in the coming weeks.

A couple of hours later, Carlos was standing in the drawing room, taking in a long last look at his soon-to-be former home. He silently walked through each room, checking that he had not left behind any of his personal belongings or any items that he felt he was owed.

Cate gave him the space he needed to say his farewells in peace. She could only imagine how hard it must be to leave somewhere you called home, and at the same time console the heartache of a lost romance.

She picked up the final box and made her way carefully down the stairs. At the bottom, she added it to the ones Carlos had already brought down.

"Here we go," piped up Carlos, as he struggled down the last few stairs with his heavy suitcases.

Miss Dior was curled up in her travel carrier, and as far as Cate could see, she looked very nonchalant about the whole thing. Cate did not have the heart to mention to Carlos that she hadn't quite managed to tell Mike about their impending arrival, and she certainly was not looking forward to Mike finding out that there was not only one house guest — but two. Mike was a dog person, and frankly despised cats with a vengeance. That was a conversation best left for later.

Carlos was on the phone with the local taxi service, confirming he was ready for pick-up, and reminding them to bring a minivan to accommodate the copious amount of baggage.

They only had to wait a few minutes before the taxi pulled up outside. The driver was a friendly man called Terry, who hailed from the East End. He was more than happy to arrange the seats in the minivan to make more space for the luggage, and, without being asked, assisted Carlos in carrying out his belongings.

Cate took a seat on-board and waited as they loaded up the last few items. She felt a twinge of sadness to witness that all of Carlos' worldly belongings fitted into a few boxes and a couple of suitcases.

Carlos dropped the envelope with the keys into the mailbox, and as he walked away, Cate could see he was fighting the urge to look back. He was trying so hard to be brave. He jumped into the back of the taxi, and they drove off.

A short while later, they stopped off at the salon — a rather ostentatious place with gold lettering swirled across the window, crystal chandeliers, and stone pots filled with large fake orchids. Carlos went in.

He returned a few minutes later accompanied by another a man, whom Cate assumed was the salon owner. He was a 'Karl Lagerfeld' character, with white hair pulled back in a neat ponytail, wearing an immaculate black suit and sunglasses. The only thing missing was the signature fan. Cate noted that he was not a happy-smiley person. From the way his mouth turned down, he looked like he had a bad smell permanently under his nose.

Cate couldn't quite hear the conversation, but she guessed that he was showing Carlos where to leave the boxes.

Terry did not hesitate in jumping out and lending a hand. He was happy to help to offload the majority of boxes, and carried them through to the storeroom.

Soon they were on their way again, this time heading to Cate's home. Of course, it was Friday evening, and the traffic across town moved slowly. Carlos sat looking out the window holding Cate's hand firmly. She had the distinct feeling that he was holding on tight in case he would fall if he let go.

Cate, still at some level, found it incredible that this adorable, funny, and handsome young man had permitted her to step into his life. She felt honoured, like a big sister. At times she worried that Carlos would wake up and see her as a fraud, and their beautiful connection would be severed forever. Why, when something was going well for her, did she always have this sense of foreboding? It was a fear she had known all her life.

***

Eventually, the taxi pulled up to the front entrance to her apartment building.

Terry unloaded the baggage, and much to Carlos' delight, he kindly offered to help them carry it inside.

Carlos paid the fare, giving Terry a generous tip in payment for all his help.

Once inside, the two friends hauled the boxes, suitcases, and the cat travel carrier into the lift. There was only room for one person to squeeze in. Cate made Carlos go with his belongings, and she pushed the lift button for the third floor. As the lift doors closed, she dashed up the stairwell. Huffing and puffing onto the landing, she made it in time to see the lift doors open, and Carlos was starting to decant his possessions.

As Cate unlocked the door to her flat, she flung it open to welcome her new friend into her home.

Carlos walked in, and she could see that he was giving the place the once-over. He didn't say anything, but something about his stance belied that he was relaxed. Cate had learnt to watch and read people over the years, and she had become quite good at it. In her mind, she preferred to have a home that felt welcoming, safe and happy — this was much more important to her than having a perfect show home like Gill's.

Excitedly, she gave Carlos a brief tour of the place. It wasn't a large flat, so it didn't take too long.

When they reached the spare room, Carlos stepped inside. It was decorated simply with magnolia painted walls, a small wardrobe, and a slightly battered antique drawer set, which Cate had purchased with the idea of sanding it down and repainting it to create a fashionable French shabby chic piece, but that had never happened.

When they had moved in twelve years ago, she had planned that one day this room would have been a nursery, and later, when that wasn't going to be the case, she had envisaged a study, decorated with feminine charm. She had even secretly been trawling eBay and the local charity shops for a chandelier. In her mind she could see it clearly; her elegant room, where she would while away the hours reading and writing her memoirs. At one point, she mentioned the idea to Mike, and he just laughed at her. He said they should make it into a mini-gym or a TV room. They had never reached an agreement, and over time, it became a junk room — a place where unwanted items were discarded, and without being aware, where Cate had inadvertently dumped her broken dreams.

Carlos tentatively walked in. He set Miss Dior's travel carrier down on the bed, turned around, and hugged Cate.

"Thank you so much. You are my number one friend, Cate. No one has ever been so generous. You have a heart of gold, and I truly mean that. You have opened your home to me, and we have only known each other for a matter of weeks. You have no idea what this means to me. Thank you, thank you, thank you!"

Cate could see tears start to well up in the corner of Carlos' eyes, but more than that, she could feel his genuine gratitude.

"You're most welcome," she smiled. "OK, here's the en suite. You can hang your stuff here, and I've cleared a few drawers for you. Sort yourself out, and when you're ready, there happens to be a bottle of something sparkly chilling in the fridge. Mike won't be back until tomorrow night. Do you mind if we order in, my treat?"

Carlos smiled, "Let's have a takeaway. No, it's my treat, so whatever you fancy, as long as it's with a glass of something bubbly."

Cate left him to it to sort out his bits and pieces and settle in. It mustn't be easy for him, but at least he was not alone, and, as far as she was concerned, he could stay as long as he liked.

Twenty minutes later, a freshly showered Carlos appeared. He was wearing a casual jogging suit, and carrying a contently purring Miss Dior. He settled down on the sofa next to Cate, who was waiting patiently for him, half watching a quiz show.

Cate disappeared and returned waving two glasses and a bottle of her favourite champagne. It had been chilling in the fridge since the fateful Valentine's night. Tonight was a fitting occasion to open it. She felt a little reticent to share it with Mike, as he was still in her bad books and had not made up for it all. Welcoming Carlos was just the uplifting excuse she needed.

"Oh, my dear sweet Cate, you are spoiling me. Keep this up, and I'll be staying forever," he joked, as he set Miss Dior onto a cushion next to him. "Cheers, my dear heart, to new beginnings."

"Welcome aboard. I hope you will be happy here, and you can stay as long as you'd like. Cheers."

They clinked glasses, and as Cate took a sip she closed her eyes, savouring the effervescent decadence sparkling on her tongue.

Together they sat, sipping the champagne and laughing as they took turns answering the various quiz show questions — mostly incorrect. The evening was already a welcome change for Cate. Over the past few months, with Mike's increasing absence, her routine had evolved into eating a ready-made meal for one while watching some game show or another. It was refreshing to have company.

As Carlos poured out the last of the champers, Cate retrieved a handful of takeaway menus. They worked their way through the various options, and after a little debate, they agreed on Thai. Cate telephoned the restaurant, placed their order, and paid.

While they waited for the delivery, Cate opened another bottle. This time it was a slightly cheeky prosecco, which seemed to meet with Carlos' approval. When the Thai food arrived, they dished up and ate on the sofa in front of the TV.

Carlos took over the TV remote and flicked through the channels.

Most of the shows ended up providing them with ammunition to poke fun at the variety of TV presenters and the numerous show contestants. Carlos was incredibly witty, and by the end of the second bottle, Cate was laughing hysterically. She was tipsy, but mostly she hadn't enjoyed anyone's company so much in such a long time.

By the time she said goodnight to Carlos, she felt tired but at the same time re-energised.

"Night sweetie, sleep well and see you in the morning," smiled Carlos, as he blew her a goodnight kiss and disappeared into the guest room with Miss Dior hot on his heels.

Chapter 14
Mad Mike

The following afternoon, the two friends were sprawled out on the sofa relaxing and watching an old black and white movie when Mike returned home.

He marched in, phone at his ear, and in the throes of a loud conversation. The one-sided exchange was all about the latest rugby results, leaving Cate in no doubt it was one of his rugby player pals. She could also tell by the strong smell of his aftershave that he had probably managed to make it back from his latest business trip in time to play in the regular Sunday morning match.

Cate stood up and walked around to greet him. He gave her a quick hug and peck on the lips, and he continued his conversation en route to their bedroom. Cate had no chance to introduce Carlos, so she followed him.

She wasn't quite sure how to broach the subject, but she had to let him know about Carlos' situation and his desperate need for a temporary place to stay.

She stood at the bedroom door and waited until Mike's call ended. She stepped in and closed the door.

Mike was sitting on the end of the bed, and he looked a little puzzled to see her walk in. Firstly, he thought she was after sex, but the look on her face told him a different story. She looked like she wanted to talk, and this made him feel uneasy.

"Hun, how was your trip? Did you win the rugby this morning?"

Mike looked at her, unsure where this was leading. "Yes, great trip and yes, we won this morning. What's up?"

"Well, we have a house guest for a few days. Erm… maybe a few weeks at most." Cate blurted out Carlos' story, summarising the key points and skirting around the fact that he was gay. She knew Mike well enough to know that this would be an issue, so best not to highlight it.

Mike sat and just stared at her with a look of disbelief mixed with rage. In fact, his face was becoming quite thunderous, and his eyes gleamed with a ferocity that Cate had never witnessed before. She was unsure what to do.

Mike stood up and walked towards her, his dark eyes fixed firmly on hers, until he was eye-to-eye. A bolt of fear shot down her spine, feeling his hot breath on her face.

"What the hell do you think you are doing, inviting someone to stay here without talking it over with me first? This is my home. You have no right!" he yelled.

Cate was shocked as she could feel the force of each word on her face. She was in part terrified and, at the same time, embarrassed that Carlos could hear their altercation.

"Look, it really isn't a big deal. It's only for a short time and you're away so much at the moment, you'll hardly notice he's here. Honestly, it won't be a problem. Hun, please, you're not being reasonable," trying in vain to appease him.

If anything, he looked even more irate.

"I might be away a bit for work at the moment, but I like to come back and relax in my home without having anyone else getting in the way. I want him out of here. I'm going out, and when I come back tonight, he'd better be gone. You sort it out now or else!"

She was left with the weight of the unspoken ultimatum hanging over her.

Grabbing his coat and phone, he shoved her aside and bulled her way through the apartment. The slamming of the front door made her jump.

Cate stood frozen in shock. Her chest heaved, labouring to catch a breath. With each thump of her heart, her anger towards Mike was rising.

What the hell! Where did that come from? I thought he might be a bit upset, but that was unbelievable. I've never seen him like that — ever! Oh no, what will Carlos think? Crap!

She turned to find a concerned Carlos peeking around the door. When she saw him, she couldn't hold back the tears.

"I'm so sorry about that. He's normally really easy going. He'll come around."

This time it was Carlos holding Cate in his arms until she stopped shaking with uncontrollable sobs.

"I don't want to cause you any problems," said Carlos. "Honestly, sweetie, it's not a problem. I'll just book into a hotel."

Cate stared up into Carlos' beautiful deep brown eyes, and she could see his genuine concern for her well-being; this served to bolster her resolve. She was not going to accept Mike's outburst. It was just not acceptable; it was her home too. She had a right to help out a friend, and Mike would have to accept it.

"No, you will not! You will stay here. Mike needs to work on whatever issue he has, and he heads off again tomorrow night for a week, so I don't see what the problem is. You're doing me a favour. I need your company. I need you here, so you are staying for as long as you want to — end of story!"

She hadn't meant to be so assertive towards Carlos, but for the first time, she could feel all the unresolved anger towards Mike wanting to rise to the surface.

Carlos nodded, but at the same time, he was conflicted. On the one hand, he didn't want to cause any problems for Cate, but at the back of his mind, he didn't want to leave her alone either. Even though he had never met Mike before, he had an intense dislike for him after witnessing his angry outburst towards Cate. Carlos' intuition was telling him something was off — Mike was hiding something. In his opinion, there was no need for hostility. It was something he disliked. He had seen enough hatred, bitterness, aggression, and violence against the gay community back in Brazil to last a lifetime.

Carlos led Cate back into the living room and had her sit down on the sofa. He went into the kitchen and returned a few minutes later with a steaming mug of tea. He handed it to Cate, sat down next to her, and encouraged her to take a sip. It was a good strong sweet tea. Cate did as he bid her, and although the sweetness was alien to her palate, after a few sips it was welcoming. Even Miss Dior jumped up next to her and curled up close; it was almost as if she was trying to comfort Cate in her own way. Cate stretched out her hand and stroked the soft fluffy fur, and it felt good.

Later, Carlos persuaded her to have a bath and then sleep it off.

"Tomorrow is a new day. Off to bed sweetie, things will be brighter in the morning, you'll see. He will calm down, and it will all blow over. Off you go. I'll clean up." He hugged her, and gently pushed her in the direction of her bedroom.

*****

Cate had a fitful night. She tossed and turned, worrying about Mike and their argument over Carlos' arrival.

Mike had not returned home.

She tried to call him, but he didn't pick up. She left numerous voice and text messages, but to no avail — just silence.

She rechecked her phone — still no response.

Her mind was awhirl with worries. It was frightening. She had never felt this way before. There was a fear in the depths of her gut, twisting and pulling. Her mind was overflowing with every possible connotation of where he was and what he was doing — many negative and dark images popped into her mind, fuelled by guilt and anger.

In the end, she had to get up and make herself a strong cup of coffee.

She was sitting on a barstool at the kitchen island when Carlos appeared. Even though his hair was ruffled from sleeping, but he still looked gorgeous. He grabbed a mug of coffee and stepped over, and while placing a caring hand gently on her shoulder, asked, "How do you feel this morning, sweetie?"

Cate couldn't quite manage to formulate an answer. The words stuck in her throat, and she could feel the tears well up again.

Her early morning start had afforded Cate a few hours on her own to reflect on her situation. Eventually, she concluded that Mike had probably rocked up to Pete's and had too much to drink. Pete had probably insisted he stay over to sleep it off. Maybe his phone's battery had died, and no one had thought to let her know. It sounded the most likely scenario.

Carlos sat down next to her, and she shared her thoughts. He nodded in agreement that it was the most likely series of events.

She shared with Carlos that she would wait until after 9am and give Gill a call to hopefully sort this mess out.

In the meantime, Cate had a quick shower and dressed. It provided her with a small boost of energy and encouragement. She then sat on the end of her bed and waited. She had a déjà vu feeling. Each time a bad thought popped into her head, she would force it back down, trying to focus on her perceived idea of what had happened; it was exactly like the morning after the fateful Valentine's Night.

At two minutes past nine, she called Gill, knowing that each Sunday morning her ritual started at 7am with yoga and meditation, followed by a massage session. By 9am, she was ready to sit down with a coffee and read the armloads of Sunday newspapers Pete had been dispatched to purchase. If anything, Gill was a creature of habit.

After a couple of rings, Cate heard Gill's voice answer.

"Hi Gill, it's Cate here."

"Oh, good morning Cate, is everything OK?"

"Yes… Well, actually I'm wondering if Mike is there?"

"No, no, he's not here. Why would you think he'd be here?"

"Sorry, we had a little tiff yesterday, and he went off and didn't come home last night. Is Pete there? Perhaps he might have heard from him?"

"I'm sure everything is fine. Pete, Pete, come here — I have Cate on the phone, and she's wondering if you have heard from Mike. He's coming now…" Gill handed her phone over to Pete.

"Hi, Cate, what's up? I hear you've lost Mike. I'm sorry, I haven't spoken to him since last Thursday at work. Look, he always could be a bit of a hothead; perhaps he got drunk with some of his rugby pals and needed to sleep it off. I'm sure he will turn up soon. If I hear anything, I'll let you know."

Cate thanked Pete and hung up. Now she felt even more confused. She didn't know any of Mike's rugby friends, so she had no way of hunting him down.

In the kitchen, Carlos was waiting for her. He saw the look of concern on her face.

"It's my fault. What if Mike has had a bad accident and is lying in a hospital somewhere, or worse still — is dead?" The tears streamed down her face. It felt like a re-run of Valentine's Night.

"The least I can do is feed you, sweetie. How does my famous special omelette sound? It's guaranteed to make you feel better," he winked. "Then I will help you track him down. I promise. And no arguments — I'll pack my stuff and go and check into a hotel."

Carlos cooked her a fluffy omelette and it was delicious. He stood over her and watched until she had eaten the last forkful. Then, true to his word again, he sat down with his phone and started the chore of finding Mike. Carlos felt awful, blaming himself for her predicament.

He started by calling Mike's rugby club, where he spoke with a helpful bar manager who claimed that Mike had not been seen since the match the previous morning. Nothing. He then called the local police station and enquired if there had been any incidents involving a man meeting Mike's description, but to no avail. No news. Next, he rang around the various hospitals in London and nearby.

By early afternoon, he had exhausted all options and drew a total blank. It was as if Mike had disappeared off the face of the earth.

"Look, at least we know that he isn't in hospital," Carlos said, trying to be upbeat under the circumstances.

Cate was looking more and more despondent, and those dark thoughts about Mike's whereabouts were looking more and more plausible.

It was a day spent oscillating between worry and anger. Cate's mind was bombarded with terrifying images of Mike's broken, dead body lying in a back street somewhere; each image more horrific than the last. It was emotionally exhausting.

Carlos and Miss Dior were both doing their best to comfort her. Carlos brewed endless cups of tea and showered her with hugs, while Miss Dior snuggled up on her lap.

***

It had just gone eight in the evening when the door opened, and Mike strode in. He stared at Cate, then glared at Carlos — his face darkened into fury when he spotted Miss Dior curled up on his spot on the sofa. Before Cate could say anything, he launched into a vicious rant blaming her for the whole fiasco.

With the onslaught, Carlos' blood started to boil. No one should speak to another person, let alone their wife, in such a callous manner. Mike's enraged him with his cruel and uncalled for comments. He loathed the man even more — he'd had enough.

"Get out! Get out! Cate does not deserve this — you're a total bastard. She was only helping me out. I'm sorry that her kindness has hit a nerve with you, but enough!" Carlos stood up, face-to-face with Mike in a standoff.

"Oh, your little boyfriend is standing up for you now? How cute. Don't worry — I'm not staying. I'm getting a few of my things and I'm outta here. Cate, you've brought this on yourself."

Cate was shell-shocked; she couldn't speak — no words would come out.

She really couldn't grasp what he was saying. It was as if her world was turning on its head and she was plunging into a nightmare.

Mike quickly packed a bag and left, once again slamming the front door behind him.

Chapter 15
Detective Work

The next few days were a blur. Cate was devastated. She was determined not to give in and call Mike. In her mind, he was the one at fault, and it was up to him to call and seek her forgiveness.

It was tough going, and after a couple of days of firm resolve, she relented. She dialled Mike's number and almost dropped her phone when he answered so quickly.

"Hi."

"Hi."

"Look, this is ridiculous. Come home and let's talk. I'm sure we can sort it all out."

"Is that guy still there?" asked Mike forcibly.

"Yes, he is looking for a new place, and I'm sure he'll find somewhere very soon."

"No, I'm not coming home. I'll call around later to pick up the rest of my things. I've found a place to stay. I don't have time for this, and I must say I'm disappointed in you Cate." He was abrupt, and there was no softening of his mood.

Cate didn't have a chance to say anything else — the line went dead. Mike had hung up on her without as much as a goodbye, leaving her feeling more frustrated and even angrier with him.

***

That evening, Carlos was working late, so she was home alone with Miss Dior for companionship when Mike appeared. He let himself in with his own keys, and without ringing the doorbell. He ignored her and headed straight to the bedroom. She heard the opening and slamming of drawers and doors. She left him to it, unwilling to put herself in the firing line again.

When he reappeared, he was carrying their large holiday suitcase and his golf bag, along with a sports bag. He certainly looked like he planned to be away longer than just a few days.

Cate watched in disbelief, hoping that he would say something so they could start the much-needed conversation. Without even looking at her, he set his keys on the kitchen bench and walked out — the air heavy with unsaid words.

Cate fought every muscle in her body to stop herself from running after him.

Is this the end? Is he not going to talk about whatever is going on here? I can't believe that this is happening to us. Am I a fool? I thought we had a good marriage. I thought we could talk. When did it all go wrong?

A few moments later, the front door opened. Cate thought it was Mike again until she realised he had left his keys. It was Carlos.

"Olá, sweetie, was that Mike I just saw?"

"Yes."

"Who was the girl in the car?"

"What girl?"

"I just saw him putting all his stuff into the boot of a car, and he seemed quite friendly with the driver."

"What do you mean?" asked a curious Cate.

"Well, sweetie, he appeared to be…" Carlos seemed to be uncomfortable in telling her. "She was quite friendly with him… Maybe she has a friendly disposition."

"Spit it out, Carlos," commanded Cate.

"OK, OK, but don't shoot the messenger. She was all over him."

Cate stared at Carlos.

"What? What did she look like?"

He looked troubled.

"Carlos, what did she look like?"

Carlos begrudgingly described the young woman, opting to play down her age and her attractiveness.

"I want to know who she is and what's going on with Mike!" screamed Cate.

"Alright, sweetie, calm down. I have a plan. One thing I've learnt over the years is how to find out information. Actually, I'm quite good at stalking. It's one of the joys of having been in a relationship with a married man for a number of years," said Carlos, as he flopped down onto the sofa beside her.

"I've some time tomorrow afternoon. Give me his office details, and I will do the rest."

"Thank you, Carlos. You're the best."

***

Cate had given Carlos all the details she could about Mike; his regular schedule when he worked in the London office, along with his favourite lunchtime haunts, and a few pubs she knew where he enjoyed a beer or two after work.

It was a long day at the office, and to say that she was distracted was an understatement. She had managed to postpone a few meetings, avoid Chris, and had spent the day at her desk under the pretext of preparing an urgent report. In reality, she sat in a trance most of the day. Her brain was swamped with all the questions forming in her head following the previous night's developments.

At lunchtime, she didn't venture out. Since this had all kicked off, she hadn't felt much like eating. She wanted to know where Carlos was and what he was doing, and even more to the point, to know who the girl was and what she meant to Mike.

She sneaked out of the office earlier than usual, even managing to avoid Kourtney's questioning. She still hadn't heard anything from Carlos. She couldn't face going home — if she could call it that anymore. Instead, she meandered through the city streets deep in thought.

Eventually, she found herself outside a bar in Covent Garden, a part of London she knew quite well, and where she used to hang out. Back, at a time, when she had first moved to the city to be with Mike. Those were the heady days of youth, love, and fun. She felt the overwhelming need for a Long Island Iced Tea, just like in the old days; and right now she just needed to be somewhere with other people and noise to help drown out her thoughts.

The bar was relatively quiet when she entered, but she knew it would be buzzing later in the evening when all the young professionals congregated. She sat down at a stool at the end of the bar, a little out of sight from onlookers, but convenient to get the barman's attention. It seemed like a lifetime ago since she was young and having fun. It had been a time when she had felt the world was her oyster and she was invincible. Back then she and Mike had been young — madly in love — and enjoying what life had to offer.

She had just finished her first Long Island Iced Tea when Carlos finally called.

"Hi, sweetie. Where are you?"

Cate told him where she was, and he promised to come and meet her, and give her a full update.

As she sat, she could feel the dark cloud of depression descending over her. She wanted to scream and shout, but all she could muster was a sigh, a deep soul-draining cry of despair. A crowd of girls on a birthday night out offered some distraction. She watched them laugh and have fun together, with shrieks of joy from the birthday girl at every gift she opened. She was jealous of their carefreeness.

Carlos arrived just in the nick of time to order more cocktails before happy hour ended, and to save Cate from falling into a deep state of self-pity.

"Here you go, sweetie," as he handed a cocktail to Cate.

"Cheers to failed relationships."

"Cheers to that!"

"OK, what did you find out?"

"Right sweetie, do you really want to know what I found out? Are you really sure, because if you want to save your marriage, you may not want to hear this?"

Cate stared into her glass and nodded.

"OK, here goes. I spoke to a few people at his favourite haunts and described the girl. Well, the girl works with Mike; she started in his department as an intern just over a year ago. Her name is Isabelle; she's in her early 20s. Apparently, they seemed to have struck up a friendship pretty quickly after she started. She is often seen with him, just the two of them, out for lunches, for drinks after work, and one of the receptionists said there had been rumours flying around the firm about the two of them since the Christmas party. The receptionist I spoke to said Isabelle is a little flirt and nobody likes her, at least the other women don't. I know you're curious to know where Mike is staying, so I followed him after work. He went to an apartment block in Islington, and it just so happened that it's where Isabelle lives."

Carlos gulped down a tequila shot. "Um… and… there is something else."

He looked Cate straight in the eyes. "Um… She's pregnant."

Cate felt like someone had punched her in the stomach, a hard and painful blow. It took a few seconds for the news to filter into her mind, and when it did, it unleashed chaos.

"What the hell? A baby… A friggin' baby! The lying cheat — it seems, after all, he did want a baby… No way, I can't believe it — he finds a pretty young thing, and I'm replaced just like that!" hollered Cate.

Bystanders turned to look at her, some in annoyance and others in sympathy.

She banged her fists on the bar top as an unholy rage engulfed her. Carlos only managed to grab her hand before she hurled her empty cocktail glass across the bar. He was partially surprised by Cate's reaction to the news. Naturally, he had expected a breakdown — more crying and sobbing — but instead, the news had brought forth a malevolent demon. Right now, Cate's behaviour was scaring him.

Only the cold hard taste of alcohol helped to suppress the rush of emotions. Cate continued to drink cocktail after cocktail.

Carlos felt helpless as he watched Cate down each drink. The more she drank, the more her inhibitions lowered, and the volume rose. He thought that she needed this time to help calm the shock. He only turned his back for a moment to check his phone, and when he turned around, Cate had climbed up onto a bar stool and was in the process of hanging over the bar waving her empty glass in the face of a not-so-amused bartender. She was shouting that she needed a refill, but the bartender knew better. He was brusquely refusing her, and this was making her more forceful in her demands. Carlos rushed over in time to prevent Cate from trying again to hurl the empty cocktail glass — this time aimed at the barman.

"Cate, sweetie, its time to go home. Now give me that glass. Let's get your stuff and get you home to bed," pleaded Carlos, as he tried to retrieve the glass before she injured herself or someone else.

It took a lot of coercion and a ton of promises to pacify Cate enough to collect their belongings and bundle her into a taxi.

The cab driver was not very happy when he saw Cate flopping around in the backseat like a rag doll.

"Hey, she'd better not puke in here, mate. If she does, you're cleaning it up and it'll cost you another £50," ordered the taxi driver, as he chucked over a plastic bag. Carlos had no choice but to agree to the terms. Much to the relief of both men, Cate passed out, and Carlos got her home without any further incidents.

Chapter 16
Crushed

Where am I? Why does my head hurt so much?

Cate's head was thumping; her mouth felt like the Sahara Desert, and her limbs had gone on strike. She lay there willing her muscles to respond, but they point-blank refused.

It took a few minutes to muster up every ounce of energy she had to drag her sorry ass out of bed. She made her way to the bathroom, leaning on every available piece of furniture to support her slow progress.

After a pee, she sat on the toilet waiting for another energy burst to make what seemed like a long trek over to the sink. When she got there, she wished she hadn't looked, as the reflection in the mirror was quite terrifying. Her hair was sticking out in all directions, her face was smudged with mascara, and her eyes were red and bloodshot. She sighed and reached into the cabinet, searching for a packet of headache tablets.

Oh hell — I need this thumping to stop!

She popped two tablets into her mouth and then cupped her hands under the running tap, drinking enough water to force down the pills. The water was cold and refreshing in her mouth. She cupped her hands again and threw a handful of water on her face. The shock of the cold water forced a sharp intake of breath. After a few minutes, she was ready to face brushing her teeth. Her morning routine was a slow, laborious process — with each step, she began to feel a little better.

By the time she pulled on some clothes and brushed and tied her hair back in a ponytail, she was ready for a strong cup of coffee; and to face Carlos.

In the kitchen, Carlos greeted her. He was already up and dressed, waiting for her.

"Ah, *meu amorzinho* has decided to surface. Here, drink this. It's a special Brazilian blend coffee, guaranteed to do the trick," as he handed over her favourite mug filled to the brim.

Cate accepted it and sat herself down on the bar stool, leaning on the counter-top to support her weak body; otherwise, she feared she would fall off.

"What happened last night? My mind is a mess," whispered Cate.

"Well, do you want the full unabridged version or the highlighted summary?" smiled Carlos.

"Just tell me what I need to know."

Carlos stood on the other side of the kitchen island and recounted the events of the previous evening. He retold her about Mike moving in with his pregnant girlfriend while opting to skim over her exploits in the bar. She needed to face the cold hard truth and not be shielded from it.

"Oh no," said Cate dejectedly, and moments later the tears were flowing down her cheeks. "I'd half-thought it was just a bad dream. What am I going to do, Carlos?"

Carlos could see Cate's brain was slowly processing the information, and he gave her a moment before walking around and sitting down next to her.

"Little sister, I'm here for you. You're not alone, and we will both get through this together," and pulled her close.

***

When her tears had finally dried up, Cate sprawled out on the sofa. She went over and over the events of the past few weeks, trying to make sense of it all and to identify the point where it had all gone wrong.

What did I do wrong? Why did he stop loving me? Was it because we didn't have kids? He must have really wanted them. Perhaps I should have made him talk to me about it. I wish I would have known; I would have changed, if only he had said something.

Her mind was filled with guilt, blaming herself for allowing this to happen. When she had said 'I do' on their wedding day, she had meant it and had genuinely believed that they were destined to be together forever. Mike had been her rock, but now he had chosen to move on.

Carlos had put on an upbeat movie for her, but it was only irritating sound competing with the noise in her head. Miss Dior had tried to curl up next to her, but Cate just pushed her away.

What the hell, he's the asshole. He abandoned me. How could he do this to me, throwing away all our years together? The bastard said he didn't want kids, and then he goes and knocks up a slut from his office. What the hell!

She could feel her face burning red with just the thought of him. She was furious.

But why didn't he say he was unhappy? Why didn't he just talk to me, we could have worked things out, but a baby? A friggin' baby!!

Her body lurched as if she had been kicked again in the stomach. She felt sick when an image of Mike standing cradling his newborn popped into her head, smiling proudly with this attractive young blonde hanging on his arm — the epitome of a happy family. She started to cry again.

Carlos heard her and reappeared armed with his cashmere blanket. He gently draped it over her. He perched on the edge of the sofa next to her and stroked her forehead.

Strange how in just a matter of weeks the tables were turned from Cate consoling him to him caring for her instead. Life could be a real nightmare at times.

He stayed until she finally fell, emotionally exhausted, to sleep. His heart was pained to see her so fragile, and he knew her raw wound only too well. When love turns and bites you, it bites hard. Sometimes he wondered if it was worth allowing your heart to be open to love, allowing yourself to be so vulnerable to another human being.

In reality, though, he knew deep down he was a true romantic. He was sure he was hardwired to believe in the power of love — after all, he was Brazilian, so it was in his DNA. For a romantic, love was more than just an emotion; it was something that seeped through to your very core — to your soul. It was all consuming, and when it failed, romantics were torn apart by the pain of love being ripped away. Carlos knew that Cate was the same; perhaps that was why they had connected so quickly, their souls called out to each other. He also knew that was why it hurt all the more when true love broke your heart.

Cate's phone rang. She looked at the number and answered it out of habit.

"Oh, hello darling, Pete has just told me about you and Mike, and I just had to call to see how you are doing? It's such a shock. You must be distraught. What can we do?"

Cate wasn't sure how to answer.

"He's such an idiot. Pete had words with him and told him to get his act together and go back to you. After all, men of a certain age do this sort of thing — it's a symptom of their mid-life crisis. You know, their heads are easily turned by a pretty young thing and all reason goes out the window. Honestly, take him back — forgive and forget, and move on."

Cate could have screamed, as a realisation dawned on her. "You knew, didn't you? Those times I called you looking for Mike, you knew, and you didn't tell me. I thought you were my friend, but no — you both covered up for Mike."

"I'm sorry darling, but we both thought it would blow over — a flash in the pan."

"Did you know she's pregnant?"

"Well, perhaps it's not his. She could just be trying to lure him in — that's what Pete thinks…"

"Damn you, Gill! Just piss off and leave me alone. I don't want your fake sympathy or your phoney friendship. I have real friends who do care about me. I don't want to hear from you ever again!"

Cate hurled the phone across the room.

Carlos was so proud of Cate, he wrapped her up in a tight hug, and she started to cry again.

Chapter 17
Love Stories

Unbeknownst to Cate, Carlos had called Luna a few days before their next knitting club meeting and explained what had happened. He didn't hold back in his storytelling, highlighting how the whole incident had destroyed Cate. As the story unfolded, his contempt for Mike was evident.

Luna listened silently, allowing Carlos to vent his anger; it was an emotion she well knew needed to be released so healing could take place. She felt that Carlos had shifted his rage from Sergei and directed its full force towards Mike. She feared, at some level, if he did not get it out, it would mess with his head, and out of his newfound brotherly love for Cate, he would do something rash. After all, he was Brazilian at heart, and he could be passionate, and all too often, a little headstrong.

"If Cate is not up to joining our next get together, do you think we could come over to you instead? If Mohammad doesn't want to come to the mountain, we will bring the mountain to Mohammad. What do you think?" asked Luna, patiently waiting for a reply.

"Fantastic — that's a great idea," agreed Carlos. He offered to prepare canapés, while Luna said she'd let the other ladies know. Carlos gave Luna the address.

***

That evening, Carlos made his grandmother's famous *Carneiro com batatas*, a family recipe handed down through several generations. When anyone in his family was ill, his grandmother made it. It was a hearty meat and potato stew.

Cate found the first mouthful was hard to force down, as she hadn't eaten in days. The second mouthful was much easier to swallow. She could taste the subtle flavours of the meat and the reassuring texture of the potatoes, and it was good.

"It's my grandmother's recipe. What do you think?" asked Carlos, as he watched her eat.

He felt sure that she was enjoying the dish, as she was undoubtedly tucking in. When she asked for another serving, he almost cried with joy.

Cate demolished the second plateful like a street kid who hadn't eaten a good meal in months.

"Well, how do you feel now?" enquired Carlos, as he cleared away the empty plate.

"Thanks, that was just what I needed. My Nanny Eileen used to say that 'a good meal cures all ills'. You know, it reminded me of her Irish stew — hearty and satisfying."

Carlos nodded in agreement; it was more or less what his dear grandmother used to say, too.

As Carlos turned around to head to the kitchen and clear up, Cate caught his hand. She looked up into his face and meekly said, "Thank you, Carlos. You are truly a godsend — an angel sent to look after me in my hour of need. Thank you."

Carlos felt that a tiny fragment of his heart had been healed, and perhaps over time, it would heal completely.

***

Carlos was buzzing around more than usual, and he had banned her from the kitchen, sending her instead to enjoy a long soak in the bath. Cate was still fragile, and she was happy enough to be ordered around by Carlos. She had neither the mental nor physical energy to object.

She was still in the bath when she heard the doorbell. She was surprised. As far as she knew they were not expecting any callers. Her heart plummeted when she realised it could be Mike. She wasn't ready to confront him, and wondered if she ever would be. The mere thought of him made the tears start to form afresh in her eyes.

She laid back in the bath and submerged herself fully under the water. She used to do this as a child, holding her breath for as long as she could, secretly hoping her legs would turn into a fishtail and she would become the mermaid she believed she was. As a child, she had always had an active imagination. Her family used to joke about it and her endless reading of fairy-tale or fantasy books. But to Cate, they had been her lifeline. She was a sensitive child, and growing up in Northern Ireland had not been easy for her. Bomb scares and shootings were commonplace on the news, and she had constant nightmares. On some level, she had not had a carefree childhood, and Cate had never realised the extent of the trauma it left on her psyche. All she knew for sure was that she could never live back in Northern Ireland. She loved her family and friends, but the complete distrust and downright hatred between neighbours was, in her mind, an absolute waste of time. She believed in the power of love and made every effort to embrace this in the course of her life in London.

She adored the diversity she found in her new home city — the vibrancy and cultural mix that had developed through generations of immigrants setting up home in the capital. She only had an issue with people who were bigoted with a chip on their shoulder. In her personal experience, the people she had met and interacted with had been friendly, helpful and welcoming. Her Nanny Eileen would have loved the rich tapestry of life woven here in this incredible city, as she had never turned anyone away from her door. She embraced everyone as a friend, choosing to see the good in people, and this was something that Cate had inherited from her.

As she emerged from beneath the water, she could hear voices — more than one. Carlos was chatting away in a friendly tone.

He'd better not have invited his friends over here. If he has, I'll be bloody angry with him — he knows how I'm feeling right now. I'm just not ready.

She dried off and threw on her jogging pants and a hoodie.

Cate marched into the living room ready for a showdown, but instead, you could have knocked her over with a feather. There seated on her sofa, baring all, were the naked knitting club ladies.

"We thought that you might like some company," smiled Luna.

"A bit of company to cheer you up, as you've been having a rough time," nodded Lady.

Cate felt terrible that she had harboured angry thoughts towards Carlos. Instead, he had been a gem and brought the girls here to support her. It was heart-warming to see them all.

"Oh, I'd best get my stuff then," said Cate managing a smile.

When she returned, she sat next to Luna. It was quite a weird feeling to be sat on her own sofa naked. In all the years she and Mike had lived there, she had only been nude in the bedroom or the bathroom. Her sex life with Mike had more or less fizzled out since the beginning of the year, and she had given up trying to get him interested. The few times she tried had fallen flat, with Mike claiming to be too tired. On one occasion she had met him on his arrival home, dressed in a sexy French maid outfit. He had only laughed — a response that left her feeling utterly ridiculous — she had never tried again.

Carlos was walking around the gathering, wearing only an apron, offering the ladies the canapés he had prepared earlier. Cate was relieved that he had put on the apron; otherwise, it would have been incredibly awkward trying to avoid his male genitalia — particularly for anyone seated.

Alice was a star. She had genuine concern on her face as she stretched across and patted Cate's hand saying, "Everything will work itself out in the end. I'm a firm believer in that. Just focus on looking after yourself, that's your first priority."

The only one missing was Jo. She had a gig with Charlie, and had sent her best wishes to Cate through Luna.

After a period of uneasy silence, Lady spoke up.

"Look, Cate, it's not easy what's happened and I'm damn sure you will go through the mill, but I just want you to know, in my experience, it is not your fault. I've been married three times, and the first one left me for his secretary. Such a *cliché*, I know. I can laugh about it now, but at the time, I believed I had done something wrong. I was left with two young children and no income. I was fortunate that I was introduced to my second husband, Philip, through a good friend. When his father died, as the only son and heir, he inherited the peerage. He became the 7th Baron Hampton, so that's how I became a Lady. It certainly wasn't love, but he was great with the boys and took care of us. Shame he died so young. He was killed in a car crash when he was forty-one. It wasn't a passionate marriage, but we respected each other. The only benefit was he left me a relatively rich widow. When we were married, I hadn't been aware of how wealthy he had been. In the end, it worked out alright for me, and indeed my boys."

Cate was listening intently, as Lady certainly had a way of telling a tale with her posh accent, drawing the listener into the story.

"What about husband number three?" enquired Alice. She hadn't meant to ask out loud, but she was hooked and wanted to know more.

"Well, my darling Alice, husband number three was a marriage for love, or should I say lust," laughed Lady. "Bertie was a lovable rogue. He was charming and a bit of a thrill seeker with a thirst for fun and adventure. He was a racing driver. I was bowled over. The boys were at university, and I was still young enough to want to find someone special to share my life with. Oh, how I adored him. He made me feel desirable. With him at my side, I felt I could conquer the world. He had such a way about him."

Lady had a dreamy look in her eye. "He was ten years younger than me, and boy did he devour life. Everyone loved him. We travelled; we partied; we made love. It was the best time of my life. Well, that was until he started losing. He started to drink, and then spiralled into an alcohol-fuelled depression. The more he drank, the more he lost, and the more he started to blame everyone around him. It was really quite sad when I think about it now. I did all I could to support him, but he didn't want to know. In the end, the alcohol killed him. It was the best and the worst time of my life, but even now I love him. He was a shining star who burned too bright to last long."

Silence.

Everyone clung to her every word, and Cate had seen Lady's story play out as a movie in her head — a love story with a tragic ending.

"And now, I just enjoy life and make the most of every day. I take love when and where it suits me. I might be a little older, but there is still life in this old girl yet," laughed Lady.

"Oh, Lady, that's such a romantic story," said Alice. "I've been with Ned since we were at school, and yes, we were childhood sweethearts. We've been together since we were thirteen and I couldn't imagine life without him by my side. I pray that I don't ever have to face that. I don't know — we're not the hot passionate types, we're just great friends who became lovers. I've always felt that Ned is the only one for me. I couldn't even think of being 'close' with anyone else. We agreed when we would get married, the number of children we would have, and it just feels like we are on track. I'm happy, and Ned appears to be very happy too. We talk, and we plan together. I guess our monthly date night is when we have time together to ourselves, and we just enjoy each other's company."

"You are so fortunate, Alice," agreed Lady. "Not everyone finds their true love, their soul mate, and you have that."

"Absolutely," interjected Carlos. "I thought Sergei was my one and only, but now I look back and realise he never was. We weren't like that; we were just two people who got something out of being together. I see that now. Next time — if there is a next time — I want to find my soul mate. I want the security and safety with someone who really loves me for who I am, and at the same time gives me enough space to be myself."

"Indeed, love and meeting your soul mate is a very sacred thing," said Luna. "Many people will endure several lifetimes before they find the person who completes them. It is a wondrous and magical thing. Most people don't value love. It's the most precious thing in this world. With love, we can heal ourselves and each other."

The ladies nodded in agreement.

Cate was curious, "What about you, Luna? Have you never wanted to get married?"

"Well, no. A long time ago, I had a romance, but in the end, I realised that I was too selfish to be bothered to run around after someone else. I prefer only to have to focus on keeping myself happy. I guess, even as a girl, when my friends were dreaming of their perfect men and weddings, I was more interested in learning about plants and animals. I never saw myself with children, a little house, and a husband coming home to his dinner on the table. No, that wasn't me at all. I'm really much happier with how things are, and my cats are my babies."

"It's funny, I always saw myself with my husband, a lovely home, and three gorgeous children, but life didn't work out like that," said Cate.

Everyone could feel her sadness.

"Carlos, what are these canapés? They are delicious," asked Lady, as she helped herself to another *amuse-bouche*.

"Just a few bits inspired by a visit to the Ritz Hotel in Paris. Not quite exact, but not bad, even if I do say so myself. You know, I never felt like cooking at my old place, but here in Cate's kitchen, I feel inspired."

Cate helped herself to a couple to try, and they were as delicious as they looked. Carlos was a very talented man indeed.

By the time the evening came to an end, Cate was starting to feel a little better. It was amazing how a handful of special friends could recharge your energy and renew your sense of hope.

She thanked each of her guests as they left. Lady told her to call her anytime as she gave Cate her business card. "I know this is a tough time, and if you need any advice or just someone to rant to, I'm here for you. I've been through it all and understand a little of what you are going through. Call me."

Alice embraced Cate in a motherly hug. No words were necessary.

Finally, Luna was ready to go. She had had a quick chat with Carlos while Cate was saying goodbye to the other ladies.

"Dearie, this is a bump in the road. If you feel up to it, and when you are ready, I would be happy to call around and do a clearing session with you. I have a few things I can do to help you get through this. Let me know, I'm here for you, and if ever you need someone to talk to, I'm a good listener." Luna squeezed Cate's hand. Her hands were warm and soft.

"Well, that was a good night," said Carlos, as he cleared away glasses, cups and empty canapé plates.

"Yes, it was good to see everyone. Thanks for that, Carlos. I'm exhausted, do you mind if I head off to bed?"

"Night, sweetie — sweet dreams." He kissed her gently on the forehead.

Chapter 18
Steps to Separation

That's it — there's no time like the present. He's made his decision — now I need to make a choice too. There's no going back now. I don't think I could forgive him — ever!

A week later, Cate was sitting in the office of the firm's HR Director. Everyone had been very supportive and understanding. Relationship breakups and divorces were becoming more commonplace, and it was in the firm's interest to support their staff and get them back to work as quickly and painlessly as possible — so much so, that their Family Law Department offered free legal support for employees. It had been one perk Cate had never envisioned herself having to use. With the news of Mike's impending arrival, though, there was absolutely no possibility of reconciliation, as she had at first secretly hoped. Instead, here she was, admitting her marriage failure to the world.

"There is no shame in this, really. I want you to know that. It is unbelievable how many marriages end up in divorce these days. From what you have told me, it's not your fault. Anyway, if you're up to it there are a couple of forms to complete, and then I'll call through to the Family Law Department and try and get you an appointment," said Linda. "If you need some time off, it is not a problem, although, maybe it's better to keep busy. If you have any concerns, you know my door is always open".

Linda was a woman in her late fifties, who was unmarried and had been with the firm since its founding, some thirty-three years earlier. She was the mother hen of the firm and the only one who could talk around the headstrong senior partner. She was the anchor in any storm, as Linda never flapped; she was the epitome of calm. She took everything in her stride, and although she could be sharp with the younger members of staff, she was the one everyone felt they could turn to in their hour of need. Cate had forged a good relationship with her, and right now, she felt comforted to know that Linda was on her side.

An hour later, Cate was seated opposite Irina Castles. Irina's office was scrupulously tidy. Her bookshelf, Cate noted, was clearly labelled and ordered with sections of books that appeared to be flagged with small coloured labels. Everything about the office, from the desk to the few discerning art prints on the wall, screamed efficiency.

Irina was, without a doubt, the best lawyer in the small family run company. She was famed as one of the best family lawyers in London, and how she hadn't been snapped up by one of the major legal firms was a mystery. Her caseload was renown, and the ease with which she recalled facts was impressive. She could readily answer a client call without the need to scramble for the respective file. She was every bit impressive up-close with her immaculately tailored suit, short dark wavy hair, and glasses. Even though she was petite in stature, she terrified most people in the firm, including some of the senior partners.

While Cate sat and waited, Irina was reading through one of the HR forms that she had completed with Linda only a matter of minutes earlier, and in which she had outlined the circumstances of the breakdown in her marriage.

Cate only knew Irina in passing, and her well-earned reputation preceded her. She was known for her acute sense of detail and her determination to do the utmost for her clients. Her list of prestigious clients, including a few celebrities, was well known. Cate was surprised to find out that Irina was going to take on her case, and sitting in her office was quite intimidating.

Irina looked up over the top of her half-rimmed glasses, perched on the end of her long slim nose like a school principal, and peered at Cate. For a few seconds, she stared long and hard at Cate, as if she was trying to divine whether she was worthy of her services or not.

There was a slight nod of the head, which Cate took to mean she had passed muster, and so the interview began.

"Right, Cate. May I call you Cate?"

Cate nodded, and Irina continued, "I've read through your details, and I firmly believe you have a strong and clear-cut case. That said, I want you to know that legally, marriages such as yours are a 50/50 split. However, there have been several cases where there may be reasons to push for damages." She stared at Cate for a fraction of a second. "May I enquire as to why you never had any children?"

Cate was quite taken aback by the question and felt like telling her to keep her nose out of it. Since the question had been posed, though, she felt inclined to answer with the truth — the whole painful truth.

Cate blurted out her story of being diagnosed with premature menopause. While she talked, she realised that tears were running down her cheeks. She recounted how her dreams of motherhood were shattered and of Mike's silence on the subject, including closing the door firmly on pursuing other options such as surrogacy and adoption.

Irina, ever the professional, indicated a box of tissues which had been strategically placed on the corner of her desk for such occasions. Never once did she avert her steely blue eyes from Cate.

Cate took several tissues and wiped her tear stained cheeks and blew her nose. She waited in silence for a verdict, and it was apparent Irina was busy computing all the information in her brain. She was sifting through every permutation to find the best solution. Cate had heard tales that Irina's IQ was phenomenally impressive and her recall of legal articles, texts, and cases was legendary. At the annual Summer Pub Quiz, all the other departments hoped that Irina was not available, as no one could match her level of general knowledge, history, geography and even sports. Her only Achilles' heel was the entertainment category. She admitted that she never watched TV, and in her opinion, movies were only for children.

"That's great. I think we can leverage that. Now, I will pass you over to Cliff, who will go through the paperwork with you. He will act as your contact person. When we are ready to proceed to the next step, we can have a quick chat."

Irina gave Cate a nod of dismissal and went back to reading another file on her desk.

Cliff was already waiting for Cate when she exited the office. She had no idea how he knew he was to meet her, as Irina has not used the telephone or her computer. Knowing Irina, she had a slick system for processing her clients — perhaps a secret button under her desk. Cate was dying to ask Cliff, but the question vanished as she followed him into a meeting room.

Cliff, a friendly young man in his mid-twenties, with an eager to please smile, had been with Irina for only two years. Cate and Cliff's paths had crossed during his first week. She had found him outside the building in floods of tears, as Irina's demanding personality was just too much for the sensitive young man. After Cate had consoled him and persuaded him to stick with it, he had found his groove and earned his place in her elite team. Although Irina was not someone to openly praise her staff, Cate had overheard her telling Linda how much she valued each team member and how she was thrilled to have such a dedicated and accomplished set of individuals on her team. She was also incredibly generous to each one on their birthdays and at Christmas. You really did have to be the *crème de la crème* to make it, and Cliff had earned his stripes.

"Oh Cate, I am so sorry to hear of your marital issues, but I want you to know that you are in the best hands. Irina might come across as a tyrant, but she's now your tyrant, and that is a good thing. She will do the best for you, and I must admit, we all will. We want to make this as painless as possible for you. Divorce can be a horrible experience. Would you like a refreshment before we proceed?"

Cate shook her head.

She had to say she was very impressed as she sat opposite Cliff in one of the newly refurbished client meeting rooms. Irina had insisted that she wanted a more professional, yet informal, setting for her wealthy clients. She had argued that, as she brought the most money into the firm by a long way, she had the right to make sure her clients had the best possible experience. Given the often high-profile status of her clients, her request had been unchallenged. In fact, she could pretty much have asked for the moon, and the firm would have agreed to keep her happy.

Cliff started to read out the questions on the collection of forms placed on the table in front of him. It was quite daunting, but Cliff's friendly demeanour made the whole experience more bearable.

Cate could answer some of the questions quickly and others, particularly regarding their financial circumstances, she could not. It highlighted to her that she had trusted Mike implicitly. She had left everything with him and had never bothered to ask about the details. As long as she had money in her account and the bills were paid, she had been happy in her ignorance. Now she realised her naivety and stupidity in taking this stance, but it was too late, and there was a lot of information she was going to have to find. It would take a while to do the research necessary to obtain the information to answer many of the questions that had been asked. She only hoped that somewhere at home, amongst the remainder of Mike's belongings, she would find the answers.

***

Luckily for Cate, Linda had kindly given her the afternoon off, almost pushing her out the door, telling her to go home — have a nice bath and come back in when she was ready.

Instead of heading home, Cate opted to take a leisurely walk down by the Thames. She couldn't face going back to an empty apartment. She needed to be lost in the melee of tourists. It was a glorious day, the sun was shining, and its warmth felt good.

After aimlessly walking for a while, she found a bench with a vista overlooking the river. She sat down and watched the comings and goings — barges, water taxis, pleasure cruisers and a police boat. As she watched, she took in a different pace of life, which was indifferent to the world on the London streets and indifferent to her personal challenges.

Who are these people? What do they do and where are they going? Do they see me? Do they feel my pain?

The view provided a distraction for a few fleeting moments before the questions started again in her head. The questions were replaced with images of Mike's smiling face when he had held her in a loving embrace, then the vicious snarl when he screamed at her on the day he walked out.

What went wrong? Why had I not realised what was happening? Why hadn't I seen the signs? They always say the wife is last to know, but surely I would have noticed? How am I going to survive without him? He was my rock. What did I do wrong?

The endless questions and self-blame whirled around inside her head until her head ached and the tears were stinging her eyes.

I'm not going to play sweet little Cate… It's time for change — time for me to change!

A switch had been flicked and her resolve boosted. Mike had been the one at fault, not her, and he was going to pay for it. She would be fair, but why should she lose out? After all, she had given him the best years of her life, and she had contributed towards all they had accumulated over their years together.

Chapter 19
Surprises

Carlos was working at a high-class fashion event in Knightsbridge, leaving Cate to trek across London on her own to Luna's. He loved doing these events, working with professional models and allowing his creative imagination to run wild. Cate was thrilled to see him so enthusiastic about it, and it was not so bad for her, either, as it gave her a little time to herself. Now that the lighter evenings were here, she was quite enjoying her journey through a different part of town.

When she got to Luna's, she just let herself in and wandered through to the living room. As usual, Lady was the first one there, and Luna was bustling around in the kitchen. Cate said her hellos and quickly undressed, claiming the armchair as her spot for the evening.

The others filed in, and before long the room was alive with the clacking of needles and conversations. In Carlos' absence, Jo sat down on the floor next to Cate. It was the first time they had talked, as Cate admired Jo's creative flair. Her current project was a beautiful soft mohair slash neck sweater in earthy hues intermingled with bright pink.

"Sorry about your trouble with your man. Carlos told me. He said that he was a real piece of work and that you're better off without him."

Cate nodded, "Well it's definitely not easy. It's hard to have shared so much of your life with someone, and then find out they cheated on you. The worst thing was not realising it. I didn't have a clue. I always thought those other wives who had cheating husbands must have known, but really, I didn't. Strange isn't it?"

"Look, I don't trust men period — my father let us down, my uncle abused me. Honestly, sister, I find it easier to trust women. I see what the men are like at the club; they leer, and they lie. It is all lust — I see them for what they are, but, hey, I feel I'm the one now using them, and it pays the rent."

"Carlos told me you have a law degree from Harvard, is that right?"

"Yes, landed a scholarship. You know, let the poor little black girl go to college so the rich white folk can all pat themselves on the back. It was a great learning experience but damn hard. It wasn't that the academic work was tough, that part was pretty easy for me. It was hard being one of the few coloured girls on the campus. That was the real challenge. I don't know if you know much about American colleges, but a number of the students get into the prestigious universities because of their parents' wealth and status. These kids are the worst. They feel that they are owed everything and can do anything they want and get away with it. You know what? The sad reality was, at least when I was there, they did. Many were racist, born and bred, and a few of the guys were sexist in the extreme.

They believed they had the right to take what they wanted without question."

Cate could feel the strength of passion about this topic in Jo's voice.

"I know of girls who were raped, but they were too afraid to speak up. It was so cruel and just not right. The verbal and unseen abuse was unbelievable, that's why I kept my head down, got my degree and at the first chance made my way here. London was a breath of fresh air. An inter-racial haven for the likes of me and I have the freedom to do what I want to do, and right now that is dancing with Charlie in the club. Who knows, if I meet the right girl, I might just decide to settle down and get a real job."

Cate had a feeling that there was more to the story, a personal experience that Jo was not yet willing to share with her. She could see the pain and vulnerability in her eyes, and Cate knew not to delve further.

A moment later, her expression changed and Jo flashed her dazzling smile.

Cate returned her attention to her knitting and had only managed to knit a few stitches when Alice's voice broke her concentration.

"Excuse me, sorry, ladies... I have some news, and I want to share it with you all."

Everyone stopped, and all eyes turned towards Alice.

Alice's face flushed a dark red; she coughed and continued, "I wanted you all to be first to know, well, the second as I told Ned first... I'm pregnant."

"Oh, I did wonder," said Luna clapping her hands. "When's it due?"

"November, all being well," said Alice, rubbing her belly. "We had a little scare, and I didn't want to say anything until we got the all-clear. "

Everyone took turns to congratulate the radiant mum-to-be, all except Cate. Every time someone made a baby announcement, it was like having a fist punched in her belly. Over the years, she had learned to steer a wide berth around family and friends having babies. Each time, it was a stark reminder of her barrenness, and it hurt as if someone was squeezing her heart — the pain was unbearable.

In the excitement, no one appeared to have noticed that Cate was quiet. She could hear snippets of conversations: "Did they want a boy or girl? What did the other children think? How would she cope with another one?"

Luna glanced across and saw Cate's face. She recognised at once the pain and suffering, and instinctively knew she had to step in and do something to ease her pain.

"Would you like to help me prepare some supper in the kitchen, Cate?"

"Oh, OK."

As they stepped into the safety of the kitchen, Luna turned around to face Cate. She held Cate's hands in her own and with a warm, caring smile, said, "I feel your pain and your sorrow. You are having a challenging time at the moment, that's for sure. Keep strong. Now, why don't I come over to visit you and bring along a few things to boost your energy? I have a feeling that your tank is running low with all that is going on at the moment."

Cate nodded, unsure of what to say. All she knew was that Luna's hands were warm and protective, and right now that was just what she needed to survive the evening.

"Are you free Wednesday night, about 7pm?"

"Yes, I'm free every night," replied Cate forlornly.

"That's a date. I'll bring my bag of tricks, and we'll do a clearing session. That will help get you back on track," comforted Luna, as she gently laid her hands on Cate's shoulders.

Together in silence, they prepared the tea and nibbles. By the time Cate walked back into the living room with supper, she felt her energy had been revived just enough to get through the evening.

"Here you go, Alice. You can have extra as you're eating for two. Congratulations," whispered Cate, as she presented the tray.

For the rest of the evening, the topic of conversation focussed on children and babies, and to Cate's surprise, she found that as the evening progressed, her pain and discomfort faded away.

The friends knitted, chatted, and laughed until it was time to go.

As they parted company, Luna made another announcement. "Next month we have a new starter. Her name is Xena; she's a student. I know I don't have to ask you all to make her feel welcome. Until next time, Namaste everyone!"

***

"Hello, Cate, it's Kourtney here. I have a gentleman here in reception, and he is asking for you. He won't give his name, but I think he's American."

"Oh, OK. I'll be right there."

No, surely not. It can't be? Oh, crap, I wished I'd worn my blue suit. Calm down; it might not be him. Oh heavens, what if it is?

Cate blushed, as she ran her fingers to tame her hair, and hurriedly rummaged in her handbag to find a mirror to do a quick check, and apply some lipstick. Since Carlos came into her life, he had encouraged her to make more of an effort with her appearance, including wearing a little makeup.

She pushed open the door into the reception area, and there was Warren, standing with his back to her reading a brochure. As he turned around to face her, she thought her heart would bounce right out of her chest onto the floor.

"Ah, there she is. May I have the pleasure of your company for a bite of lunch? I just happened to be in the neighbourhood and had some time on my hands, and I thought I would love to spend it with you."

Cate could see Kourtney straining to overhear.

"Let me grab my bag. Kourtney, can you put my calls to voicemail until I get back? Thanks."

A few minutes later they were strolling along the pavement. It was awkward, the tension between them like two magnets desperately trying to pull together.

"So, what do you normally do for lunch around here?"

"Well, when the weather is good, I usually grab a sandwich and sit in a little park near here. I love to sit and watch the world go by."

"Sounds great, lead the way."

Cate bought sandwiches and drinks at her usual mobile sandwich van, and together they walked towards the park. It was a day when summer was starting to burst through, still a little chilly with the sun streaming down. They sat down on a park bench, and Cate divided the picnic.

"Well, I can't remember the last time I did anything like this." Warren took a bite of his sandwich and looked around.

"I find it helps me think clearly and allows my stresses to disappear — a least for an hour."

"I like it. I can see the appeal. Perhaps I need to do this more often. What do you think?"

"Yes, why not. Erm… Warren, I have a question. I hope you don't mind me asking — but how did you know where I worked?"

"Ah, the joys of having a team of experts on hand. They can find out anything," he laughed.

Cate relaxed and enjoyed chatting away with him. They watched and talked about the goings-on around them. Cate loved the way Warren tilted his head back and opened his mouth when he laughed.

The magic was broken when his phone buzzed. He checked it and said he had a meeting across town.

They walked back to Cate's office in silence, and as he said farewell, he kissed her.

She felt her legs go weak at his touch, and she longed for more.

Chapter 20
Clearing & Cleansing

Wednesday night arrived and as promised, Luna was there at Cate's door with her carpetbag in hand at just gone 7pm. For a fleeting moment, Cate thought of Mary Poppins; only the umbrella was missing.

"Come on in," welcomed Cate, as she helped Luna with her heavy bag. Cate led Luna into the living room, where Luna plonked herself down on the sofa. Cate set her handbag on the floor next to her, but couldn't resist having a quick peek inside. She caught a glimpse of bottles, bags of what looked like dried herbs, feathers, and the spine of a battered old book. She tried a little harder to read the title, but couldn't — immediately she felt guilty for snooping into Luna's personal belongings.

"Sorry, would you like a drink?"

"Yes, that would be lovely, dearie. Here, I brought my own teabag. You know, I find that I need some fuel when I do clearing work as it burns up so much of my energy. You don't happen to have any cake do you?" asked Luna.

Ordinarily, there would have been a few sweet treats stashed away. However, since Carlos moved in, he had been quite strict with her. He was fastidious about how he looked and told her off for having anything naughty indoors to tempt him. In fact, right now, the cupboards were practically empty — mostly because she couldn't be bothered to go shopping, and partly, as she didn't feel like eating much these days.

"Oh, we don't have any cake or any treats. I think there might be an apple strudel and some ice cream in the freezer. Would that do?"

Luna's face said it all with the mere mention of apple strudel and ice cream.

Cate went off to sort out dessert, while Luna fussed around setting up for the clearing ritual.

From the safety of the kitchen, Cate watched as Luna cleared space on the coffee table and set up a pattern of coloured stones and crystals. She then produced a small stone bowl, which she proceeded to fill with dried herbs. Next, Luna set up some green candles, and then she set out a bundle of feathers tied together with a ribbon. What intrigued Cate the most was what she could only describe as a sizeable rolled-up 'joint'. Immediately, Cate had visions of sitting with Luna, taking puffs of this supersized 'joint' as they passed it back and forth, just as she and Mike had done on the odd occasion as students.

By the time the strudel was ready, and Cate was scraping out the last of the ice cream into the dish, she could feel her nose start to twitch. There was a strange smell wafting through from the living room. The smell was emanating from the bowl of dried herbs that Luna had positioned in the centre of the crystals. The candles on the outside of the formation were flickering.

"Do you need me to turn off the lights or do anything special?" asked Cate, as she handed Luna the dish and a spoon.

"Well, if we turn off the main lights and leave a few lamps on, that would make for a lovely warm glow. It's not necessary, just a feeling I quite like, if that's alright with you, dearie?"

Cate dimmed the lights, and with the glow from the candles, it looked quite cosy. Her nose was also adjusting to the aroma and she could faintly detect a lavender note in the mix.

Luna wolfed down the dessert and patted her belly as she released a sigh of satisfaction.

"Now, let's get to work."

"Just one quick question before you start: what's that for?" asked Cate, pointing at the roll-up.

"Oh, that? That's a smudge stick — lots of special dried herbs rolled up together. I will light it and use it to clear away the bad energy around your home."

"Oh, thank goodness! I thought I'd have to smoke it," laughed Cate. Luna looked at her a little perplexed.

"Anyway, let's get started."

Cate watched with interest as Luna picked up the bunch of feathers and said an incantation, as she wafted the feathers back and forth over the smoking bowl. This continued for several minutes. As Luna worked away, Cate felt a shiver run down her spine. Perhaps it was just her imagination at work, but there was a feeling of calmness passing over her in waves.

Oh, that's weird — am I being drugged? Boy, this feels good. I don't want it to stop. I feel so light — as light as a feather floating on the breeze.

Cate stared into the flickering flame, and she could see images of the traumas of the past few weeks with Mike. Visions danced silently in the flames, each one disappearing as another formed. She was transfixed, watching each one unfold telling her story. She felt a strange feeling of disconnect with the events. It was as if she was watching a movie being played out that had nothing to do with her; she was merely a voyeur. Strange flashbacks of her life appeared, working back in her timeline, things she had long forgotten emerged and then faded away.

She was not sure how long she had been sitting in this trance-like state. Her awareness gradually returned to the room, back to the present. She witnessed Luna lighting the smudge stick and wandering around the room waving it and singing some mystical chant.

Luna worked her way clockwise around the room, and into each corner. She then motioned for Cate to join her. They went around all the rooms in the flat together, including Carlos' bedroom. Cate felt a little uncomfortable about going into Carlos' room as he wasn't there, and she felt as though they were invading his privacy. She didn't say anything; deep down she had a feeling that his space also needed this clearing as much as hers did.

All in all, Luna had been working away for an hour or so, and they were wrapping up the ritual when Carlos arrived in.

"*Ai meu Deus*! What's that smell? Own up, what have you two been smoking here?" he said with a playful grin, pretending to hold his nose.

Luna replied, again oblivious to Carlos' innuendo.

"We've just done a clearing and cleansing ritual to remove all the negative energy and create space for positive energy to flow in. By the way, we did your room too. Hope you don't mind, dearie."

Carlos playfully rolled his eyes at Cate.

"As long as you haven't set fire to the place, then that's OK. I think I need some positive energy to flow my way, although I have a feeling since meeting you Cate, it is. Anyone want a glass of wine?"

Luna opted for another tea, again retrieving her special homemade teabag from the recesses of her bag, and dangling it in the mug of hot water Carlos handed her. Cate reached out and grabbed the chilled glass of prosecco being offered.

"May good energy flow our way always. Cheers, my gorgeous ladies," toasted Carlos. "You don't happen to have your cards with you, do you, Luna?"

"Cards?" asked Cate, again her curiosity piqued.

"Yes, I always carry a set with me. They're my angel cards, similar to tarot cards, but I feel calling upon our angel guides is more positive. Would you like a reading?"

Carlos nodded eagerly.

"OK, let's do it. I'll clear some space here."

She produced the pack and then proceeded to bless them with one of the crystals, explaining that she needed to clear any old energy and connect with her guides and angels to channel their message. She turned to face Carlos.

"Focus on your question and call upon your guides and angels for their guidance. I don't need to know the question. You just need to be clear about what you'd like to know," she instructed Carlos.

Carlos closed his eyes and Cate could see his lips moving as he did as he was told.

"Next you need to choose ten cards. As I work through them, you can point at the cards that call to you," said Luna, as she shuffled the pack.

Slowly she worked through the cards, and as she did so, Carlos chose his ten. As each card was selected, Luna set it face down in a specific formation, which she explained was known as the Celtic Cross.

When the ten cards were laid out, she started with turning over the first card. Slowly she worked her way through and explained each card's meaning and its relevance to Carlos' situation.

Cate found herself both intrigued and a little frightened. As a child, a few older girls at school had been caught playing with a Ouija board, and all hell had broken loose. Cate had failed to see how pretending to push a glass around a few letters on a board was dangerous, but there had been an almighty uproar over it. She had even been taken aside by her mother and made to promise that she would never play with such things. Now, here she was. She felt she was breaking that promise, but at the same time, it didn't feel wrong with Luna. Everything about Luna's vibe was caring, motherly, and deeply invested in other people's well-being. To Cate, Luna was like a light shining the way through the darkness. She couldn't quite explain what it was, but that was how she felt.

By the end of the reading, Luna summarised that the way ahead for Carlos was looking positively rosy and that his soul mate was on his way. She also mentioned that

Carlos would be moving overseas, where his dreams would come to fruition.

"Wow, if that all happens — how wonderful — but I really don't see how it can come true."

"Trust that the Divine Source has a plan for you. All you need to do is believe and watch out for the opportunities when they are presented to you. I have a strong feeling you won't have to wait long now," smiled Luna, as she gathered up the cards. "What about you, Cate? Would you like a reading?"

"Yes, she does," piped up Carlos, as he reached out and grabbed Cate's hand.

Luna repeated the blessing and clearing of the cards, and Cate focused on forming a question in her mind.

Will my heart ever heal? Will I find love and happiness again?

Cate chose ten cards, and Luna carefully laid them out, again turning them over one by one, explaining the meanings.

Cate was drawn to the cards she had chosen. To her surprise, Luna also explained that Cate would indeed marry again, and she would also find her soul mate and happiness in a foreign land.

Cate was a little sceptical, as it sounded too similar to Carlos' reading, but only time would tell.

"Luna, it's getting late. Do you want to crash out here for the night?" asked Cate.

"Oh dearie, no, thank you. I need to get home to my little ones. They like mommy to be there; otherwise, they play up and can make quite a mess, but that's kind of you. Cate, you don't know what a wonderful kind heart you have. Help me pack up, and I'll be on my way."

Together they gathered up her belongings and waved Luna into the night.

"Well, what do you think?" asked Carlos, as he poured out another glass of wine.

"Certainly was an interesting evening for sure. I think we need to open a few windows to let that smell out. I've never done anything like that before. It's frowned upon where I grew up. I can still hear our priest call it 'the devil's work', but I don't feel that with Luna. She makes me feel safe in a strange way. I can't explain it, but it's the feeling when I'm around her. Do you know what I mean?"

"Yes, Luna is a special kind of soul. You do know that she is a Wiccan, a white witch? She only practises magic to help people. I have grown to love Luna as a mother. She is the one who has and will always be there for me without judgement, and that is very special indeed. Now I have a mother and a new sister," smiled Carlos. "I'm excited to know who my soul mate will be and where I will be moving to. What about you?"

"I don't know. It's way too hard to think about meeting anyone else with the way I feel right now. As for the hint of foreign lands, the way I feel about it, I'm already in a foreign land. I guess only time will tell. By the way, don't you have a birthday coming up?"

"Yes, but I'm not looking forward to it. I'll be turning thirty-three, and I'm single. Not sure I feel like celebrating."

"You might not, but I think we need an excuse to get some friends together, get dressed up and go out on the town. How about dinner in Covent Garden and then maybe hit a club? It's been forever since I danced the night away. Come on! I can't believe I'm saying this, but it will be fun

— something we both could do with. You never know, 'Mr Right' might be waiting out there for us."

"OK, OK, but I get to choose the restaurant and the club, and you let me give you a makeover. Tell you what, if I meet 'Mr Right,' I'll buy a bottle of champers for you and me to celebrate."

"Agreed. I'm off to bed. I need my beauty sleep; I've got work in the morning."

Chapter 21
Birthday Celebrations

All the ladies from the knitting club were thrilled to be invited to celebrate with Carlos, and it was agreed that this outing would replace their regular monthly meeting. The only one who declined was Alice, who was finding it difficult to cope with the soaring temperatures, claiming pregnancy and hot weather did not bode well for her swollen ankles. She wished them all lots of fun and made them promise to send her tons of photos.

In the end, Carlos chose a trendy restaurant where he had been before with Jo. It was in Soho, near where she worked. He felt that it would be perfect: not too fancy, not too pricey, and more importantly, in his book, they did fabulous cocktails. Once booked, Cate swung into gear and made some birthday arrangements of her own.

***

The big day arrived, and Cate got up early to make Carlos an extra special birthday breakfast, which delighted him. She then watched as he opened the cards she had secretly retrieved from the mail over the past few days.

"Here, this one's from me," said Cate, as she handed over an envelope and a giant gift box, wrapped in gold and white paper with masses of gold curly ribbons on top.

"For me?" screamed Carlos, as he grabbed the box from Cate's hands.

Like an excited child, he opened the card, smiled and set it up with the others. He then proceeded to rip off the wrapping from the package, opened the lid and peered inside.

"What on earth?"

He pulled out lots of gold-coloured shredded packaging and there, hiding at the bottom, he found an envelope. Retrieving it, he looked at Cate with a puzzled expression.

"Just open it!"

"Oh! You did, didn't you? You star, I will love you forever! I've always wanted to learn how to make my own cocktails, but how did you know?"

"Well, I vaguely remember you mentioning it at some stage. Now you can tick it off your bucket list — and there are two tickets so you can bring a friend."

"Um... I wonder who I could bring along?"

"Yes, I wonder... hint-hint! It includes an afternoon tea, too — cocktails and cakes, know anyone who might like that?"

"Cate, do you know anyone I could invite?"

"Well, if you're asking, I happen to know this wonderful redhead who will kill you if you don't invite her."

"Guess I'll have to ask around."

"Damn you Carlos — you know I want to come too," Cate said while delivering a playful slap around his head.

"OK, stop that — yes, you can come too."

"Just to let you know, I've to go out this morning and will be back early afternoon. Then you can work your magic on me. I've put a bottle of fizz in the fridge, and I'll bring a few nibbles back. The taxi is booked to pick us up at 6.30pm on the dot, and the girls are meeting us at the restaurant at 7pm. All you have to do today is chill out and prepare for a fabulous evening. Deal?"

"Deal, Miss Bossy Boots. Think I'll head back to bed, followed by a long leisurely bath. Don't mind if I use your bathroom, do you?"

"No, go ahead, and I'll even let you use my expensive bubble bath — only as it's your birthday," laughed Cate.

"By the time you return, I'll be one hot mama's boy," he said, touching his butt and making a sizzling noise.

"Then I'll need my magic wand to turn Miss Frump into Cinderella." Carlos crossed his arms and looked Cate up and down.

***

It had just gone 4pm when Cate let herself back into the apartment. She could hear loud funky music playing, and if she was not mistaken, Carlos was warbling along too.

The living room had been transformed into a mini salon, and Carlos was still dressed in his bathrobe. As soon as he saw her, he picked up a hairbrush and rushed towards her.

"Finally! I thought you were never coming back. An artist needs time, and this is going to be tight."

"Seriously, let me get in you crazy man. I need a pee and a quick shower before you start."

"Quick, quick and don't wash your hair. I know what I want to do to you."

"OK, but anyone listening would have thought you meant something else," scolded Cate, wagging her finger, in jest, at Carlos.

She quickly unpacked the nibbles and set them out. She uncorked the bottle of champagne and handed Carlos a glass.

"Happy Birthday, my darling Carlos. May all your dreams come true — love you. Cheers!"

"Thank you, sweetie. Now go and have your shower."

Cate showered and quickly dried off before slipping on her cotton dressing gown, and joining Carlos back in the living room.

Carlos motioned for her to take a seat and he set to work. He pulled and teased her hair; straightened and curled; pinned and twisted. Finally, he stood back, satisfied with his work.

"OK, can I see it?" He handed her a mirror.

"That's the hair done — now for the face, sweetie."

Carlos had borrowed a makeup set from work — it was packed with lotions, potions, brushes and palettes, from muted browns to neon pinks. Cate was the canvas and Carlos was the artist at work.

After what felt like an eternity to Cate, Carlos stood back and admired his handiwork.

"Here, take a look. I have taken a beautiful woman and created a goddess."

Cate gazed into the mirror Carlos held up.

Cate took a sharp breath in; shocked by the woman staring back at her. He had worked magic, as the reflection was of a truly stunning woman — her red hair braided and curled like a Greek goddess, while the makeup highlighted her blue eyes. The long fake eyelashes felt odd, but the result made her eyes big and bold.

"Well?"

"Carlos, I don't know what to say. You really are an artist! I look incredible — you've worked a miracle. Thank you."

"Great, now what are you wearing?"

Carlos followed Cate into her bedroom, where he curled up on the bed watching her as she retrieved a black baggy pants suit.

"I was thinking this and a pair of black boots and my gold clutch bag."

Carlos was shaking his head, "I have created a goddess, not an 80s reject. Let me have a look."

Carlos rooted through Cate's wardrobe and continued to shake his head in disbelief at the uninspiring garments on offer. Finally, he found the little black dress she had worn on the fateful Valentine's night.

"This is the one, um… the only one. Seriously, I need to take you shopping."

Carlos helped Cate into the dress, handed her a pair of gold strappy sandals and her gold clutch bag. He then delved into her jewellery box and found a gold and diamond costume necklace.

When she was fully dressed, he clapped his hands and smiled at her.

"Now we have perfection, well, as close as we can get with your crappy wardrobe," laughed Carlos.

***

Cate and Carlos strolled into the restaurant, arm-in-arm. Heads turned as the attractive couple walked in. To their amusement, a table of Japanese tourists whipped out their phones to take photos as if they were some celebrity couple.

Cate waved at Lady and Luna, who were already seated at their table situated towards the back of the restaurant.

"Oh, my heavens, what have you done?" exclaimed Carlos, when he spotted the table and a mass of golden balloons tied to the chair in the middle, and the tabletop adorned with streamers and confetti.

"I love it, thank you." He hugged and kissed Cate, Lady and Luna.

As Carlos took a seat at the head of the table, Jo and the new girl, Xena, arrived. Jo looked stunning in a red off-the-shoulder figure-hugging dress, and the Japanese tourists got very excited again. Cate was sure one of the group had jumped up pointing at Jo, shouting, "Grace Jones."

Xena was dressed in black trousers, a pair of chunky laced-up boots, and a washed out Van Halen T-shirt. The ensemble highlighted her pale skin and mousy brown hair. Immediately, Cate felt Xena could benefit from a Carlos makeover. Everything about her styling was unflattering. From what little contact she had had with her, she thought that the poor girl was desperately trying not to be seen. Although, she had seemed to have no issues in getting undressed in front of the others at her first meeting.

Jo and Xena sat down next to Carlos on one side, with Luna, Lady, and Cate on the other. They ordered drinks and chose from the menu.

It was a fun evening. Conversation flowed along with the wine. Cate enjoyed talking with the others and getting to know them better. Lady was recounting endless tales of her travels and numerous affairs, which seemed to be making Xena's head spin. Luna sat quietly, and Cate suspected she felt a little out of her comfort zone, and had only made an effort because it was for Carlos. Jo's raucous laugh resounded above the din of the restaurant. Cate noted that many of the other diners kept looking in their direction, some in annoyance and many others with curiosity.

The companions chatted, ate, and drank the night away.

Cate looked over at one point during the evening, and Carlos smiled and mouthed 'thank you'. Indeed, the tables had turned, and it made her feel good to see how happy he was.

After they had finished eating, the waitress cleared the table. Cate pretended to slip out to the toilets. Instead, she ordered a bottle of champagne and gave the manager the heads-up.

To Carlos' delight, the waiters appeared with a birthday cake, complete with sparklers, and everyone sang happy birthday.

"What a fabulous birthday with my special family. This means so much to me, and I thank you all from the bottom of my heart," said Carlos, as he cut the cake.

"Here's to you Carlos, you are one special young man. On behalf of everyone here, we wish you a very happy birthday and many more to come. May joy and happiness always be with you," said Lady.

***

"Where to next?" asked Jo, after Lady had kindly paid the bill, and the group were loitering outside on the street.

"What about *The Flamingo Club*? It's not far from here," suggested Carlos.

"Excuse me, ladies and gentleman. I'm going to call it a night; my babies need me. Carlos, have a wonderful birthday. I have a feeling that you will get a special gift tonight, keep your eyes and ears open, my beautiful birthday boy — 'Mr Right' may be around," said Luna, as she squeezed him tight before disappearing into the night.

"OK, *The Flamingo Club* it is," said Jo, as she linked arms with Xena.

***

The Flamingo Club certainly lived up to its name. There were fake palm trees, and everything from the wallpaper to the cushions on the booth seating had an array of flamingo designs. It was gaudy, ostentatious and over-the-top; precisely as it should be. Loud Latin music was pumping out of the speakers set up around the place, and although it was early in the evening by club standards, the dance floor was already packed.

Jo waved across at one of the waitresses — who it turned out worked with her part-time at the strip club — and the friends were shown to a VIP booth towards the rear of the establishment. It was a little less noisy and was slightly raised with a good view of the dance floor and the stage, where Jo promised there would be a live band and entertainment later in the evening.

A round of the signature 'Flaming Flamingo' cocktails was ordered.

Cate couldn't quite decide what type of club it was. There was a woman in a flamingo-coloured dress embellished with crystals and feathers; the flamboyant outfit was finished off with matching fake feather eyelashes. Cate suspected the woman was a drag queen. Another man sported a Victorian morning coat and top hat; while a group of beautiful Asian women wore matching flamingo-coloured chiffon dresses.

Carlos lent across and whispered in Cate's ear, "It's a gay and drag queen club. I hope you don't mind?"

Cate smiled back, unsure how she felt about it.

After the first round of cocktails, came a second; then a third.

Cate's head was starting to feel a little fuzzy, and she was glad they had eaten.

The next thing she knew Carlos and Jo were dragging them up to dance. Lady insisted she was happy to sit and watch, while the young ones enjoyed themselves.

Cate squeezed onto the dance floor amidst the gyrating mass. It had been a very long time since she had been dancing. A few tracks later and the music stopped, and somewhere in the background, someone clanged a gong. The dance floor cleared and everyone returned to their seats. The air was abuzz with anticipation.

The band stepped out on stage. They took a bow and struck up a lively upbeat melody. The woman in the feathery dress stepped out to join them, and to loud applause, began to sing in a voice that could have rivalled Dame Shirley Bassey. She sang a few songs, including one while lying across the top of the transparent glass grand piano, batting her long feathery eyelashes at the pianist.

What followed was the group of Asian women or, as Carlos later told Cate, 'lady-boys'. They danced and performed terrific acrobatic feats in sync to the beat of the music. It reminded Cate of a visit to a *Cirque de Soleil* show many years ago with Mike. She had loved it, whereas Mike had wanted to leave at the end of the first act.

The entertainment drew to a close with the diva singing a couple more songs, and as she left the stage, the dance floor filled up again.

Carlos headed off to order more drinks, while Cate sat and surveyed the scene unfolding before her. Lady had struck up a conversation with an attractive elderly gentleman seated at a small table nearby. Jo and Xena were getting into the groove on the dance floor, and it might have just been Cate's imagination, but it looked like Xena was blossoming; she seemed to be having fun.

Where is he? He only went to order some drinks. He's been ages. I hope he's all right.

Cate decided to go looking for her missing friend, and after negotiating a melee of revellers, she found Carlos at the bar talking with an attractive looking fair-haired guy. Carlos spotted her and waved her over.

"This is my best friend — Cate. May I introduce you to Scott Marsden, a movie director from Los Angeles. We're just chatting about London."

"Charmed, I'm sure," said Scott, as he gently kissed the back of her hand. His accent reminded her, with a jolt, of Warren.

"What can I get you to drink — a cocktail?"

"I think I've had enough for tonight, but I'd love sparkling water, please."

Scott turned around to catch the bartender's attention, and Carlos lent over to whisper in Cate's ear.

"I think he's 'the one'."

Cate smiled, and part of her wished deep down that he was, indeed, 'the one'. She wanted to see Carlos with someone who deserved him and would make him happy.

She thanked Scott for the water and made her way back to the booth, leaving the two lovebirds cocooned in their new little world. She could see they certainly had chemistry, but the big sister in her wanted to protect her baby brother.

Back at the booth, she found that she could keep an eye on them from a distance. It provided her with a perfect vantage point to oversee the comings and goings. She felt like a monarch overseeing her realm.

As the evening progressed, Cate noted that Lady had now joined the man at his table and they were engrossed in conversation. She could see that the slow dances had started and Xena was happily being held in Jo's arms, swaying to the music. Across the room, she could see Scott and Carlos engaged in the first throes of romance, as Scott put his arm around Carlos and drew him in close for their first kiss.

Why does it feel like everyone around me is moving forward, and I'm stuck in the same spot?

Chapter 22
Summer Lovin'

The sun was streaming in through the gap in the curtains, caressing Cate's face with its warm rays, gently coaxing her out of a deep sleep. She turned over, stretched, and willed her eyes to open.

It had been an uneventful few weeks since Carlos' birthday, filled with routine and everyday tasks. To be honest, that suited her just fine. A sense of normality had descended upon her — comforting and reassuring. Her body was finally able to release the built-up tension, and relax. Even the occasional run-in with Creepy Chris at work had been a welcome interlude from all the drama of the past few months. Carlos had settled into his new home, and their living together was a blessing. They both had fallen into a comfortable routine. She had heard nothing from Mike.

Cate prised herself from the bed, slipped on her robe, and shuffled into the kitchen.

"Good morning, gorgeous," chirped Carlos, as he handed her a morning coffee. "Isn't today just wonderful, filled with so much joy and love?"

Cate accepted the mug. "Someone has the love bug, methinks? Bitten bad — real bad!"

"Oh, sweetie, if only you knew. My heart has taken flight and is soaring in a sky of angels."

"Enough of the poetic claptrap. Can't you be more sensitive? I'm still nursing a wounded heart here," replied Cate, as she stretched out her free hand and playfully slapped Carlos around the head.

Since the night at *The Flamingo Club*, Carlos' romance with Scott was blooming. There were frequent Skype chats stolen in the early hours, accommodating the time difference along with Scott's demanding work schedule. Cate was delighted to witness Carlos' renewed vigour for life, and it lightened her mood to listen to his upbeat banter. His positivity was infecting her through osmosis, seeping into every pore and willing her to lighten up.

"What are your plans for the weekend? I was thinking of heading up to Hyde Park and bringing a picnic and a book. Want to join me?"

"Oh, well, I'd love that and would have said yes, but I think you missed the important word — *champers*, sweetie!" laughed Carlos. "Why don't I grab a chilled bottle on my way home from work and meet you for an evening in the park? How does that sound?"

"A girl can't say no to an invitation like that, can she now? I'll stop on the way and pick up a few nibbles, and meet you in the park, near the boathouse by the river. Do you know where I mean? Not far from the Hyde Park Corner entrance. Call me when you're on your way, and I'll let you know exactly where I am. Off you go, or you'll be late. Shoo, go!"

"OK, Miss Bossy Boots! Love you, sweetie. See you later."

***

Cate was strolling through the park, enjoying the peals of laughter from a nearby group of kids playing tag on the lawn. The Serpentine certainly created a beautiful setting for a summer's day picnic. She smiled to herself as she merrily swung her woven summer basket filled with goodies. A little further along the path, she found the perfect spot for their picnic. It was close enough to enjoy a view of the lake and far enough away from everyone else. To boot, there was a little shade offered by a nearby tree.

One of the drawbacks of having such fair skin, as much as she loved the sun, was the sun did not entirely love her back. In half an hour, her skin would be screaming red if she didn't wear the highest sunscreen protection she could find. In the past, when she and Mike had splashed out on exotic beach holidays, she was often found covered from head to toe under the largest beach umbrella they could find. Too many times suffering the misery of sunburn had taught Cate that it just wasn't worth it. Now she covered up, lathered herself in sunscreen, and when required, she would splash out on a good spray tan at the beauty salon. Even if she might have liked a bit of a tan, pale skin was sought after by a number of women across the world — with some going to great lengths to lighten their skin colour. Cate had been horrified to learn that some of these women even used body creams containing bleach.

Cate had settled down on the picnic blanket, kicking off her sandals and stretching out. She fixed her sunglasses and tilted her straw hat down over her face, allowing a few minutes to enjoy the sun, justified by telling herself it was necessary to get a dose of vitamin D. She was relaxed, and life was good.

A ringing next to her made her jump up with a start. She answered quickly.

"Hi, sweetie. Where are you? I've just come into the park; I'm walking along the path."

"Keep going for a few minutes, and you'll find me by the river bank. I'll keep an eye out for you. See you in a minute."

A moment later, she spotted Carlos striding along the path. She waved to him. He raised his hand to wave back; just as a frisbee hit the back of his head. He was not amused, and although she couldn't quite hear what he was saying, she had a fair idea from the angry scowl on his face.

"Poor hunny bunny. Shall I kiss the boo-boo better?" mocked Cate, puckering up her lips in jest.

"Funny, ha ha," huffed Carlos. "Kids are dangerous; they shouldn't be allowed in the park. The park should be a kid-free zone, or at the very least they should have a small part sectioned off with warning signs," as he sat down next to her.

"Here, this might help cool down that hot head of yours," said Cate, handing Carlos a glass of chilled champagne he had brought along as promised.

"Thanks," replied Carlos, as he took a long sip from his glass. "Much better now. OK, so what do we have to eat? I'm starving."

Cate rummaged through her bag and carefully set out all the bits and pieces for their picnic on the end of the blanket. She had even remembered a set of colourful non-breakable picnic plates, cutlery, and matching napkins.

When everything was set out, she felt quite proud of herself. It looked perfect.

"Wow, not bad. Top me up, and I'm going to tuck in. It was a long day at the salon — one of my VIPs dropped by without an appointment, and that threw my schedule completely off. Guess who didn't have time for lunch? How was your day? You look chilled."

"Fine. It's the first time in ages where I feel quite content. The waves of sadness and anger seem to be washed away by the sun. I hope it's a sign that things are starting to look up. Now, that's enough about me. I want to know all about your budding romance with Scott. Is it love? Is it true love? Are you going to leave me for your new man?"

Carlos leaned back on his elbows, tilting his head up to the sky; his aviator sunglasses mirroring a large white cross created by aeroplanes that had passed a few minutes earlier.

"Ah, if only I knew. My heart wants to dive in and swim in the sea of romance, while my head is telling me to hold back and avoid being hurt again. I do love talking to him. We can talk for hours, and it only seems like minutes. It's so different from my relationship with Sergei — we talked very little, and it was more about the physical side, and if I'm honest, the money. With Scott, the distance means that the physical side is a non-starter, right now anyway. But I guess it means that we're getting to know each other, and I have to say, I like him a lot. He's a great guy, so intelligent, so interesting. He also has a wicked sense of humour — I love that about him. He makes me laugh, and he just gets me. I want it to be more, but it's probably just a passing phase. For goodness' sake, he lives in L.A. — he has plenty of pick and choice, so why would he want me?"

Carlos paused in thought.

"You know, I would love for him to be 'Mr Right'. I never thought I would ever say this, but I'm fed up hanging out in bars and trying to find someone, and the idea of checking out an online dating site fills my soul with horror." Carlos turned to face Cate, shifted his sunglasses down his nose, and peered over them, "What about you? When are you going to get on the dating horse again?"

"Well, I haven't given it a thought. I'm too raw to even think about it. I can't see myself putting on glad rags and hanging around bars trying to pull a bloke. No way am I doing that. I'm more likely to end up being a lonely old spinster, doing my naked knitting to get my kicks. Can you imagine, me with all my old white saggy skin, sitting in an old people's home, still knitting squares in the buff?"

"On some sad level, I can," laughed Carlos.

The two friends sat together and enjoyed the relative peace while they drank their warming fizz and wolfed down all the treats.

The sun was starting to drop, and a chill was creeping into the air. Cate looked around, and many of the families had disappeared, with only a handful of lovers clutched in each other's embrace left.

I wonder how many people have walked by and thought we were a couple? If only they knew.

"I think it's time to head home. It's getting a little chilly, and I don't want to miss Scott's call. He said he'd Skype me later, and he had some news to share with me. Wonder what that could be? Come on, girl, time for home."

"Yes, time for home. I'm feeling tired all of a sudden. I think it's drinking champagne in the heat. Here, you shake the blanket and fold it up while I clear away the rest."

"Um… Cate, did you put sunscreen on?" asked Carlos, as he stared at her with a look of horror.

Cate looked down to see that half her body was a lobster-red. She had forgotten to put sunscreen on her legs, and as the sun had moved around, her legs and feet had suffered the consequences. It looked like someone had spray-painted them red, complete with a sizeable diagonal line just above her knees. As she gazed down in wonderment, she could feel the pain push its way through and the tightness with the swelling.

"Oh crap! It hurts."

"Can you walk?" asked Carlos, concerned and a little fascinated to witness that someone's skin could become so angry-looking in such a short time. It made him thankful for his olive skin that tanned easily.

"I'll try," winced Cate with the searing pain, as she hobbled forward.

Carlos carried her belongings and acted as a crutch for her to lean on. The pair slowly inched their way to the park exit, where Carlos flagged down a taxi. There was just no way Cate could negotiate a packed Tube in her fragile state.

Back at home, Cate sat on the edge of the bathtub soaking her severe sunburn in a lukewarm mixture of water and oatmeal. It was a solution her mother had used on her as a child once when they had holidayed on the north coast near the Giant's Causeway. Who would have thought it was possible to get badly sunburnt in Ireland? That year, though, had been one of the sunniest summers on records.

All the other kids had loved it, and she had been the one left suffering. Having such pale skin and red-auburn hair had been her curse.

On one holiday to Morocco, Mike had to step up as her bodyguard, as everyone, from the stall traders to the children on the street, wanted to touch her hair and her pale flesh. It reached the point where she had been afraid to venture out of their hotel room. Even the tour agent had suggested she cover up as much as possible and be wary, as there had been cases where western women had been kidnapped and sold into slavery. Over the years, she had gotten used to people commenting on her blue eyes, which positively shone a brighter blue if the light caught them at a particular angle. Cate had inherited her colouring from her grandmother.

While her mind drifted in the haze of nostalgia — her aching limbs thankfully forgotten — her thoughts turned to her grandmother. Nanny Eileen had been an impressive lady. She had raised her five children on her own, as her husband had died with consumption in his late-twenties. His meagre pension had not been enough to feed and clothe the family, so Eileen Mary McKinley had found a job as a housekeeper and cook for a local doctor and his family, where she had single-handedly run a tight-ship. If that was not enough, she had also taken in washing for several other well-to-do families. Eileen was a woman on a mission; no one dared to cross her, and anyone fool enough to do so soon learned it was not a wise move. She did not suffer fools gladly and used all her connections to leverage suitable jobs for each of her children — who, by all accounts, were more afraid of the wrath of their mother than any hell-fire and brimstone. Eileen was a proud and resourceful woman, who undoubtedly paved the way for her offspring — and future generations.

Cate had adored her grandmother. Perhaps age had softened Eileen, as her own scarce memories were filled with wonderful snippets of activities like baking apple pies, knitting, and lemonade with home-baked shortbread. Even now, tears were welling up in the corners of her eyes. She wished her grandmother was there right now, to give her one of her big-bosom hugs and whisper in her ear, "There, there Kitty. All will be fine. Just you wait and see".

Carlos caught her wiping her eyes with the back of her hand and assumed she had been crying from the pain. The big-hearted soul helped her swing her lobster legs out of the cooling bath and gently patted them dry. Then he proceeded to lather on a generous coating of natural yoghurt; yet another remedy handed down from Cate's mum. As he worked away covering each burnt leg, Cate sat quietly and never once flinched.

Carlos then carried her into her bedroom and laid her down on top of the bed, where he had already placed a clean towel. He had also set up a fan, which oscillated back and forth, sending out a much-needed cooling breeze across the room.

"Night, my little red lobster. Just call me if you need anything," said Carlos, as he kissed her gently on the forehead.

As Cate drifted in and out of sleep, she could hear voices and muffled laughter in the distance, and it was comforting to her, lulling her back to sleep.

***

It took a few days applying soothing balms and ointments to get her legs back to normal. Apart from the dry skin and endless flaking, Cate was feeling right as rain again. She even found herself humming the tune she heard on the radio before she left for work that morning. 'Happy' by Pharrell Williams was a sure way to start the day on an upbeat note. Even the thought of another meeting with Irina Castles did not make a dent in her mood.

Carlos was remarkably upbeat too, and indeed his budding romance was lightening his mood. Cate was sure that, in spite of Carlos playing down his relationship with Scott, she could see the signs of love blooming. He would rush in at night and disappear into the recesses of his room. Cate felt like a mother to a teenager.

The only positive side effect of the solitude was the fact that it gave her time to focus on her knitting. After having knit enough squares, Luna had carefully stitched them together to create a blanket, which Cate kindly donated to a local hospice. At the last meeting, Luna had finally deemed her experienced enough to start work on the shawl pattern she had chosen all those months ago at Mr Yamamoto's wool shop. She had cast on the stitches, and Alice had helped her get started understanding the pattern. Once the hieroglyphics were explained, it made sense, and it was quite simple. As she worked away stitch by stitch, the yarn changed from a deep blue to marine, then from a soft green to turquoise. The result was quite striking, reminding Cate of the Aegean Sea where she and Mike had spent their belated honeymoon island hopping.

Mike had hired a sailing yacht, skippered by a leathery-tan Greek man who only spoke only a couple of words of English. It had been magical, lying stretched out on the deck with the white sail taut in the wind, the boat slightly heeled to one side, and the bow ripping through the turquoise waters. Her happiness at that moment was unbound, watching Mike's tanned body pulling ropes under the watchful command of the skipper. When he was allowed to take over the helm, he stood tall like a Viking; seeing him, at that time, in his element made her feel dizzy as a wave of unbridled love coursed through her veins. It was hard to believe that, after just a few years, here she was — alone and in the throes of divorce.

Why does love die? What happens? Was it my fault? Did I not do enough to keep the flames burning bright? Was not being able to have children the nail in the coffin? I wish I knew what I could have done to make it better. I loved Mike, and I know, in his own way, he loved me too.

Knit one, purl one, knit one, purl one — the simple repetition was soothing, calming like a meditation. It was just what she needed to focus her mind and push the self-blame out.

Cate was just about managing to suppress the urge to cry, focussing intently on each stitch when Carlos bounded in and sat down beside her.

"Hey, watch it buster. I could have stabbed you with a needle! You frightened the bejesus out of me."

"Sorry, sweetie, but I'm feeling so buzzed, and I have to tell someone. Guess what?"

"What?"

"Oh, I'm so excited!" exclaimed Carlos, smiling from ear-to-ear.

"Go on then, tell me."

"Scott is coming over to the UK to film part of a movie he's working on somewhere up North, and he wants me to join him. I can't believe it. I'll get to spend time with him and hang around on-set. There will be a couple of Hollywood stars, and I'll be there hobnobbing with them. How cool is that?"

Cate thought Carlos was going to keel over with excitement and from lack of oxygen, as he managed to pour out the entire spiel without taking a breath. He was one excited bunny.

"Lucky you, sounds like fun. How long for? Will you be able to take time off work?"

"Oh, you are a party pooper. I hadn't thought about that. I do have about one week's holiday due to me, and I could see if I could take a bit longer as unpaid. Right now, I would happily resign to spend time with Scott. It's a once-in-lifetime opportunity, and I'm not going to miss it."

"Yes, it certainly is a once-in-a-lifetime opportunity. Do you know who the actors are?"

"No, Scott is keeping the lid on that at the moment, and no matter how much I coax him, he won't tell. But hey, a Hollywood movie star is a Hollywood movie star. I'd die if it is Angelina Jolie. Now I'm even more excited. How am I going to sleep now?"

"Carlos, come on. They're only people. No matter who it is, won't it just be good to have some quality time with Scott?"

"Yes, as ever, you're right. Scott is such a hunk, and it will be great to see him again and get up close and personal — nudge-nudge, wink-wink," smiled Carlos.

"That I don't need to know. I'm off to bed — work tomorrow. I need to get some beauty sleep, even if you don't." Cate hugged Carlos, put her knitting away, and went to bed.

Chapter 23
An Artist's Muse

The summer was well underway.

It was a time of year that made Cate's heart sing. The days were lighter, with the warmth of the sun a welcome respite from the long grey, wet winter. She had to stop herself from skipping up the street to the office; smiling to herself every time she spotted one of the cheerful floral displays that had sprung up around the city. At lunchtime, she would take her sandwich to one of the small parks dotted around, hidden away from the hordes of tourists, and enjoy the pleasure of reading in the shade of the trees.

Life was tootling along. She faced each day, one day at a time. She no longer focussed on the future. She had no idea what the future would hold, and it was just too disturbing to think about it. Her daily routine provided a safe-haven for her fragile heart, and she was OK with how things were right now.

Divorce proceedings were well underway with the *decree nisi* filed, and a court date in the coming weeks. Irina had explained that it was a formality and Cate was not expected to attend in person, which had been a relief.

Still, the idea that her marriage was being undone made her heart feel heavy.

Reflecting about her marriage made her think back to the last knitting club night when she had misread the pattern, and Alice had spent half an hour unravelling her work. Watching Alice rip back the stitches had made her angry with herself — sad to know all the hours she had wasted by making one small mistake. Alice, being a kind and gentle soul, had said it was necessary, and it wouldn't take Cate long to re-do the section.

That was how she felt right now, like her marriage and life with Mike were being ripped back to fix a mistake they had made many years previously. There was nothing to be done, as Mike had made his choice and she was no longer part of his plans. He had chosen a new love and together they were weaving a new life: a new life with a child.

Her lip trembled with the image of Mike standing with his arm around Isabelle and them smiling down at their newborn. To stop the floodgates from opening, Cate bit down hard on her lip, closed her book, and slipped on her sandals, ready to head back to her office — her sanctuary.

***

One evening a week or so later, she found Carlos was bouncing around the flat, waving an envelope and card. They received an invitation to a Summer Party from Lady. The invitation was a formal stiff card with gold-embossed trim. The handwritten note accompanying the formal invitation explained that Lady was inviting the knitting group around to her Notting Hill home for a summer get-together. The idea of swanning around Lady's garden in the buff made Cate chuckle to herself. She never in her wildest dreams would have imagined being the recipient of such an invitation, and even more surprising, she was excited about it.

Carlos' mood flattened when he realised that he would be up in Yorkshire on location with Scott on the date in question. His disappointment quickly disappeared, as he shared with Cate the names of the Hollywood stars headlining the movie — his constant pleading had managed to wear Scott down in the end.

**

Cate hugged Carlos. His suitcase was at his side, and the car service Scott had arranged to drive him up north was waiting.

"Have fun — be good. Say hi to Scott, and I hope that I'll meet him again soon. And tell him he will have me to deal with if he doesn't look after you."

"Oh sweetie, I will, and you have fun at Lady's. Say hi to the girls from me," said Carlos, as he hugged her again.

The driver put the suitcase in the boot, and Carlos slipped into the back seat. The car pulled off, and as it drove into the distance, Cate waved. Her heart felt a little heavy. She would miss Carlos over the next three weeks, but at least Miss Dior would be around to keep her company, and she had a new TV show on Netflix she was itching to watch. Right now, though, she needed to go and get ready for Lady's summer party. It would be lovely to catch up with the other ladies and enjoy a little friendly gossip.

The invitation stated that the event would start from 4pm onwards. Cate, who was usually extremely punctual, decided to err on the side of arriving at least half an hour late, in the hope that some people would already be there and she would not be left standing on her own. Another reason she missed Carlos, and in a strange way, Mike too. Having company meant she did not have to attend parties on her own. Anyway, it was what it was, and she would have to deal with it.

***

By the time she stood at the front door to Lady's home, she was just over thirty-five minutes late.

Lady's house stood in the midst of a row of Victorian townhouses, tall and proud. It was painted white with numerous planters and hanging baskets dotted around adding a splash of vibrant colour. In the centre of the small front garden, stood a manicured topiary in the shape of a heart.

Cate climbed the stone steps to the front door and rang the doorbell. As she waited, she stared at the grotesque face leering back at her from the ornamental doorknocker. It was as if he had given her the once-over and found her unsuitable to gain entry. To Cate, he looked like she was a bad smell under his snooty nose.

Fortunately, she didn't have to wait too long before the door swung open, and a mature gentleman dressed smartly in a pressed black suit, white shirt, and black tie greeted her.

"Welcome, Madam. Please follow me through to the garden. Please, this way."

He directed her with a wave of his arm and marched her along the hallway. Cate only managed to catch a quick glimpse of the interior and was impressed with the bright, colourful paintings amassed on the wall climbing the stairs. Further along, a door had been ajar, and she had a quick peek into what she assumed to be the living room, where her eyes were immediately drawn to a magnificent portrait of a woman in the nude hanging over the fireplace.

After accepting a tall glass of Pimm's from a tray offered by a young woman, Cate stepped through a set of French windows onto a small patio area, with stone steps leading down into the main garden. She noted there were quite a few people were milling around, or standing chatting in groups — she realised her error in wrongly assumed it was just an invitation for the naked knitting club ladies. Nervously, she edged her way down the steps and joined a nearby group to whom Lady was animatedly telling a story.

On seeing Cate, Lady interrupted her tale to introduce her. Cate smiled and shook hands, promptly forgetting each name as her nerves kicked in. Lady embarked again on her storytelling. Cate stood on the edge of the group, half listening while searching around trying to spot her friends.

"Hello, goddess of my heart —Venus reborn and walking amidst us mere mortals. May my heart be stilled as my eyes gaze upon thy divine beauty? May I have the honour of introducing myself? I am at your service — and just who might you be, my eternal heavenly star?"

Cate jumped, startled by the man. He stepped forward, bowed slightly, reached out and took her hand and kissed it. As he bent down, his bald head reflected red in the sun, clashing with his garish Hawaiian shirt. She didn't know whether to be flattered or repelled by him.

"Oh, the colour of your fiery hair. You are a demon from the depths of the underworld here to steal my heart. Let me look at you in this light."

He walked around her studying her, and as he did so, the more uncomfortable she felt.

"Over here," a voice called out to her. She put her hand up to shade her eyes, and she could make out Luna waving at her from across the garden.

"Excuse me, my friend is calling me over," whispered Cate.

"I will find you, my dear muse, for you are stirring my creative soul. The gods have sent you to me to end my drought of inspiration. You will be the fuel to rekindle the fire. Please tell me your name, so that my lips may taste its sweet form. Wait, no, don't tell me, for I will call you *Circe,* as you have bewitched me. *Adieu*, my dear one — I will find you again my fair *Circe*."

The man stood blowing kisses to her as she made her escape to join Luna, Alice, Jo, and Xena at the far end of the garden.

"Who was that man?" asked Jo.

"I've no idea. He was extremely odd and kept insisting on calling me *Circe*."

"Ah," interjected Luna, with a nod of knowing. "That is the famous artist Percival Davenport. Some of his artwork hangs in the Tate Modern. He's considered a genius of this era. His use of colours and light are considered to be quite transcendent. He's a good friend of Lady's. I think she told me once that she has a few of his paintings, including one he did of her when she celebrated her fiftieth birthday. Oh, I think he is actually a 'Sir'. I suppose you should be quite flattered that he has taken a shine to you. You never know, we could be seeing paintings of you hanging in the Tate Modern next."

Cate blushed at the idea of becoming a muse to a well-known artist and her body being captured on canvas to be ogled by art lovers.

Xena was standing next to Jo. She looked changed, softer and happier. She smiled as they chatted with Luna. If Cate was not mistaken, she kept looking at Jo with a glint in her eye, the sort of look stolen between lovers in the early bloom of romance. Jo must have, on some intuitive level, sensed Cate's knowing. She reached out, took Xena by the hand, pulling her closer, and then announced to the ladies that they were now officially a couple. Xena looked as if she was going to burst with pride at their secret being revealed at last. Everyone wished them well, and Luna gave her little nod of approval, almost indicating that it was something she predicted and was pleased to see come to pass.

Alice was starting to show, the roundedness of her belly just beginning to bulge under her floral summer dress. She was glowing, and Cate couldn't be sure if it was the pregnancy or if she was enjoying being out, away from her brood. Either way, she seemed confident and relaxed in the social situation, unlike Cate.

The afternoon seeped into early evening, the heat of the sun softened into a warm shimmer, and the few remaining revellers were settling in for the evening. Luna and Alice had gone, Jo and Xena were cuddling in the wisteria-covered summerhouse, and Cate felt it was time to head home. She found Lady talking to Sir Percival on the patio. Cate would have preferred to slip away unnoticed, but she had no choice, as they were blocking her exit.

"Ah, here she is — the light of my world, the fire in my soul," shouted Sir Percival upon seeing Cate clamber up the stairs. "This is my *Circe*, my muse, the one to ignite my creative juices. Isn't she magnificent?"

Lady turned around in time to witness Sir Percival embrace Cate in his chubby grasp and plant a wet kiss on each cheek.

"Now come on, you drunken old fool. Cate is a beautiful woman, but I'm sure she doesn't want a lecherous old man spouting poetic claptrap at her. Isn't that right, Cate? Give her your card, and if she's interested she'll contact you," winked Lady, coming to Cate's rescue. Sir Percival released Cate with a look of a mischievous schoolboy having been told off, and dug his hand into the pocket of his garish shirt to produce an engraved silver case from which he extracted his business card.

"Forgive me, I am but a poor artist driven by my passion and I can't curb my enthusiasm when I see something, or someone, who inflames my heart. Please take this. Forgive an old fool, and I bid thee farewell, my red-haired beauty. Until we meet again, my *Circe*."

Sir Percival made such a theatrical sweeping bow in his inebriated state that he wobbled and almost fell off the patio. Thankfully Lady caught his arm just in time to save him from injury.

Lady walked with Cate back through the house to the front door. "He is a dear but gets so excitable. It's his artistic temperament, and when he's had a bit too much to drink, he is quite incorrigible. But do think about his offer to paint you. He is extremely gifted, and it is a liberating experience. Don't worry; he's harmless. He is a gentleman through and through, and his partner keeps him in check normally. Unfortunately, Arthur had another engagement today, so Percy came here on his own — he only drinks, as he is quite shy in company. Before you go, come and see the painting he did for me."

Lady ushered Cate back through to the hallway and into the room she had peeked in earlier. As she walked in and could see the portrait, she was blown away by the detail created by the colours, and the use of light added another dimension to the piece. It was strikingly beautiful exuding a sense of warmth and love.

"It's stunning," admitted Cate.

"Yes, he made me a very happy woman. I've had photos taken over the years by all sorts of wonderfully talented photographers, but this is the piece that I feel is my legacy. It will be here in the world when I am long gone, and that pleases me. It is like my soul still living on, even when my body returns to dust. Think about it, and if you are interested, let me know, and I'll make the arrangements. He lives only a few doors up from here; he has converted the loft into a light, airy studio. I can always come along for moral support; we could make a day out of it."

Cate left with her head filled with the notion of becoming an artist's muse, and secretly, it gave her self-confidence a much-needed boost.

**

A few days later, Cate's phone rang. When she answered it, she was a little surprised to hear Lady's voice.

"Apologies for calling, Cate, but I have a rather distraught Percy here. He has been begging me to call you and talk you into doing a sitting for him. He really has a bee in his bonnet about painting you, to the point where he is getting very agitated. He has an exhibition coming up, and he feels that the main piece should be of you. He says he has had dream after dream of the painting he wishes to create, but he needs his 'Circe'. I know you work, but would there be any chance you would be willing to come this weekend? And, of course, you're welcome to come and stay here as my guest. Please say you will, as this mad old fool is driving us all crazy."

"Oh, well… I don't happen to have any other plans this weekend, so I could do it, as long as you come with me. The only issue is, Carlos is away at the moment, and I'm taking care of Miss Dior, his cat… Well, our cat now, I suppose. I can't leave her on her own."

"No problem. Miss Dior is welcome to come along too. There's plenty of room here and my butler, Henry, can keep an eye on her. He is a real softy for animals. So that's a yes, then?"

"I guess so. Yes, why not."

"Come Friday evening, and we can have a little dinner together first. Could you be here for before 7pm and we'll have a bite of supper together? I'll invite Percy and Arthur."

"Yes, that sounds like a plan. Oh, I'm nervous and excited, but at least I've had some practice taking my clothes off for strangers already," laughed Cate, feeling butterflies rising in her tummy.

***

Friday evening arrived; Cate was back at Lady's front doorstep with her overnight bag, and carrying Miss Dior in her travel carrier.

Henry answered the door and took Cate's bags, leading her to one of the guest suites. The room was freshly aired, with a sizeable four-poster bed, a mahogany wardrobe in one corner nestled between the sash windows and the door to the bathroom. The room was painted magnolia with accents in a pale eggshell blue, which was complemented by a cover in the matching colour with delicate white flowers and small birds.

"Shall I take Miss Dior down to stay in the pantry with me?" asked Henry, holding the travel carrier at eye level where he was checking Miss Dior, who appeared to be very nonchalant about the whole ordeal.

"Why not? She seems happy enough," and, as if she agreed, Miss Dior purred contentedly.

"Drinks will be served promptly at 7.30pm in the drawing room, with dinner for 8pm. Shall I collect Madam?" enquired Henry, making Cate feel that she had been transported into an episode of *Downton Abbey*.

"No, no, I know where it is. Thank you, Henry."

Cate had been in such a rush to get home and pick up Miss Dior that she hadn't had enough time to tidy herself up. She had a quick shower, enjoying the array of lavender-scented soap and shampoo on offer. She quickly towel-dried her hair, opting to leave it down to dry out naturally. She applied some fresh makeup and pulled on a floaty chiffon top, that Carlos had insisted that she purchase the last time they went shopping, teamed with elegant black palazzo trousers, new strappy sandals and matching clutch bag. There was a mirror just behind the door, and she smiled at her reflection in approval.

In the drawing room, Cate was greeted by Lady and, not two, but three men. Sir Percival stepped forward and kissed her hand, and then introduced her to the tall, slim man with receding grey hair and a bushy grey beard. This was Sir Percival's long-term partner, Arthur. Arthur kissed her lightly on each cheek, making her giggle as his beard tickled her face. Lady introduced the other man as Antoine de Chasseron, an extraordinarily well-groomed and very handsome Frenchman in his late fifties. He shook her hand while apologising for gatecrashing their dinner, explaining that he was only in town for a few days and wanted to spend time with his beloved Lady before he flew off again to oversee a book launch in New York.

The company was quite convivial, and Cate enjoyed an incredible night hearing many tales of adventures and exploits in foreign lands. It was the sort of evening she had only been privy to in movies, with intellectuals, artists, aristocrats and adventurers sharing stories, laughter, and friendship. As she slipped into the bed and felt the cool fresh cotton sheets against her skin, she fell into a contented slumber, like a well cared for infant.

***

The following morning, there was a knock on her bedroom door. It was Henry; he had prepared her a breakfast tray. He explained that her ladyship was having a leisurely morning, which Cate took to mean that she was still in bed with her handsome lover. He advised Cate that he would personally escort her to Sir Percival's house, and to be ready for 10am. Cate ate breakfast, showered and dressed, and made her way downstairs to the drawing room.

Right on the dot, as the grandfather clock in the hallway struck the hour, Cate followed Henry out the door and down the street to No.137. Arthur answered the door, and Cate was handed over into his care. They chatted about the previous evening as they climbed the stairs up to the converted loft space. Sir Percival was already there, setting up and fussing around. When he saw her, he rushed over.

"Welcome, welcome, my beautiful *Circe*." They all had tried but failed, to convince him to call Cate by her real name, but he was insistent as an artist he should be granted his whimsical ways. Cate considered it more stubborn than playful. Anyway, here she was, ready or not.

"Call me Percy, my radiant goddess. If you change into this behind the screen, we can get started. I know exactly what I want, and the light is perfect."

Cate stepped behind the screen and changed into the flimsy chiffon garment. It was a little on the skimpy side in parts, mainly around her bust, and it was most definitely see-through. There was a mirror behind the screen. She grabbed a couple of hairpins from her bag and clipped her hair up in such a way that it cascaded in waves over her shoulders. She had hoped it would help hide her breasts but to no avail. However, the overall effect was quite pleasing, and she had to admit that she certainly looked more like a goddess than a dull office worker.

Sir Percival, or Percy as he insisted she call him, was nearly moved to tears when she stepped out. He clasped his hand to his chest like his heart was going to explode. For a fleeting moment, Cate worried that he was having a heart attack. Percy directed her into position, sitting in a high-backed chair with different props and throws strategically placed around her. He stood back and admired his handiwork. Arthur agreed that it was perfect and left them to it, promising to bring refreshments on a regular basis.

At first, Cate felt awkward and a little uncomfortable holding the pose, but as she relaxed, her mind wandered, and they chatted as Percy worked away behind a vast canvas. He was a genuinely lovely man, and Cate recognised a kindred introvert; one who drank a little too much to cope with the anxiety of social situations. He was quite a dear, but also a taskmaster who barely gave her time out to eat, drink or use the bathroom.

***

The weekend ended up being great fun, and it given her self-confidence a much needed boost.

Sir Percy had refused to allow anyone to see the fruits of his labours; insisting that he wanted the piece to be his *pièce de la résistance* at this next exhibition. He proclaimed to Cate that, "the world shall bow at your feet in awe of your divine beauty my *Circe*".

On returning home late Sunday evening, she felt exhausted, yet her mind felt invigorated. Miss Dior also appeared to have enjoyed her sojourn being mollycoddled by Henry. Before heading to bed, Cate checked her phone and was pleased to receive a photo from Carlos showing him on-set sitting in the director's chair with

Scott laughing in the background. He looked genuinely happy, and that made her happy too.

Chapter 24
Man Trouble

Carlos returned home full of stories, making Cate laugh with his anecdotes and his impersonation of the leading lady. By all accounts, she was a diva in the truest sense. Even Carlos was impressed by her constant demands on the poor on-set assistants — she had to have a fresh bottle of mineral water opened each time she wanted a drink, and it was not just any mineral water, it was one that had been imported specially from some tiny mountain village in Swiss Alps. He talked about the hard-working crew behind the scenes, and when he talked about Scott, Cate could see a twinkle in his eyes. Whether he knew it or not, she could see that he was in love.

Carlos reluctantly fell back into his routine, and Cate was relieved to have him back at home. As much as it was good to have a little space, she had missed him more than she cared to let on. He had his fair share of annoying habits, but it was these little peccadilloes she had missed around the place. Even Miss Dior was thrilled, in her own way, to have him back home.

Cate thought that Carlos might be unbearable after his Hollywood experience, but mostly he talked incessantly about Scott.

***

The two friends were falling back into the groove when Cate returned home one evening to find Mike sitting on the steps at the front of the building. Far from looking happy and content, he looked like he had aged a decade in a matter of months. He stood up when he saw her and walked down to meet her.

Oh hell, what's he doing here? OK, Cate, be cool, don't cause a scene — you're worth more than that. Keep it together — you can do this.

"Hi Cate, do you have time to talk?" He sounded flat.

"I guess so. Is it about the divorce?"

"Yes... No. Well, I guess so."

"Come on up for a drink. Carlos isn't back until later, so we have the place to ourselves. But I'm warning you now, no funny business or any of that crap like the last time. I have the police on speed dial. OK?" demanded Cate, as she opened the door and he followed her to the apartment.

Inside, he waited to be invited to sit down.

"Coffee, tea or a glass of wine?" asked Cate from the kitchen.

"I think I need something stronger, so wine would be fine."

Cate handed him the glass, and he took a gulp.

"So, what is it that you want to talk about?"

"Erm…. After everything, it is hard for to me to admit this… but I want to come back. I miss you. I miss us, and our life together. Being with Isabelle hasn't been what I expected. She nags me most of the time and never lets me out of her sight for two seconds without accusing me of having an affair. I miss the life I had with you. Will you take me back? I'm sorry — really, really sorry. Sorry for all the hurt I've caused you, and I promise you that it will never happen again. Cate, give me — us — another chance. Please."

Mike looked worn down, battle-weary, and for a fleeting moment Cate's heart went out to him.

What the hell? Is he joking? Does he honestly think I would take him back after all the hurt he caused me? No way. No way! Maybe if there wasn't the baby, but there is.

"What about the baby?"

"You know, after everything we went through, I didn't really wanted kids any more. I was quite happy just being the two of us; we could do our own thing and travel. Now I feel hemmed in — trapped. I'm not cut out to be a dad. I don't feel like I've had a night's sleep since we split up. Isabelle is baby mad and already planning my life around the baby. She drags me along to her baby birthing class, and I hate it. Cate, how did I mess up so bad? I'll admit I was weak. I allowed my head to be turned by her flirting; I was a fool. I realise now what I had with you, and I want it back. I want my life back."

Keep calm — keep it together, you've come too far to lose it now!

"When's the baby due?"

"End of October. I suppose it's only a matter of weeks now, but I don't want it. I want you!"

"Mike, you made your choice, and you chose her. She is having your baby. You have to grow up and face your responsibility. I'm sure once the baby comes along, you'll be fine. You'll make a great dad; I know that. It's probably her hormones, and once she has the baby, she'll settle down.

It's scary for both of you — you need to support each other. Go home and talk to her right now."

Cate took the glass from Mike's hand and pointed towards the door.

"Go home and talk it over, tell her that you are scared and work it out together. Our time together is over. You and me, we're the past. I'm moving forward with my life; you should do the same."

Mike looked deflated.

He left with a heavy heart knowing how much he had lost. Cate closed the door behind him, and although she felt sorry for him and their loss, she also felt a weight had been lifted. She felt a sense of liberation. Facing Mike and hearing he wanted her back was the catalyst she needed to know in her heart that it was over — there was no going back now.

***

Later that week, Cate was on her way to the office, enjoying the early morning sun and the relative peace. She was only a few steps from the entrance when she thought she heard someone call out her name.

"Hello, Cate."

Cate swung around to see a silver car with darkened windows parked beside her. The back window nearest to her was down and there, smiling at her, was Warren. Cate's heart skipped a beat. The car door opened and he stepped out.

"You're looking gorgeous. No, actually, you look even more delectable since our last meeting. You are positively beautiful. I hope that's the effect that I have on you," he laughed. "Look, I'm back in town for a few days, and I would be delighted if you would join me for dinner this evening. My driver will pick you up at 8pm at your home. I have been looking forward to spending more time with you. Say yes, and you will make an old man very happy."

"Yes, I'd love to." Her acceptance poured out of her mouth before she had time to think.

Oh, hell, yes! What harm could it do? I think my bruised ego needs a little attention, and after all, I'm a single lady now — or at least, I will be very soon. Come on, how could any woman not want some of that!

"Great, see you later." He leaned over and lightly kissed her cheek, remaining long enough for her to get a good deep whiff of his aftershave. He got back into the car and it drove off into the deluge of London traffic. The intoxicating aroma of his aftershave lingered in her nostrils, even when she sat down at her desk. It was a mix of sophisticated fresh citrus, with a strong masculine oriental note; and right now, it was triggering heightened senses in her body which had been dormant for the last few months, and were not at all suitable for the office.

Cate was hard-pressed to concentrate on anything. All she could think about was Warren's dinner invitation, and how she wished she had spent some time on personal grooming. She'd have to make up an excuse to take the afternoon off, giving herself more time to get ready for her hot date.

***

At 8pm on the dot when the buzzer rang announcing the arrival of her transport.

"Well, what do you think?"

Miss Dior looked her up and down, and if Cate was not mistaken, she gave her a haughty nod, which Cate took to mean that she was good to go.

She grabbed her pashmina and handbag, checked that she had her phone, and locked the door behind her. Carlos was working late, so she had sent him a quick text informing him that she had plans that evening and would be back late, so as not to wait up.

It was a balmy summer evening, and the city's pubs were packed, with many of their clientele, drinks in hand, spilling out onto the streets. Cate sat in the back with her window down, soaking in the passing sights and sounds, keeping her mind occupied lest she would panic about the evening ahead with Warren. After last time, she felt that it would not take much encouragement to give in to his devilish charms and spend the night. It was driving her crazy just thinking about it — should she or shouldn't she? There had only been Mike for the last seventeen years, and the prospect of having sex with someone else was both frightening and exhilarating.

The car pulled up outside a modern apartment block. The driver walked around, opened the door for her, and handed her an envelope. Inside was a card with a logo, Kennedy Property Developments, and a handwritten note: Code 4571A — take the elevator to the 44th floor, Warren.

Cate did as directed on the note. As the lift signalled she had reached the 44th floor, the door opened directly into the apartment, and Cate stepped out. She admired the muted tones of the walls and the furnishings, all perfectly matched to the modern open-plan space. Walking a few steps further into the room, she could see a set of French windows leading onto a large terrace. Warren was standing there, his back to her, enjoying the city view over the Thames. She watched him in silence, drinking in the scene. He only turned around when he heard her high heels tapping along the wooden floor.

"Oh, you are a sight for my weary eyes. Please come in, or should I say come out and join me. Isn't this the most fabulous view? You know, London is one of my favourite cities in the world, and now even more so since finding you here." He stepped forward and gently placed his hand at the base of her spine and ushered her through onto the terrace.

"Oh, it's stunning," murmured Cate, as the nearness of him was playing havoc on her senses again. Part of her just wanted him to pull her body into his embrace, kiss her and take her, like in a trashy romance novel.

"I hope you don't mind; I thought we could dine here tonight. I've hired a private chef for the evening, and he is under instructions to cook whatever your heart desires," said Warren, as he handed Cate a glass of chilled champagne.

It was perfect — the setting, the champagne, and Warren — almost too perfect. Cate had that feeling in the pit of her stomach that something was about to go wrong. Warren held the chair for her to sit down, and as he took his seat, a waiter appeared with a plate of *hors-d'oeuvres*. He stood aside and waited patiently to hear her dinner request to pass onto the chef.

"Oh, I don't know. I can't think... Warren, why don't you decide?"

"No, this evening is for you. What is your favourite meal? Do you enjoy French, Italian or Mexican? Cate, you surely must have a dish you adore."

"OK, well, I do love Italian, and my Mum used to make lasagne followed by a peach pavlova for my birthday treat. OK, lasagne, but I think if I have a choice, I would prefer a berry panna cotta tonight. What do you think?"

"Sounds perfect," said Warren.

The waiter nodded in agreement and left, while Warren topped up her glass and struck up a lively monologue about his time spent in Italy. He told her about his first visit to Rome, Florence, and Venice as a teenager. His father had sent him off to explore Europe for the summer, and it had been the best thing for him. He had learned about fine wines, good food, music, dancing and love. As he recounted his long-forgotten trip, Cate noted the glint in his eyes.

Cate talked of her own brief experience of visiting Rome on a school trip; her own story was quite a stark contrast to the romantic portrayal painted by Warren. It had been her final year at Convent School, so there had been no wine, music, or dancing, and no scope for love. It had been endless stuffy museums, with a visit to Vatican City, where they had been crushed amongst the crowds assembled to receive a blessing from His Holiness. Since then, Italy had not held much appeal, although she did love Italian food and prosecco.

"If you had all the time in the world, what would you do?" asked Cate, who was feeling more relaxed thanks to a few glasses of champers.

"Well, it is not something I have ever thought about before. Let me see; I guess I would take Loren, my daughter, on a world tour. Together we could explore and experience every country. I guess having time with her would be a good thing. I do feel guilty since her mother passed away as we don't spend enough time together, but I am tied down with running my business. There's no one else who can do that for me."

"Oh, surely you have a team of people who could manage a couple of weeks at least without you? I'm sure your daughter would love you to spend time with her. What age is she, again?"

"A teenager, she'll turn sixteen on her next birthday. I find it hard to connect to her even when we do spend time together. I took her to dinner in her favourite restaurant in New York a few months ago, and she just sat glaring at me or glued to her phone. I wanted it to be enjoyable, but we fell out on the drive back home. Kids today don't have the same level of respect. I wouldn't have dared to step out of line around my parents. Anyway, she has Maria, our live-in housekeeper, who takes care of her. Now enough about Loren, I want to know more about you, Cate. You captivate me with your beautiful Irish accent. My ancestors come from Ireland, a small village in Limerick. Tell me about where you grew up."

Warren listened, as Cate explained about her childhood growing up in Belfast. She amused him with tales of their sibling rivalry; he listened intently about how 'The Troubles' had touched her life, and he laughed when she relayed stories of the pranks they played on the nuns.

They wined and dined, chatted and laughed into the early hours. Standing together at the railings, they gazed out over of the city's illuminated skyline. With the comfortable silence between them, Warren reached out to Cate, and she willingly folded into his arms. His kiss was warm, exploring and it sent a shockwave that ignited every nerve in her body. She was his for the taking, and he knew it. He led her to the bedroom, where their lovemaking was unhurried and deeply sensual.

Cate had not had an experience like it in a long time; not since Louis. Warren was an accomplished lover; reawakening a primal passion that had long been buried. She ached with pleasure, and her body yearned for more.

They made love again, as the early morning sunlight streamed into the bedroom. Warren cradled her in his arms and kissed her forehead as he brushed her cascading curls from her face.

"You are the sweetest woman I have ever met. Delores, Loren's mum, was a fiery person and never entirely settled into the role of wife and mother. She became ill at a time when I was building the business, and I'll admit that I didn't take time to spend with her, and then she was gone. I regret that. Cate, if I had a wife like you, I don't think I would ever leave our bed." He kissed her forehead again, then slid his arm out from under her head and got up.

"You stay as long as you want. I, unfortunately, have an appointment, and then I fly back to New York tonight. I promise next time we will spend more time together, and I hope to see a lot more of you over the next few months. By the way, how's your divorce going?"

Cate was quite taken aback by his candour about her divorce. It was a word she couldn't even manage to say to herself.

"Yes, it would be lovely to spend more time together, and regarding the other thing, my solicitor is dealing with it."

He nodded, kissed her again and left.

Cate lounged around the luxurious apartment while the private chef, who was still there and who looked exhausted, prepared her a lavish breakfast.

I could get used to a life like this, a lady of leisure being waited on hand and foot. Oh, yes, indeed — an attractive, wealthy, and successful husband like Warren would do nicely.

Chapter 25
Cornish Retreat

Luna had announced that the knitting club was on a sabbatical over August, as everyone was busy with holidays and other commitments. Luna, herself, had planned time in the West Country at a little picture-perfect cottage, complete with a rambling rose garden, to spend some time researching herbal healing. She had rented the cottage for a few weeks and was excited about the prospect. As the cats were happier at home, she had arranged that Xena would move into her house to cat-sit. This arrangement was mutually welcome to Xena, who was becoming more self-assured under the watchful and loving eye of Jo.

Carlos' romance was growing stronger day-by-day. His mood was lighter and brighter, and Scott's influence had a settling effect on him. He spent more time reading books recommended Scott, and he was now the one instigating cultural trips to a range of museums and art galleries across the city. There were no longer girlie chick flicks and evenings spent drinking too many cocktails. He had taken up a fitness regime and become vegetarian, like Scott. Sugar was also off the menu, along with alcohol and pizza. One positive side effect, at least for Cate, was that Carlos was quite happy to prepare meals for them both, and she also felt healthier. His morning routine had also been transformed — he now began each new day with a short yoga and meditation session. Cate had to admit that she was seriously impressed with his devotion.

The summer was long and hot. As the temperatures rose in the city, Cate found herself longing for a break. The idea of time by the coast — by the sea — certainly had appeal. Since she had split with Mike, she had not taken any official holidays, and she had plenty to use up. She thought of Luna and wondered if she would be brave enough to go off on her own, something she had never done before.

One particularly stifling day in the office when the fan on her desk blew only hot air at her, she spent the afternoon searching for the perfect get-away spot in Cornwall — somewhere away from the oppressive heat.

After much searching, she found a small family-run hotel in Fowey that fitted the bill perfectly. She could easily travel by train, and the accommodation was located right in the centre of the small coastal town. It was somewhere she had always wanted to visit since reading Daphne du Maurier's book *Rebecca* and watching the *Poldark* series. Mike had never been interested, so now was the perfect time to go. The idea of strolling along the rugged and windswept coastline appealed to the romantic in her, and before the day was out, she had made a reservation and purchased her train tickets.

Oh, look at me being all grown up and doing it. Can't wait. Yay, go me! What a fun way to spend my birthday this year, walking the coastal paths with the wind blowing through my hair, as the waves tumble ashore — the shores where ships were wrecked, and smugglers buried their plundered loot.

Then in the next breath —

Oh hell, what have I done? I've never gone anywhere on my own. I'm mad. I'll get murdered walking on my own or fall off a cliff, and my body will be washed out to sea, and no one will miss me until my bloated body washes up on some beach weeks later. What the hell! Just what are you thinking? Seriously Cate, don't do it!

When she told Carlos what she had done, he was extremely encouraging.

"Just go and do it for you. You'll have a great time. Cate, you're only going to Cornwall, not backpacking in the Amazon jungles. Go — and if you don't like it, jump on a train and come home. Look, if it makes you feel better to check in with me each night, send me a text, and if you don't check in, I'll call the hotel to send out a search party. Sweetie, you will love it, and you'll enjoy the fresh sea air."

"OK, yes, deep down I'm excited; just the whole doing-it-alone thing is terrifying. Oh, the one thing I will enjoy for certain is the Cornish cream tea. I'll have to walk for miles to burn off all the calories," she laughed.

"I wish I could come with you, but I've got some grovelling to do at work to make up for my time off with Scott."

***

A few weeks later, she was on the train trundling her way across the south coast of England. Given the bad reputation for British rail services, she was pleasantly surprised to find her journey ran quite smoothly from start to finish. Cate sat near the window and enjoyed watching the world fly past. She was happy to sit hidden behind her book watching the antics of her fellow travellers. One older couple was very put out by a young Australian backpacker, who insisted on nestling down on his backpack across the two seats opposite them and slept for most of the journey to Plymouth. Undoubtedly, the most upsetting thing was that the young man had kicked off his hiking boots, causing a pungent stinky-feet smell to waft around the carriage. Cate opened her window, and the welcome breeze eased the situation, at least for her.

She arrived in the village of Par, where she was due to change to a connecting local bus service to Fowey. She was tired and hungry, and irritated to discover that due to a slight delay on the final stage of their train ride, the bus had already left.

Carrying her bags and suitcase, she found a number for the local taxi service. She dialled the number, and a helpful woman advised her to sit tight, there would be a taxi with her in a few minutes. True to her word, there was, and soon she was sitting in the comfort of an air-conditioned car travelling through the scenic countryside to her final destination.

On arrival at the hotel, she was welcomed by a friendly young woman who informed her about the hotel facilities and breakfast arrangements while showing her to her room. The room looked recently redecorated in a nautical theme of blues and whites — it was fresh and appealing. There was a double bed, and the room offered a view out across the harbour. Cate allowed herself a few moments at the open window to drink in the warm sea breeze and watch the seagulls ride the thermals over the town. It was as charming as she had hoped.

Cate, just look — isn't that view breathtaking. You are going to love it here. Just sit back and enjoy it.

Her rumbling stomach reminded her that it had been a long time from her early morning breakfast. She quickly freshened up in the bathroom and made her way back to the reception area. The young woman was absent from her post; however, the welcome aroma of food beckoned from further along the hallway. Cate followed the smell like a bloodhound and was thrilled to find it led her to a lovely little bistro, with a terrace overlooking the harbour. She took a seat and enjoyed the shade provided by a blue and white striped umbrella. The cares and fears she harboured faded away as she was mesmerised by the sunlight glinting on the water.

After lunch, she explored the small town. It was just what she imagined; quaint with bags of charm. There were still a good number of visitors ambling around, but not enough to spoil the experience. She discovered a row of artsy boutiques filled with handmade jewellery, pottery, and paintings. To her delight, there were lots of little bistros and cafés. There was a lovely little museum in one of the oldest buildings in Fowey, and down by the harbour, there were boat tours. In the small tourist information office, she learned that a literary tour of the area ran every Wednesday and Friday, with the daylong bus trip visiting many of the famous local sights that inspired many writers, including Daphne du Maurier. Cate booked her seat immediately, as this was one thing she did not wish to miss, and to crown it all, the tour included lunch and a Cornish cream tea — perfect.

Over the next few days, Cate enjoyed the sights and sounds around her new temporary home. She sampled several famous Cornish pasties at the hut by the beach, and she dined on a freshly caught fish each evening. She relished the Cornish ice cream and even had her first cream tea at The Fowey Hotel, in the drawing room overlooking the estuary. Choosing to add to the luxury and to celebrate her birthday, she pushed the boat out and ordered a chilled glass of champagne. The luxurious setting deserved the decadence, and as it was her birthday, there was no excuse not to. Today she celebrated her thirty-eighth birthday, and although she was alone, she was happy to celebrate her newly found self-confidence — daring to spread her wings and enjoy the sensation of soaring.

Right Cate, it's time to let go of the past and be open to the future. I'm not wasting any more time hanging onto the 'what ifs' — I'm choosing, right here, right now to be thankful for all the opportunities coming my way. Who would have thought little old me would have posed for a famous artist, and made this pilgrimage here on my own? Life is wonderful, and I am going to enjoy the fantastic ride!

By the time Wednesday morning arrived, Cate had difficulty dragging herself out of her bed early enough to grab a quick breakfast before heading off to the tour pick-up point. At 8am, the town was just about coming alive, and the rising sun was starting to warm the fresh morning air.

Cate had already spent many hours in the Fowey museum learning about the local area which inspired Daphne du Maurier's writing, and she had even managed to visit a few of the highlights in and around Fowey.

At least twenty plus people were loitering around, most within groups of twos or threes and all looked like keen book lovers, or like they were being dragged along by one. The coach arrived, and Cate was relieved to find it was a luxury air-conditioned coach. She boarded and took a seat by the window towards the back of the bus. Once all the literary enthusiasts on board, the tour began. Carol, their young tour guide for the day, introduced herself and explained that she had studied literature at university and was now a writer and part-time editor herself; with summers spent acting as a tour guide in the area.

As the coach negotiated some narrow country roads and bumbled along the coast, Carol pointed out various sights. She talked about many of the well-known authors and poets who were inspired by the region.

Their first point of interest was Menabilly where Daphne du Maurier had lived. The 17th-century manor house had been the inspiration for the fictional Manderley Estate in her famous first novel *Rebecca*, one of Cate's all-time favourites. Unfortunately, the estate was not open to visitors, but as the coach drove around the area, Carol pointed out other places that had featured or at least inspired some of the writer's other works, including *The Birds* and *My Cousin Rachel*.

The next port of call was Charlestown Harbour. The picturesque harbour was used to portray Truro harbour, as it would have been back in the late 1700's, for the latest TV series *Poldark*. Cate enjoyed strolling around and secretly hoped they would be filming, but alas no.

The tour then continued down the striking Lizard Peninsula, where they were told tall-tales of smugglers and pirates. Cate, along with many of her companions, lapped it up. Her nose was pressed to the window as she watched the rugged coastline unfold punctuated with small bays and coves. They stopped for lunch in a charming restaurant overlooking the Atlantic Ocean, before continuing the tour back inland through the wild expanse of Bodmin Moor; where Cate was thrilled to see a herd of the famous wild horses. Finally, they ended up a Bolventor, where the Cornish cream tea would be served in the famous *Jamaica Inn*.

While they ate, Carol told them about du Maurier being inspired to write her book of the same name, after staying at the inn. They heard tales of smugglers and how many who stay at the inn report strange happenings and ghostly sights in the hours of darkness.

By now, all the literary lovers were giddy with the romance of it all. Lots of photos had been snapped, and even Cate had managed to grab a few selfies along the way to send to Carlos as part of her daily check-in.

By the time she arrived back to Fowey, she was weary. Instead of dinner at the nearby restaurant, she frequented most evenings; she decided to enjoy a glass of wine and a sandwich on the terrace at the hotel. It was the perfect setting to spend time re-reading a copy of *Rebecca*, which she had purchased at the small bookshop in the town. As she read, her thoughts turned to the twisting plot of her own life. She felt a tinge of sadness over the ending of her marriage to Mike, and the enchantment of her budding romance with Warren, along with the excitement of her new eclectic friends. Sometimes real life could be stranger than fiction.

The week went by quickly, and soon she was boarding the train for her journey back to London, and her life again. At least her batteries were recharged, and she felt renewed. Her retreat had given her space to breathe and think. She was returning stronger and ready to face life again. This time, it would be on her terms.

***

When she hauled her bags in through the front door of the apartment, Carlos leapt up to her aid. She was exhausted from a day's worth of travelling in the searing heat; it hadn't helped that the train from Plymouth back to London had no air-conditioning.

"Sweetie, welcome back! Well, my little explorer — how was it?"

Cate poured herself a glass of water and told Carlos of her retreat; painting a picture of her experiences in language that would have made Daphne du Maurier herself proud.

"You look different. You look relaxed, but it is more than that — like you've made inner peace with yourself. I like it," said Carlos. "Now for my update."

There was a pause as Carlos took a deep breath and Cate knew there was something big coming.

"When you left, Scott and I talked, and I said you had gone and I was a little lonely without you. So, the next evening, I arrived home to find guess-who standing at the door. Can you believe it? He was missing me too and decided to jump on a plane over to visit. So, guess who called in sick for a few days? Anyway, we had a great time. Did you know he is a fabulous cook and wine connoisseur? We explored London together, did all the sights — London Eye; London Film Museum; Madame Tussauds; a movie bus tour; and even the Jack the Ripper walking tour. It was amazing."

"Wow, that sounds great."

Carlos put his hand up to stop her.

"I'm not finished. Now sweetie, don't be angry with me. You know the vouchers you bought me for my birthday? Well, I know that we said we would do it together, but Scott wanted to do it, too. So, we did that together on his last day. It was great fun, and I promise I will take you another time. Oh, we laughed the whole time. He said he had never enjoyed himself so much. Well, after the mixology and afternoon tea, we ended up in a little bistro, very romantic, and guess what?"

Carlos stopped and looked at her with his eyes wide, waiting for her response.

"You ate prawns and ended up with food poisoning? I don't know. Tell me," replied Cate.

"Are you ready for this — he said he loves me."

"Oh, Carlos, do you feel the same?"

"Absolutely, but wait, there's more…"

The suspense was starting to irritate Cate.

"He asked me to marry him!"

"What did you say?" said Cate bouncing up and down, hanging onto Carlos' arms.

"What do you think I said? YES, of course!"

"You're getting married; you're engaged? I don't believe it. I leave you on your own for one week, and you go and get engaged," screamed Cate, as Carlos swung her around in his arms.

"Yes, and we have six weeks to arrange the wedding."

"Holy crap, are you kidding me? Six weeks? Can it be done?"

"Yes, as long as you agree to be my bestie and help me. Although, Scott did say he'll organise a wedding planner to sort everything out. It's going to be at his home in Malibu on the beach. How cool is that — how bloody Hollywood, right?"

What the hell — Carlos and Scott? Getting married? He'll go off and leave me. Crap — I'm turning into that old hag sitting alone with my knitting and my books. No, no, no — Carlos, please don't leave me!

"Sweetie, are you free next Saturday? We need to go shopping for my wedding outfit. I know just what I want. There is a tailor on Savile Row who is incredible. I'll call and make an appointment, and we will need to get something suitable for you, too. Cate, will you be my bridesmaid, matron of honour, witness, whatever they call it?"

"Yes, yes, yes — and by the way, I guess that means you owe me a bottle of champers, as he is your 'Mr Right'."

"Yes, I definitely do," said Carlos grinning from ear to ear.

Tears trickled down Cate's cheeks. In her heart, she was filled with joy for him, but also felt a little twinge of sadness.

Chapter 26
Wedding Plans

On Saturday morning, Cate invited Carlos to breakfast at Papa Jean's café before heading to his appointment with the tailor.

Papa Jean came bustling over as soon as he spotted Cate, leaving a customer waiting for his coffee order, and greeted her with his signature bear hug. When he released her from his grip, he noticed her companion. He looked at Carlos and then at Cate and exclaimed, with a mischievous glint in his eye, "*Ma chérie*, who is this handsome young man?"

"Oh, Papa, this is my dear friend Carlos. We are living together. Well, I mean that we are sharing an apartment together. Erm… Mike left me."

Papa Jean looked even more confused.

"No, I mean to say it's not like that. Carlos is getting married," and then as an afterthought, she blurted out, "Mike left me for another woman who is about to give birth any day now."

Jean nodded as he grasped the situation. Seeing the tears starting to well up in Cate's eyes, he gave her another quick hug; then turned to Carlos and shook his hand congratulating him on his impending nuptials. Papa Jean returned to his station to finish serving the now irritated customer, who was still waiting for his coffee. Carlos and Cate sat down, and as soon as they did so, a waiter brought over a range of pastries, courtesy of Papa Jean.

Carlos was in awe of the delicious pastries, claiming that the aroma alone was adding pounds to his lean pre-wedding frame. The coffee was strong and invigorating, and Papa Jean came over with a glass of champagne for each of them to toast Carlos' forthcoming marriage.

"Cate, why haven't you brought me here before now? It's just divine," exclaimed Carlos, tucking into his third pastry. As he brushed away the crumbs, he laughed, "Perhaps it's a good thing, otherwise I would be the size of a mountain. Treats today only, as it's a special occasion."

When Cate tried to pay the bill, Papa Jean insisted it was on him, and he said he hoped that it would not be too long before he would see them both again. As he hugged her farewell, he whispered in her ear, "I like that young man, shame he's taken, but you will find someone who deserves you, *ma chérie*, and he will be lucky to have you. *A bientôt*."

Cate led the way from the café, cutting down back streets to avoid the growing crowd of Saturday shoppers on Oxford Street. In less than ten minutes, they were on Savile Row.

Cate knew that Savile Row was famous for having some of the best tailors in the world and from what she gleaned from reading celebrity magazines; it was popular with the young royals, a handful of A-list celebrities, and quite a few premiership footballers. As they walked down the street, each window displayed their craftsmanship. Carlos stopped a couple of times to admire the elegant handmade suits, pointing out details. She was happy to admit she was a philistine on the topic of fashion, and even more so when it came to men's fashion.

They arrived at the shop a few minutes before Carlos' appointment. Rather than killing time outside, Carlos went in.

"Good morning, sir. May I assist you?" asked a smartly dressed salesman. He was wearing a tailored suit, which fitted his lean frame to perfection. His hair was sleeked into the style popularised by many of the well-known footballers, with a neatly trimmed beard. To Cate, he looked like he had just stepped out of a glossy magazine.

"Hello, my name is Carlos Santos. I have an appointment at ten-thirty. I'm a few minutes early."

"Of course, Mr Santos, we have been expecting you. Please step this way."

Carlos and Cate followed the man into an area towards the back of the shop. Fortunately for Cate, there was a comfortable brown leather sofa, and she was happy to install herself there for the duration, while Carlos was guided to an area with racks of suits: from black to eye-catching reds and a few trimmed with gold. There was an ornate full-length mirror to one side, and the fitting room had a heavy midnight blue velvet curtain secured with a large gold tassel. Next to the sofa was a table with a selection of men's fashion magazines. Cate picked up one to flick through while the man and Carlos discussed his requirements.

The appointment lasted almost two hours, and Cate was bored out of her mind. She had browsed through all of the available magazines, several times, and played with her phone until the battery was almost flat. Carlos, meanwhile, tried on a range of styles of jackets, waistcoats, trousers and shirts. The salesman measured Carlos thoroughly, which Carlos didn't seem to mind. Cate could see he was relishing the experience.

She had never imagined that men's suits could be so involved. There were jackets with tails known as *morning suits*; there were dinner jackets; Nehru jackets; double-breasted; single-breasted. Then the trousers were with pleats, tucks, or flat-fronted; straight leg or tapered leg; relaxed fit or slim fit.

Wow, Mike just went to M&S for his casual wear and Moss Bros. for his suits for work. I never knew there were so many options to choose from. Please, Carlos, pick one and let's get out of here. I'm bored and a little peckish!

Under the expert guidance of the salesman, Carlos finally settled on an ivory dinner jacket, with a tuck-fronted trouser with a slightly tapered leg, which to all accounts was very en vogue at the moment, along with a soft gold brocade waistcoat, matching cravat, and pocket handkerchief. Cate had to admit he looked as if he had stepped straight from the pages a magazine.

"Carlos, you look amazing. Did anyone ever tell you, you could be a model? It looks perfect on you."

"Yes, indeed sir. The style is perfect on you, and when it is altered to your fit, you will certainly cut a dash on your wedding day."

Carlos stood in front of the mirror, straightened himself up, and asked the salesman to take a photo.

The suit would be ready in four weeks; fortunately, they had one in stock, which only needed altering. They would call and notify Carlos to arrange the final fitting as soon as the suit arrived back, and small alterations could be done within a day. Carlos also spoke with the salesman to arrange for a similar style suit to be made in a dove grey for Scott, assuring the anxious salesman that Scott would call in, in-person, in the coming week.

Carlos handed over his credit card details and didn't flinch at the cost, which initially shocked Cate. She had been used to Mike purchasing his suits from shops where an expensive suit cost only a few hundred pounds.

"Now, let's get you sorted out," said Carlos, as they stepped out of the shop.

"I think I need a bite to eat first. What about tapas?" replied Cate, trying to suppress the grumbling noises from her stomach. "There's a bar around the corner from here where we can regroup and decide the next step. How does that sound?"

"Seriously, you have room after that breakfast?"

"You know me: when I get low blood sugar, I get my *Cate-bear* on. I think it's best I eat something. Just a wee bite — come on, Carlos, it's literally just two minutes from here," pleaded Cate.

"OK, you win. Lead the way, my hungry little bear."

The tapas bar was cosy. Carlos ordered a bottle of cava to wash down the various plates of tapas. They were both more than happy to set aside their healthy eating regime for the day.

"While we're this far, I think we should go to Selfridges to find something for you. I hear from many of my clients that they do a great range of evening and occasion wear.

If we don't find anything there, we can jump in a cab and head over to Harrods. OK?"

"OK, let's do it," replied Cate, although secretly, it was not something she was excited about doing. After her last embarrassing experience in Harrods, she was a little reluctant to go near any elegant dress shops.

"Carlos, are you sure you know Scott well enough to get married? You don't think you're rushing in?"

"Oh, I know it has only been a handful of months, but I know. I love him and feel that I've known him forever. He makes me laugh; we have fun together. We could talk forever. It's like he completes me and makes me a better person. It's totally different from my relationship with Sergei. With Scott, I feel it here." Carlos put his hands to his heart.

"You know, you're like a baby brother to me, as well as my best friend, and I wanted to check. I've got a good feeling that you guys will make it work," said Cate, as she reached out and grasped Carlos' hand in hers.

"When is Scott next across?"

"He should be here early next week. I'll speak with him tonight to find out the details, as I'll need to set an appointment with the tailor. My heart races at the thought of seeing him again and holding him in my arms. He is my best friend, my lover, and my soon-to-be husband. Cate, you do know that you are, and will always be my number one girlie best friend, don't you?"

"I'll miss you, Carlos. I'm bursting with happiness for you, but I will miss you… and Miss Dior."

"Yes, I'm glad you brought that up, because I didn't quite know how to broach that topic. Scott will arrange for my personal belongings to be shipped back to his home at the end of filming next month. He has invited me to fly back with him when he goes back at the end of next week. He already has an attorney working on all the paperwork for my visa. Apparently, it won't be an issue for us to get married and me to join him. I probably won't be able to work for a while, but I'm OK to be a kept-man for a bit." Carlos shifted in his seat and turned to face Cate, eye-to-eye. "Promise me you will come to visit. I couldn't bear to have you come into my life and then lose you. Please say you will come and stay, and Scott will pay your airfare. I believe there is a guest room, and I'm putting your name on it."

"Oh, Carlos, of course, I'll come to visit. I've never been to California, and it would be great to explore it with you."

***

A short walk back through the side streets and in no time at all they were standing in the makeup and perfume area of Selfridges. Carlos read the store guide, and soon they had pushed their way through to the ladies eveningwear and bridal department. Cate felt like a fish-out-of-water as Carlos explained what was needed. The pretty young sales girl walked them through to a private shopping area, explaining that usually an appointment was required. However, they were in luck, as the person who had been booked just called and cancelled.

The sales girl tried to ask Cate about her preferences and did not get far, so Carlos stepped in and described what he felt would be suitable. The girl instructed Cate to step into the plush fitting area and strip down to her underwear. Once Cate had done so, the girl stepped in and took some key measurements. Unlike Carlos, Cate felt uncomfortable, until the girl announced that she was a dress size-12. Cate was shocked; she hadn't worn a twelve since she married Mike, and that was only after practically starving herself for months in an effort to squeeze into her wedding dress.

A few minutes later, the girl appeared back with an armful of dresses to try on. She explained that, given that the wedding was in less than two months time, there were limited options available. She kindly informed them that some of the dress samples were on sale and if there was anything suitable, the store also offered an alteration service, for a small fee, to ensure a perfect fit for madam's wedding day

Carlos laughed, and before Cate had a chance to explain that it was not her wedding, she was whisked back into the fitting room to try on the dresses.

The first dress was too full and flouncy, and as soon as she stepped out, Carlos shook his head. The next dress was tight with a fishtail in gold lace. Again, Carlos shook his head. The third was an off-the-shoulder dress with a fitted bodice embroidered with a gold floral design, and a soft tulle skirt. Carlos nodded but was still not convinced.

"No, getting better, but still not right."

The last dress was a two-piece outfit: a boatneck gold lace top with cap sleeves, teamed with an ivory chiffon skirt. When Cate put it on it felt more comfortable, and with a quick peek in the mirror, she knew she liked it. When she stepped out, Carlos stood up and clapped.

"That's the one! It's stunning on you and looks fabulous with your hair. Yes, sweetie, I can see your hair piled up with a subtle tiara and soft curls cascading down. Yes, we'll take that one — it's a perfect fit. How lucky is that?"

"Yes, I love it too. It feels comfortable being a separate top and skirt. It makes me feel elegant like Audrey Hepburn in *Breakfast at Tiffany's*."

Carlos followed the sales girl back to the register while Cate changed back into her regular clothes.

***

With all the excitement, Cate was exhausted by the time they returned home. She excused herself. Carlos didn't mind as he had plans to Skype Scott with all the updates of their day.

In the bedroom, Cate hung up her outfit, following precisely the instructions issued by the sales assistant.

I can't believe how beautiful it is; it's like a wedding dress. If I ever got married again, it would be perfect.

Cate ran a bath and stepped in. The bubbles were soft on her skin. As she lay back, she remembered the thrill of buying her wedding dress for her marriage to Mike. She had spent the day with her mother back in Belfast, trawling around the two main bridal boutiques. She had tried on so many dresses, and most of them made her look like she had stepped out of a Disney princess movie. In the end, she had found an understated dress in an off-white embossed satin, with a sweetheart neckline, fitted bodice fastened with a row of pearls down the back, and a skirt that hung softly over her hips. Her mother and the lady in the shop had wanted her to choose one of the big princess-style dresses, but in the end, it was Cate's decision. She had also opted for a very simple veil. Cate felt she had been an elegant bride, and even the last time she had pulled out their wedding album, she believed she had made the right choice.

Well, I certainly made the right choice with the dress, if not the man. All that planning, cost, and the vows we made, all gone — or at least will be in a matter of weeks. Would I do it again? Probably not — I don't think I could put myself through it again. I would find it hard to trust someone completely, and a marriage must be built on love and trust.

It was all hype, and from what she could see, you end up being the one left with your heart in tatters. Although she hoped that Carlos and Scott would live happily ever after, she realized that not all marriages stand the test of time. Up until her sister, Tara, had gotten divorced, no one in her family had dared go down that route. Marriage was for life, or a 'life sentence' as her father used to say. Now, she would be the next one admitting defeat, and she guessed she would — sometime soon — have to let her parents know of her failure. After what her mother had said when she heard about her sister, it was a conversation she was not keen to have. Her parents adored Mike, and she always got the feeling they were ashamed that it was her fault they didn't have more grandchildren.

Anyway, this isn't about me; it's about Carlos' happiness. I'm just pleased to be part of it and to be there for him. Wait 'til the ladies find out; they'll be thrilled. Guess I'll have to get my thinking cap on for ideas for a hen night. I wonder what we should do?

***

A few evenings later, Cate received an unexpected telephone call from Warren. He was calling from Tokyo. Unable to sleep, he called wanting to hear her voice. He chatted about his dislike for the busy chaotic city, with its endless neon signs and raw sushi bars. She, in turn, told him about Carlos' news, and excitedly invited him to be her plus one at the wedding. She found it hard to hide her disappointment upon hearing that his schedule was packed with meetings relating to an upcoming property deal. Warren, sensing her mood change, promised to make it up to her next time they met.

Cate was just thrilled to hear from him, and looked forward to seeing him, and secretly wishing to be held in his arms again.

Chapter 27
Naked Knitting Hens

With everyone still getting back into their routines following the summer period, Luna sent all the naked knitters a quick text message to let them know that the first club night was the upcoming Wednesday evening. Cate read the text and admitted to herself that she was excited to catch up with everyone again. It seemed like a lot had happened the last couple of months, and by all accounts, the next few would also be busy.

***

"Welcome back, ladies — and gentleman, it's been a busy summer. How are you all doing? How are you, Alice? Oh my, that bump is fairly growing... the baby is due late-November, is that right? I think you might want to prepare for it coming earlier," said Luna, placing a hand on Alice's swelling belly. "How are you, Xena? Thanks for looking after the place while I was away. I see that being in love is agreeing with you."

Xena was cuddled up next to Jo, and they both looked extremely content together.

"Cate, you are looking well rested. I heard you enjoyed a little break down to the Cornish coast. It looks like it has done you good. And what about you Carlos? Is there something you want to tell us?"

Cate looked at Carlos a little surprised. How could Luna know? But then, it didn't take a psychic to see that Carlos was bursting to share some news.

"Well, Carlos, we're waiting," said Luna, smiling.

"I'm getting married!"

The room exploded into a mass of people sharing congratulatory hugs and kisses with Carlos. The room was abuzz with the high-octane energy of excitement.

Once everyone settled down, Luna invited Carlos to share the details, as everyone wanted to know who the lucky man was, when the wedding would be, where it would be, and who would be invited.

Carlos shared all the details, telling them about his summer with Scott; how Scott had turned up at his door because he was lonely without Cate, and how he popped the question. Carlos told them about the fitting for his suit and how Cate also had the most beautiful dress to wear, as she would be his 'best woman'. He went on to tell them that there would be a hen night, yet to be arranged, and if anyone had any suggestions, please speak with Cate. He hinted that a pampering spa experience would be great in a fancy hotel with good food and lots of champagne. He told them that the wedding would be in California, at Scott's Malibu home on the beach.

Jo piped up, "Oh, Carlos, that just sounds so romantic. I often thought if I ever got married that I would love a beach wedding." She smiled at Xena and gave her a kiss on the cheek.

"Carlos, I know just the place for your hen party and I'll talk it over with Cate. Congratulations, and may I be presumptuous to ask; are we all invited to the wedding? And if so, may we bring a plus one?" enquired Lady.

"Ladies, you are my family. How could you not be invited? I sincerely hope you will all come, and of course, you may bring someone," replied Carlos, looking around the room at all his dear friends.

"Sorry, Carlos, I won't be able to be there."

Everyone turned to stare at Alice. Of course, her baby was due, and there was no way she could fly.

"You'll definitely be there for the hen night, and we will have to see if we can rig up a live video link for you to join on the day. I'm sure that Scott will know someone who can do that. You might not be there in body, but I'll damn well make sure you are there remotely. How does that sound?" Carlos knelt down next to Alice, put his head on her extending girth. "Both of you."

Alice patted Carlos' head, then started to cry, citing hormones as her excuse.

"So, there's no point in trying to organise a surprise for the groom-to-be, or is that bride-to-be? Anyway, while we are all here together and Carlos obviously has some idea of what he would like, we may as well bounce around some ideas," said Cate, taking charge.

"Absolutely," agreed Luna. "How about a spa day? Although, I have to admit, I've never done that sort of thing."

"How about a goddess weekend down in the New Forest?" suggested Xena enthusiastically. Jo hugged Xena and thanked her for a great idea, but suggested that as it would be October, it might not be suitable for Alice in her delicate condition.

"Lady, you mentioned you have an idea. Let's hear it," asked Cate.

"OK, my dears. I have a friend who owns the most wonderful little manor house in the Cotswolds. They have a small spa facility and a wonderful gourmet restaurant; he used to be a chef in a Michelin-starred restaurant in London. I could contact him, and I am sure we might be able to rent the entire place just for us in October. I think he also runs some gin workshops too, as well as cooking classes. Here, I'll find his website on my phone, and you can have a quick look and see what you think, as we don't have a lot of time to organise."

Lady found the website and passed her phone around the group. Carlos grabbed the phone from Cate, eager to see.

"I love it. It's just perfect! I'll talk to Scott as he has offered to treat us all, and he has left it completely up to me. If it's available, we could go up the Friday and come back on Sunday. Make a weekend of it — time for lots of spa treatments. I have my wedding suit to fit in, so I can't indulge too much, though. Cate, you've always said you'd like to make your own gin. What do you all think?"

"Count us in," answered Jo, with Xena nodding excitedly beside her.

"My feet and legs are swelling and get quite sore, so a lovely spa treatment and some pampering would be heavenly," replied Alice.

"Oh yes, I'm in too. We could bring along our knitting projects and have a mini-hen knitting night too," suggested Luna.

"Do you want to give your friend a quick call now and just check availability before we get too carried away?"

They all replied, 'yes' in unison.

Lady disappeared into the kitchen, already dialling the number.

When she reappeared a few minutes later, she was smiling and nodding.

"He usually closes end of October through to early December, but as it is me, he said he would keep the manor open. Would the weekend, before Halloween, suit everyone?"

Everyone nodded in agreement. Lady said she would liaise directly with Archie, the owner, and keep Cate in the loop.

***

"Come on Carlos! Get a move on. The car is waiting. What the hell are you doing?" shouted Cate, as she stood bag in hand ready to lock the front door behind them.

Carlos' life was a whirl; he had only returned a few days previously from his visit to California and could not stop raving about it. He'd handed in his resignation, but his boss got so shitty with him that they fell out and he demanded Carlos leave immediately; which to all intents and purposes suited him. He still hadn't recovered from his jetlag, although he had no complaints flying in first class. He had a million and one things to do, or at least that's how it felt. Right now the idea of heading away for three days to his hen party all felt too much. He just wanted to curl up and go to sleep for a few days.

"Carlos, I swear, we will go without you if you don't get a move on!" shouted Cate.

"Coming, Miss Bossy Boots. You can't go without me; I'm the *hen*."

Finally, they clambered into the back of the white stretch limo, a surprise that Cate had organised. The rest of the group had already been picked up and were waiting inside.

"Let's get this party started — time for a glass of champers," said Lady, waving a bottle in her hand. The limo was well stocked with mini-champagne bottles and a few non-alcoholic drinks for Alice.

"Time for some music to get us in the mood," said Jo, connecting her phone with a party playlist to the limo sound system.

Two and a half hours and three pee stops later; they pulled up the drive to Wold's End Manor. The manor house was a 16th-century building in a honey-coloured stone with an expansive garden. To the right-hand side, Cate spotted an old stone archway covered in ivy that led into another part of the garden. She made a mental note to explore it later. The place was idyllic.

As the ladies stepped out of the back of the limo, the heavy-set front door opened and a tall willowy man stepped out. When he saw Lady, he rushed over and greeted her like a long-lost friend, showering her with affection. Cate secretly wondered if this was another of her past lovers. Archie was introduced to the ladies and to Carlos. He bid them welcome and promptly arranged for each guest to be shown to their assigned room.

Cate's room did not disappoint and reminded her of her weekend stay at Lady's home.

She unpacked her overnight bag, hanging up her dresses and arranging her underwear and other clothes in the drawers of the antique chest. She showered and put on the fluffy white bathrobe and slippers, courtesy of the hotel, and wrapped her wet hair in a towel. She had at least thirty minutes to enjoy some knitting time before getting ready for dinner.

Who would ever have thought I would be sitting in such a beautiful place with such wonderful friends and be knitting? Let alone being at a hen weekend for my gay best friend. I would never have believed it in a million years.

***

Archie whipped up a sumptuous four-course dinner, which lived up to his Michelin-starred acclaim, with each course paired with a wine grown locally. Poor Alice was disappointed that she was so heavily pregnant she could only eat a little of each dish. Carlos looked at Cate during their culinary experience and shook his head as he patted his stomach. Cate felt the same; she wanted to enjoy each and every succulent morsel, but she held back knowing that she had a size-12 dress to fit into.

Even when the others were beaten, skinny Xena devoured every mouthful and sent back each plate cleared. At one point, Archie came out and commended Xena, saying that she was every chef's dream.

By the time coffee and chocolates were being served back in the bar area, one by one, the friends drifting off to bed. When it was only Cate and Carlos left, he admitted he was shattered and needed his rest too.

***

The following morning started with a leisurely breakfast, and the friends trickled in, meeting again. Cate had never seen such a breakfast menu before. There were kippers, kedgeree, smoked salmon, brioche French toast, pancakes, an array of freshly baked pastries, and a full English breakfast to order. In the end, still sated from the previous evening's extravaganza, she chose to enjoy a steamy hot coffee and nibbled on a warm buttery croissant, which she had to admit rivalled Papa Jean's.

After breakfast, they were given their time slots for treatments in the spa. Unfortunately, it was only a small area and could not accommodate the group en masse. However, most of the party were happy to either disappear back to their rooms or to enjoy a stroll around the gardens. Carlos was off for his massage treatment, so Cate decided to explore the grounds. It was a beautiful October day with a mellow autumnal sun. Through the ivy-covered archway, she discovered a topiary garden, filled with perfectly sculptured trees in the shapes of an elephant, a flower, a dog, and one she felt sure was an aeroplane. Interspersed were rose bushes that had now been trimmed back for the winter. Cate could only imagine how spectacular the garden must be at the height of summer.

After a while, she wandered back into the hotel and sat down in one of the large sofas near the original stone fireplace in the reception area, in which there glowed a real log fire. She picked up a magazine from the coffee table and enjoyed leafing through the pictures of magnificent historic properties in the area. She was in awe at how many of the old listed buildings had been renovated to retain their charm and original period features, and yet updated to offer all modern comforts.

Cate allowed herself a few moments to imagine living in such a beautiful place. She visualised living here at Wold's End Manor and hosting the most spectacular Christmas parties. Friends and family would arrive and step in from the wintery cold to relish a hot mulled wine standing in front of a roaring fire. She could see the massive real Christmas tree, decked with traditional trimmings, tucked into the corner beside the fireplace. She could see a long dining table set up for the Christmas feast in the dining room, and how everyone would gasp as the turkey was brought out and set before them — it was Warren's face she could picture, smiling at her as he carved the turkey.

The sudden image of Warren in her daydream yanked her back to reality. Strange she hadn't heard much from him since he called her from Tokyo.

Whoa – where did that come from? I guess I'm surprised I haven't heard from him lately. I wonder if he ever thinks of me. It's a shame he can't come to Carlos' wedding. It would have been lovely to have him there with me. Oh Cate, maybe that was it — one night of passion and poof! Gone, moved on to the next woman.

***

After a quick lunch in the bar, Cate and Luna went off for their appointments. The area was quite compact, and as Cate enjoyed her luxury pedicure, she couldn't help but listen to Luna's running commentary about her massage experience. From the perspective of an outsider listening in, it could be easy to misunderstand what was going on, and what exactly Luna was enjoying. All you could hear were exclamations like: "Ohhh, a little more... Harder, harder... Aggghh that's so good, don't stop."

At one point, Cate thought Luna was purring, or perhaps she had fallen asleep and was snoring. Either way, she could barely contain her urge to laugh, and couldn't wait to share the story with Carlos.

As they had some time before dinner, Luna suggested they all get together in the reception area for a bit of knitting and nattering. Cate was happy to join in; she was at a point in her pattern where she needed a little assistance to fathom the next part. As usual, Alice was ready to offer her help, and with a few minutes' explanation it all became clear, and Cate could carry on. The group sat together knitting and chatting — fully clothed, even though Lady had insisted that Archie wouldn't mind. Cate glanced across and was pleased to see Carlos looking relaxed chatting away with Jo and Xena; with his own knitting project practically untouched. It gave Cate an idea.

Dinner, thankfully, was not such a gastronomic affair as the previous night, but delicious all the same.

Afterwards, Archie had arranged for a singer to come in and entertain them in the bar. The guy was good, singing a repertoire of Sinatra and Bublé songs. The atmosphere was perfect, although Cate did wonder if it was the type of hen party Carlos had wanted. She needn't have worried, as Carlos was enjoying the cocktails and the company of his friends; people with whom he could just be himself, exactly how he felt with Scott. Towards the end of the evening, he ended up singing a duet with the entertainer, and to be fair, it was pretty good.

***

The following morning, after breakfast, the final day's activities kicked off with a gin workshop. This event was the part of the weekend that Cate had been looking forward to the most.

The bar area had been set up for the workshop, and Archie introduced his friend, William, who ran an artisan gin distillery in the nearby village. William was a charismatic man who was very passionate about gin. He told them about the history of gin; explained the distilling process; and talked about the botanicals used to give the gin its unique aroma and flavour. He explained that they would be making something known as 'bathtub gin'.

Each of the friends received a small bottle of the basic alcohol, and was invited to add their preferred botanicals — based on some recipes William personally recommended. Cate opted for lots of juniper berries, black peppercorns, orange peel, and half a cinnamon stick. William advised them to remove the botanicals in approximately twenty-four hours, and then the gin would be ready to drink. Cate could hardly wait to try hers, and she thought it was a lovely touch that Lady had gotten labels designed especially for the occasion; each one personalised with their name.

As a farewell gesture for the ladies, Archie had wanted to do a special lunch, and had decided to create a menu based on Carlos' Brazilian heritage. There was *moqueca* — a fish stew; followed by a plate of *brigadeiro* — handmade chocolate bonbons.

Carlos over-indulged and commended Archie on his ability to prepare each dish as well as, if not better than, his grandmother.

"Thank you, thank you so much, *muito obrigado*... You have no idea how happy you make me..." He said, choking back the tears. Soon everyone, including Archie, was crying and hugging.

Chapter 28
Births, Deaths & Marriages

Carlos was in his element; he had turned into 'bridezilla', and was enjoying every moment of it. He was in constant contact with the wedding planner in L.A. discussing various details of the wedding to the nth degree. Cate felt a little sorry for the wedding planner, but at the same time, Carlos was right to insist on the wedding he wanted. When Cate overheard about a flock of doves being released to celebrate their marriage, she had to say something.

"Carlos, what the hell? A flock of doves, are you mad?"

"What? I think it would be romantic seeing the white mass ascend into the blue skies across the ocean. In the promo video the planner sent me, it looked incredible."

"Think about it for a second; those poor doves are stuffed into cages and then let loose to dear knows what. It's downright cruel."

"OK, sweetie, I didn't think of it like that, but I guess you're right. What about each guest releasing a white heart-shaped balloon with our initials on it?"

"Erm... No. Again, think about it — the balloons float off and then end up in the sea where some poor unsuspecting dolphin eats one and dies. Do you want to have that on your conscience?"

"OK, no doves and no balloons. Since when did you turn into such an animal activist?"

"Since seeing horrific videos on Facebook. Look, this wedding is going to be amazing, but just think about some of the consequences. That's all I'm saying. By the way, did you sort out about Miss Dior being the ring bearer?"

"Yes, all in hand. She will be gorgeous. You don't mind looking after her on the day of the wedding; do you?"

"No, we're your best girls, isn't that right Miss Dior?" Cate answered, as she picked up Miss Dior and gave her a quick cuddle.

***

A few days later, the two were en route to the airport, along with Miss Dior in her travel carrier. Scott suggested that it would be advisable for Carlos to be there a week before the wedding to do the last-minute preparations, and Carlos had insisted that Cate come too. Scott's PA had worked a miracle to find them a flight on which Miss Dior was permitted to fly in the cabin; otherwise, Carlos had refused to go.

The three of them sat in the first-class lounge enjoying the hospitality on offer. It was the first time that Cate had been in such a place, and she loved it. Carlos was acting as if he did it all the time, and from now on, he would. The luxury service continued when they boarded the flight, meaning that the journey flew by. The cabin crew fussed over Carlos, Cate and Miss Dior, ensuring that all their wishes were fulfilled.

On arrival in the Los Angeles airport, Scott's driver was there to meet them. Scott sent his apologies for his absence, as he had hoped to be there in person to greet them, promised to see them for dinner back at his home.

Cate was amazed at the buildings, people and cars, as they cruised along the highway down to Malibu. She had been to New York with Mike once, and that had been impressive, but this was spectacular.

They pulled up at Scott's — and now Carlos' — home, a modern three-storey building with stunning views of the ocean. Valentina, the housekeeper, was there to greet them, and it was apparent how much she adored Carlos already. She also came from Brazil, and the two of them chatted away in Portuguese like long-lost family.

When Valentina showed Cate to the guest suite, she could hardly believe it; her bed faced a huge glass window overlooking the sea. She could have sat on the end of the bed forever enjoying the blue expanse; it was calming.

Suddenly finding her energy levels recharged, she quite happily abandoned her bags and rushed back downstairs to find Carlos perched on a stool at the kitchen island, while Valentina was fixing him a snack.

"Welcome to my new home, sweetie. What do you think?"

"It's incredible. I love it."

"Valentina, we'll be out on the terrace," said Carlos, as he escorted Cate onto the outdoor area just off the open plan living room. A gentle sea breeze rolled in, and Cate could taste the slight saltiness on her tongue. It was beyond stunning, looking out across the vast never-ending stretch of ocean, with the constant waves gently lapping the shore. The two ate in silence.

Carlos' phone rang. He excused himself to deal with the call from the wedding planner, leaving Cate in a state of bliss.

***

Scott breezed in around 7pm, and it was apparent how thrilled he was to see Carlos. He welcomed Cate, while apologising profusely for not making it to the airport to meet them as planned. The three sat down to a fabulous meal prepared by Valentina. They chatted easily about their flight, Cate's first impression of L.A. and Malibu, Scott's latest project, and the wedding. Scott was so relaxed and quite happy to let Carlos have what he wanted, but Cate did notice if there was something he didn't entirely agree with, he would talk Carlos around with sound reasoning. Scott and Carlos made a great team, and their love for each other ran deep. It was different from her relationship with Mike. She had been the one to compromise, and Mike's needs always came first, something she had never recognised before now. Cate left the two lovebirds together and retired to her room, where she was surprised to find all her clothes neatly put away, her wedding outfit pressed and hung up. Her bed was turned down with the remote for the shutters set on the bedside table.

As she slipped into bed, she stared at the stars twinkling over the ocean, and made a mental note to thank Valentina in the morning.

***

The following morning, Scott and Carlos had gone off to meet with the bakery in charge of their wedding cake, and Matteo, the wedding planner, would meet them there.

Because of the meeting, Cate had plenty of time to have a walk along the beach. Her hair was blown in the light wind, and she felt truly alive for the first time since her visit to Cornwall. The sea spoke to her heart.

As she walked, she saw several people out with their dogs, and she lost count of the number of people running past her. People were friendly, wishing her a good morning, and one elderly lady dressed in a velour jogging suit power walking, stopped and struck up a conversation with her. Cate had this preconception that people would be standoffish, but so far, they had been open, warm, and friendly.

By the time she returned, Carlos and Scott were back with Matteo in tow. She met them on the beach at the front of the house, where Matteo was explaining how the wedding area would be set out, and he assured Carlos that the weather would be perfect, as he, personally, had checked with the local meteorological office. Scott walked Cate back up to the house, leaving Carlos and Matteo to wrangle out the last few details.

"Cate, may I have a quick word, please?"

"Yes, sure."

"I wanted to say a huge thank you to you. I appreciate how much you mean to Carlos and how you have been there for him. I want you to know that I love him with all my heart and I will do everything in my power to care for him and make him happy. I have never felt this way about anyone. I'm glad he has you, and I want you to know our guest room is yours to use anytime. After all, we'll soon be family," said Scott, as he turned to face Cate.

"Thank you, Scott. Carlos is like a baby brother to me and it makes me happy to see him happy, and he is, without a doubt, very much so with you. I can see how different your relationship is from how mine was with Mike. You bring out the best in each other — that's special. And thanks for the offer of the room, but you'd better be careful, or you might find I move in too. This place is unbelievable."

Carlos returned in time to join Scott and Cate for lunch on the terrace, with the news that everything was sorted, and he just couldn't wait for the big day. Miss Dior sauntered in and without any coaxing jumped up onto Scott's lap, where she purred contentedly.

If Miss Dior approved, then all was well.

***

That evening, just before dinner, Cate received a text message from Luna with some good news. Alice had been rushed to the hospital, and after a relatively smooth labour, had given birth to a bouncing baby boy whom she named Carlos Santos Price, after a dear friend. When Cate told Carlos, he was moved by Alice's sweet gesture to name her newborn after him, and the soppy pair cried.

Luna's message had confirmed they would all be arriving two days before the wedding, giving them time to recover from jetlag and acclimatise. She also explained that her cat, Trouble, had died, and she felt guilty about leaving Soot. Lady had been the one to persuade her that she had to put her grief behind her — for now — and think of Carlos.

Scott had arranged, through a friend, the use of a nearby holiday home for the ladies. It was perfect, only a few minutes' walk further along the beach.

Cate offered to go with the driver to meet them at the airport. Carlos would unfortunately be unavailable, as Scott had arranged a special surprise for him — a pre-wedding honeymoon night at a 5-star hotel in L.A. They would return the morning before the wedding. Valentina had been instructed to cater to the ladies' needs, and she did. The ladies were exhausted from their transatlantic flight and retired to bed early.

Cate enjoyed the short stroll back from the ladies' temporary home along the beach, enjoying the sunset.

Oh, it's beautiful here. I love it and can see why it will be perfect for Carlos in every way. I hope that I will find my 'soul mate' someday soon, but in the meantime — there's a bed with an ocean view waiting for me.

***

Cate was enjoying the luxury of solitude on the terrace. She soaked in the early morning peace, being gently hypnotised by the rolling waves breaking on the beach, with Miss Dior curled up on her lap sleeping. She closed her eyes and breathed in the calm — the calm before the storm.

Her phone beeped, telling her she had received a text message. When she looked, she couldn't believe it — it was a photo of Mike cradling his newborn baby. He looked so happy, so proud, exactly as she had always pictured he would be. It was a boy, named Noah — both mother and baby were doing well.

Good for you. I hope that you will be a great father to this little man. Mike, you had better shape up, but I think this little lad will be the making of you. You have to grow up now.

Looking out from the terrace, it was hard to believe that, by tomorrow, the place would be transformed into Carlos' dream beach wedding.

Miss Dior, do you want to know a secret? I'm officially a divorced woman. Just before we left, I got the 'decree absolute'. No fuss, just the end of an era; the official death of my marriage. Miss Dior, I'll tell you this, but don't tell anyone. I'm scared — petrified. I know I can do this. I can do it alone, but it's damn scary and now Carlos is moving on. Yes, I'll have to dig deep — let go of the past and focus on my future. I guess I have no choice. What is that mantra? I can and I will. Yes — that will be my mantra from now on. I can and I will. Thanks for the pep talk. Remember, this is our little secret, so don't tell anyone. I'll tell them when I'm ready.

***

As predicted, Matteo's team descended on the place and set to work like a well-oiled machine. There was a team of guys setting up the beach area; there was a team installing a make-shift kitchen for the caterers in the area under the terrace; and much to Valentina's disgust, they were lugging some of the larger items through the house, as the side alley was too narrow. Cate had a good guess as to what she was shouting at the men in Portuguese.

Carlos and Scott arrived home in the midst of the onslaught, and Carlos was immediately nabbed by Matteo to ensure that the set-up met his approval. Scott waved his arms in surrender and disappeared into the sanctuary of his office, claiming that he had some work to do. Matteo took command like a general directing his troops. With his clipboard in hand, he wielded instructions with ease and precision. Cate watched in awe as the scene unfolded like a picture in a pop-up book.

In a matter of hours, the first part of the wedding preparations was complete. Matteo and his crew left, promising to back by 9am the following morning to do the final preparations. The caterers would start work around midday, with the florist adding the floral decorations in the early afternoon. The stylist team would arrive at 1pm, with the photographer turning up around 2pm to capture shots of everyone getting ready. The string ensemble would set up and start playing for guests arriving from 5pm; the ceremony would start promptly at 6pm.

Carlos collapsed onto the sofa and sighed, "What hellish monster have I unleashed? Why did I want all this fuss? I just want Scott and me, with all my dear ladies to witness our union."

"Come on, it's all coming together, and it will be amazing. Have you seen the menu for the buffet? I just wish my skirt was elasticated," laughed Cate, reaching out and holding his hand, offering support and encouragement.

"Yes, it's an amazing buffet, and no, you are not going to change into your 'all-you-can-eat' trousers."

"Tell me everything — well, the bits you can tell me — about your surprise night away."

"Oh, Cate it was amazing, another world..." Carlos perked up, sharing the lavish details of the resort until it was time to go and get ready for dinner with the ladies. Scott wanted to take them all out to his favourite little bistro.

Scott was a massive hit with the ladies, who had arrived all together in time for drinks on the terrace before dinner.

Over dinner, the ladies were all vying for his attention and keen to get to know him better. Like Cate, they were all eager to ensure that Scott was good enough for their Carlos; and by the end of the evening, there was no doubt that he truly had earned the seal of approval from each and every one of them.

The bistro was only a twenty-minute walk along the beach, and as it was such a beautiful evening, they decided to walk back. Everyone took off their shoes, and together they strolled back allowing the full moon, reflecting on the sea, to illuminate their way.

After leaving the ladies off at their house; Cate, Carlos and Scott walked the few hundred metres back to Scott and Carlos' home. Cate slipped away, as Carlos and Scott shared a tender moment looking out over the ocean. Hand and in hand, they made their solemn vows to each other with only the moon as their witness. Cate could still see them from her bedroom, and unbeknownst to them, she took a photo of their moment, planning to get it printed and give it to them as a token of their private ceremony.

Dear Moon, I ask you to hear my wish. I pray that these two precious souls will live a long and happy life together, sharing and caring for one another with love as their compass. I ask you to bless them with profound joy and abundant happiness. I call upon you to witness and honour my wish. Let it be.

Cate climbed into bed and fell asleep under the watchful gaze of the moon.

***

The morning of the wedding arrived.

Cate had expected Carlos to be a total mess, but no, he was calm and relaxed. He looked like he had the best night's sleep ever. Even when the first batch of Matteo's workers showed up, he nonchalantly waved them out to the beach.

"What have you done with Carlos?" Cate eyed him with suspicion.

"Carlos is cool, calm, and collected. This is the biggest, most important day of my life and I'm going to chill out and enjoy it. Now, sweetie, do you want some coffee? Valentina only uses the best Brazilian beans."

"Just as long as you do; and yes, to the coffee. Has she made any of her amazing pancakes? I'm starving."

"I've told her to watch you — you can have one. You still have a dress to fit into," said Carlos, as he hugged his friend close. "I will always love you. You know that, don't you? And I believe Scott told you that the room you're in is now basically yours. I want you to come and visit as often as you like."

"Thank you. I love you, too — forever."

***

The stylist team turned up a little late, but managed to work their magic with ease. Cate sat in her silk kimono, a small thank you present from Carlos; it reminded her of her visit to Mr Yamamoto's wool shop and his knitted kimono. Hard to believe that so much had happened since then.

Cate sat back and enjoyed the luxury of having a tribe of stylists working on her from head to toe. Under the watchful guidance of Monsieur Antoine, Cate was transformed into a movie star. They helped her into her dress, and Monsieur Antoine guided her over to the full-length mirror in the corner of the room. If she had been amazed at what Carlos had done in the past, she was blown away at the beautiful goddess looking back at her. Perhaps Circe was deep in there, trying to get out.

Right Cate, it's time for action, time to step up — you can do this. Remember, you're doing it for Carlos. I can and I will. Try to not cry, and don't do anything to ruin his big day.

The photographer was teasing Carlos — who was already dressed and groomed to perfection — into a range of poses when Cate arrived. Carlos looked up, and because of the look on his face, everyone turned to see what was holding his gaze. Cate gracefully glided down the wooden stairs, unaware that all eyes were transfixed on the goddess descending into their midst. The photographer grabbed his camera and took a few shots. Scott, who was standing in the wings, walked over and took her hand, leading her safely down the last few stairs.

"You know, if I weren't gay, and head over heels in love with Carlos, you could easily steal my heart," whispered Scott in her ear, causing her to blush.

The photographer called upon Carlos and Scott for pose after pose. Then Carlos had a few taken with Cate; some with the happy couple, and finally a family one with Miss Dior, who had also received a pampering session of her own. She was happily strutting around wearing a gold ribbon tied in an enormous bow, looking every inch a diva.

***

By 5pm, all was ready, and the first guests were arriving. They were happy to mill around enjoying a welcome cocktail, chatting and laughing. Cate found the ladies in the midst of the crowd and invited them to come and have their photo taken with Carlos.

The photographer staged the ladies, in all their finery — complete with feathery fascinators and a few wide brim hats — with Carlos and Cate in the middle. He took another with the ladies standing, and the happy couple sat in their midst.

The wedding ceremony went off without a hitch, and when the couple said their vows, it was perfect in every way. Cate noted that many of the guests reached for their tissues. She bit hard on her lip to fight back the tears: partly as she didn't want to ruin her makeup, and partly because she didn't have a tissue at hand — plus, she didn't think Miss Dior would be too happy if she used her fluffy coat as a makeshift handkerchief.

Afterwards, the rows of chairs were quickly replaced with tables for the evening buffet. The atmosphere was relaxed. Cate found herself seated next to a set designer called Morris, and his partner Stevie, a cameraman, who kept her amused with their tales of on-set mishaps.

The speeches were short and emotional. Scott's words and tenderness toward his new husband were touching and heartfelt. Cate was called upon, and although she had written out a speech, she set it to one side and spoke from her heart.

"Dear Carlos and Scott, I wish you a world of joy and happiness together. The wedding is the easy part; the marriage will take a lot of trust and respect for one another. There will be times to compromise and times to say sorry. There will be ups and downs. As my grandmother used to say, never go to bed on the back of an argument. Talk and make up. Enjoy the precious moments, big and small. Finally — and most importantly — allow love to be your compass to guide your path, and all will be well." Cate smiled over at Scott and Carlos, "Please join me in raising your glass and together let's wish these two beautiful souls a lifetime of joy and happiness together. To Carlos and Scott."

Carlos thanked everyone, and instead of a speech, he called all the single ladies and men to line up as he was going to throw his bouquet. Cate shuffled forward with the other singles in the crowd. Carlos turned his back to the small line-up and tossed the flowers high into the air. Cate reached out and grabbed the prize as it tumbled back down towards the earth. She hadn't meant to catch it, but here she was with the bouquet in hand.

"Oh Cate, sweetie, looks like you'll be next!" shouted Carlos.

***

A dance floor had been set up and the band struck up music for Carlos and Scott's first dance together.

"Would you care to dance with a lonely old Yank?"

Cate swung around in disbelief; it was Warren.

"What are you doing here? I thought you said you couldn't make it."

"I wanted to see you again, and I'm glad I did come. You look sensational. So, would you care to dance with this old fool who has flown hundreds of miles to be here with you?"

"Of course, let's dance."

Warren embraced her in his arms and they danced, swaying to the soft melodic beat. It felt right, as if they were meant to be, and at that precise moment Cate was deliriously happy.

"Marry me."

"What did you just say?"

"I said, marry me."

"You can't be serious."

"I have never been more serious in all my life. Marry me, Cate. I love you, and I want you to be part of my life. Marry me."

Perhaps it was the moonlight, a few glasses of champagne, or Cupid weaving his own unique romance, which influenced her reply.

"Yes," Cate answered.

"Come with me."

Cate allowed herself to be led by Warren to his chauffeur-driven car, which was parked up on the road. They kissed as the car drove along. Cate didn't care where they were going. She was with Warren, and it felt so right. She felt safe and protected.

The car pulled up next to a small private jet, and without asking, Cate followed Warren up the steps. In just over an hour, they landed at Las Vegas airport. Warren had made a few calls, and a white stretch limo was waiting for them. It was surreal — like a movie in which she was willingly playing a leading role.

Before she knew, they had pulled up at a small church. The neon sign outside said 'Cupid's Wedding Chapel'. They signed some paperwork before the marriage officiant led them through the ceremony, with Warren and Cate repeating their lines on cue. The ceremony ended with each affirming their commitment to the other with 'I do.'

Warren slipped a diamond ring on Cate's finger, and when the officiant pronounced them man and wife, he pulled her close into a tight embrace and kissed her.

"Well, you're mine now," declared Warren, as he kissed her again and again.

They flew back to L.A., where Cate stayed the night with her new husband in his suite at the Waldorf. They made love throughout the night, consummating their marriage, and reaffirming their love for one another.

Cate was now officially *Mrs Warren Fitzgerald Kennedy.*

Chapter 29
The New Mrs Kennedy

"I love you, Mrs Kennedy."

Cate awoke to see Warren standing over her. He was already dressed.

"I'm sorry, my darling. I have to fly back to New York. My chauffeur will take you back to Malibu this morning, and we will talk later. We have plans to make. I can't live a moment without you and want you at home, with me, where you now belong."

"Oh, OK. Talk later."

"I'm the luckiest man alive this morning. I love you."

"Love you, too," said Cate, as Warren stooped to kiss her before leaving.

Cate lay in bed.

I can't believe it. I'm only divorced, and I'm married again. Oh no, what will Carlos and the ladies say?

Cate held her hand out and studied the rock on her finger.

She surfaced slowly: partly because of a headache from too much champagne, and partly because she didn't quite know how she would break the news to Carlos, let alone her parents, who didn't even know she was divorced.

What a mess. She could imagine Nanny Eileen looking down and saying, 'Well, Kitty, too late to change your mind. You've made your bed now!'

A hot shower and three cups of coffee later, she slipped back into her outfit. It didn't quite feel the same. It reminded her of seeing women slinking back home after a one-night stand, doing the 'walk of shame'. That was how she felt as she made her way out of the luxury hotel and into the car, feeling all eyes were watching her.

***

"And just where did you slip off to last night?"

Cate had only just stepped in the front door to be greeted by Carlos. He stood with his hands on his hips and a stern look on his face.

"Did you sneak off with that handsome man?"

"Erm... Yes. That's Warren."

"Oh — that's Warren!" shrieked Carlos, running over and leading her to the table where Scott was already seated and waiting for breakfast.

"OK, spill the beans. I want to know everything." Scott watched the interaction between the two friends with amusement; this was a side of their lives he had never been privy to.

"O-M-G, what is that on your hand?" Carlos jumped up and stretched Cate's hand out for Scott and Valentina to see the ring. Valentina gasped.

"Come on, tell us," commanded Carlos.

"Well... I don't know how to tell you this..." Cate pulled her hand away.

"You're engaged! Look at you only just divorced... I take it that you are now divorced, or as good as? Oh, Cate, I'm so happy. I guess he's your 'Mr Right'?" Carlos was bouncing up and down with excitement. "Oh, we have a wedding to plan. I love it!"

"There's no wedding to plan," whispered Cate.

"What? You mean you're waiting for your divorce to finalise, and then you can, right?"

"No. I mean... Yes, I'm already divorced."

"Well, then what's the problem?" asked Carlos, confused.

"Warren and I are already married."

Carlos and Scott looked at each other bewildered.

"You can't be. You were here yesterday at our wedding. How could you be single one day and married the next? It's not possible."

"We flew out to Las Vegas and got married in a wedding chapel there last night. I am now officially 'Mrs Warren Fitzgerald Kennedy'."

Carlos looked at Scott, his brow furrowed with concern, and his eyes wide with disbelief.

"Is that Warren Kennedy, the New York property mogul?" asked Scott.

"I don't know. All I know is he has a property development business, and he lives in Connecticut."

"Well, that's interesting," said Scott rubbing his chin.

"What do you mean interesting?" blurted Carlos.

"Well, he is one of the wealthiest men the East Coast, and he's consistently listed as the most eligible bachelor in the country. I believe he lost his first wife to cancer and has never remarried; although, he has been associated with some of the most beautiful models and actresses in the world." Scott paused to look at Cate.

Carlos grabbed his phone and did a quick Google search. "Is that him?" as he showed Cate a photo.

"Yes," she whispered.

Cate was shocked. Shocked, at learning she had landed a multi-billionaire husband, but the way her stomach churned was more than just excitement and hunger.

What have I done? Oh, Cate, just who do you think you are to step into the role of wife to a multi-billionaire? Oh crap.

Carlos sat looking at Cate in total disbelief, dumbstruck by the shock of Cate's news.

***

Cate went up to her room, took off her dress, and climbed into bed. She should have been happy and celebrating, but she didn't feel like it.

I'm sure it will all work out. It's just the shock, *the suddenness of it all. Warren loves me, and together we will work it out. It's a new adventure. I can and I will.*

***

A few hours later, Carlos knocked on her door. He let himself in and sat down on the bed next to her.

"I'm sorry, sweetie. I think it was the shock. If you're happy, then I'm happy. He certainly is a handsome guy."

Carlos brushed the hair from her face and kissed her on the forehead. "I'm here for you, always— remember that. Now, it's time to get yourself tidied up and come downstairs. The ladies are coming over for a barbeque, and we're opening presents. Come down when you're ready. I think it best you tell the ladies your news yourself."

Carlos left, and Cate, for the second time that day, dragged herself out of bed and had a shower. This time she had suitable clothes to change into.

When she was ready, she stared at herself in the mirror, took a deep breath, and bolstered the courage to face her friends.

***

Downstairs, the ladies had gathered on the terrace, looking a lot more relaxed in their comfortable attire. They were swapping stories about the wedding: people they had talked with and things the happy couple had missed. Cate stepped into their midst. The energy shifted, and they all looked at her.

"Cate, well done on your speech. It was beautiful, spoken from the heart," said Luna, sensing the need to break the strange atmosphere.

"Yes, indeed it was, and a good message to all married couples," added Lady.

Carlos walked over and put his arm around Cate. "Yes, it was, and it meant a lot to Scott and me. Cate has another piece of news to share. Go on, tell them," he encouraged her, giving her shoulder a little reassuring squeeze.

"Well, I've something I need to tell you all... I'm married, too."

Silence.

"Yes, it would seem that Scott and I weren't the only ones to tie the knot yesterday," laughed Carlos.

"Who, what, when, where?" asked Lady.

As the friends sat and listened intently, Cate retold the story of her whirlwind wedding in Las Vegas.

"Oh, it's like a fairy tale," squealed Xena, with delight at hearing that Warren was an extremely wealthy man. Jo looked a little less excited and more concerned about her friend's impetuous action. It was one thing to get engaged, but another to run off and get married to a man she hardly knew.

"Well, congratulations to you and I hope we will get to meet the lucky man very soon," said Luna with a smile.

"I guess now is the right time for gifts," yelled Carlos, grabbing the biggest package.

Carlos and Scott worked their way through a pile of presents. Carlos ripped them open with the enthusiasm of a child on Christmas morning. There was a myriad of household items, gift vouchers, and photo frames. When the last of the gifts were opened, Luna stood up and handed Carlos a neatly wrapped box with a huge gold bow.

"This is a little something from us for you both — something to bring you luck and remind you of all of us."

Carlos opened the gift, and from the box, he pulled out a throw in soft cream, beige and gold, with hearts and the word 'love' embroidered across some of the squares.

"We all knitted squares and made it for you. Do you like it?" asked Luna.

"I love it," replied Carlos, wrapping it around his shoulders. "It means I'll always have a part of each of you with me."

"Here, this one is from me," said Cate.

Carlos opened it.

"Oh my, it's my sweater. Did you finish it?"

"Yes, with a lot of help from my friends."

"I love it. When I wear it, it will feel like you're hugging me. Thank you, Cate."

***

Warren called Cate that evening and discussed arrangements for her to move to join him and Loren. She felt a sense of relief chatting with him, and was excited to meet her new stepdaughter.

Isn't it all unfolding just as Luna predicted, all those months earlier, with her angel cards — that both Carlos and I would meet our 'soul mates', move overseas and live happily ever after?

Chapter 30
Fond Farewells

A few days later, post-wedding, Cate returned to her apartment in London.

It was empty without Carlos and Miss Dior. At least she was back to sort out a few things, and then she, too, would be off to start a new life.

First things first, she felt she owed it to Mike to let him know that she was married again; it was one of a few difficult conversations she had to face.

She dialled his number.

"Hi Mike, this is Cate."

"Hi Cate, how are you? Did you get my text about the baby?"

"Yes, he looks gorgeous. Look, I've something I want to tell you, and I thought it was better coming from me than you finding out."

"Oh, what's up?"

"I'm married again."

"Sorry, did you say you're getting married again?"

"Erm... No. I'm already married again."

"Hellfire, Cate, you didn't let the grass grow under your feet for long."

"Well, it was all a bit sudden, but there you go. I did it. Look, I'm putting the apartment up for sale as I'm moving to the States. So when the sale goes through I'll make sure you get what you are owed. OK?"

"Yes, I was going to ask you about that. Anyway, who is the guy? Is it anyone I know?"

"No, you don't know him. He's a businessman I met recently in London."

"Seriously Cate, you do surprise me. Sorry, I've got to go. The baby is fussing, and Isabelle has gone out for the day. Come and meet Noah before you go, if you'd like."

"Thanks for the offer, but I think it best if I don't. I'll be in touch about the sale when it goes through... Mike, I always thought it would be you and me forever, but sometimes life has other plans. Take care."

"You take care too, and I hope that this marriage works out for you, Cate. You deserve a good man."

One call down — the next would have to be with her parents.

I think I'll do that one face-to-face. I believe I owe them that.

***

Cate handed over her resignation letter directly to Linda, who was surprised when Cate filled her in with all the news. She wished her all the best, and agreed that as it was a quiet time of the year, Cate could pack up her belongings and leave by the end of the day, if she so wished.

"We'll miss you, Cate. You have been a valued member of the team, and well respected by everyone in the company. Even Irina was impressed with you and was angling to get you on her team. It has been an interesting year for you, and you deserve some happiness. It sounds inspiring, starting a new adventure. They often say, as one door closes, another opens. Keep in touch. I would love to know how you are getting on, and if your new husband ever needs a good law firm in London, perhaps you will put in a good word for us."

"Thank you, Linda. I will."

As the news spread throughout the office, there was a steady stream of colleagues popping their heads in to wish her all the best, and many saying how much they would miss her.

"Hi, Cate, I believe you're leaving us. Was it something I said?" laughed Chris, thinking he was funny. "I heard you've gone and snagged an American billionaire. Now how did you manage to do that? Married to poor Mike, divorced him, and then married this Warren guy? I didn't peg you for a gold-digger, but guess I was wrong. Well, good luck — I think you'll need it, and by the way, I'm taking over your office when you're gone."

Chris was one person she would be happy to see the last of, and he was welcome to her office.

Kourtney stopped her in the reception on her way out. "Hey, Cate, sorry to hear that you're leaving us, but I'm glad for you. Well done, you give me hope. Congratulations, I will miss you."

To Cate's surprise, Kourtney ran over and gave her a big hug, and as Cate left, she was sure that Kourtney was dabbing her eyes.

***

There wasn't much to sort out at the flat, as Warren's London office had taken charge of the sale, and would arrange for all her belongings to be put temporarily into storage until they received further instruction. They had also delivered a packaging crate for Cate to pack the items she wanted to have immediately upon her arrival in the US, including clothes. Additionally, they were organising all her documentation, leaving Cate little to worry about. Once her updated passport — complete with visa — was returned to her, she booked a flight back to Belfast.

She had opted not to tell her parents of her impending arrival, choosing instead to stay at a hotel in the city centre, which seemed a little odd. She had decided it was the safer option, just in case they didn't handle the news too well.

Cate paid the taxi driver and walked up the driveway to the front door. It wasn't the house she had grown up in. Her parents had moved the year she spent in France, so it never felt like her home. She rang the doorbell and waited.

"Oh, heavens above, Bronagh, come quick! You'll never believe who it is."

Cate hugged her father as she stepped into the hallway, just as her mother appeared out of the kitchen.

"Blessed Mary and Joseph! Cate, is that you?" Wiping her hands on her apron, she then hugged her daughter.

"Come on in and let's get the kettle on. Michael, bring in her suitcase and put it in the guest room." Then to Cate, "If I'd known you were coming, I'd have made it up for you. Oh, this is a surprise."

"Mum, I'm not staying. Well, I'm only here for a few days, and I've a room in town."

"Oh," said Bronagh, looking a little dispirited. "We see so little of our children and miss you all. Take a seat in the living room, and I'll make a wee cuppa. Then we can catch up... I have a feeling you have something to tell us. You're doing that thing you used to do as a wee girl; you chew the side of your lip. Go on through, and I'll be there in a moment."

Even after all this time, Cate's mother could still read her like a book.

Michael was sitting in his lazy-boy chair, and the TV was on with a re-run of a show they had watched years ago.

"Well my girl, you're looking well. How's life treating you in the big bad city?"

Father and daughter chatted about the weather and then about the football, until Bronagh appeared with a tray.

Once they had tea in hand, Cate recounted her exploits of the past year. She felt it was best to be open and honest with them.

They sat and listened in silence, with her mother shaking her head on hearing about Mike's affair. By the end of the account, they both sat in silence — their brains desperately trying to make sense of the affair, the divorce, and the news that Cate was now married to someone else. To crown it all, he was an American billionaire whom they had never met, and he was stealing Cate away to live in the States.

Bronagh cried; it was all too much.

"Don't worry pet, I'm sure she'll come round. You certainly don't do things by half, do you? Just as long as you are happy, then we will be happy for you. Things have moved on, and divorce happens a lot now. Perhaps it's best you call us tomorrow. Give us a night to sleep on it and let's talk in the morning."

Cate let herself out, annoyed that she had caused her mother and her father so much distress.

***

The following morning, the telephone rang in Cate's hotel room. It was the receptionist calling to let her know she had two guests in the lobby — a Mr and Mrs Rafferty.

Cate stepped out of the lift, and saw her parents standing waiting for her. It almost broke her heart; they looked so small and out of place in the fancy hotel lobby.

"There she is," smiled her father.

"Let's sit here and I'll order some coffee. Have you had breakfast?" asked Cate, ushering her parents over to a quiet corner.

"Of course, we have. I'll have a cup of tea," snapped Bronagh, still rattled from the previous day's bombshell.

"Now, Bronagh, we haven't come here to get all snippy." Michael held Bronagh's hand. "We're here to say that we understand it has been a hard year for you. We wish you would have spoken to us sooner, as it must have been hard for you, with one thing and then another. We are happy for you about your marriage, as long as you are happy. It all seems just a little too rushed. That's all. Hearing it all in one go yesterday was a little overwhelming. Isn't that right, Bronagh?"

"Yes, indeed it was a shock. Cate, you have always been a sensitive one, and as long as you are sure that this man will make you happy, then we are happy for you both. Perhaps you can tell us a bit more about him. Do you have a photo?"

Cate ordered teas and scones with strawberry jam, knowing that they were a favourite of her mother's.

"Here, this is a photo of us getting married."

"Oh, heavens above. He is a handsome man; like one of those American film stars… and Cate, you look beautiful too. What a stunning couple, don't you think, Michael?"

Cate told her parents what she knew about Warren, about the death of his first wife and that he had a daughter.

"Cate, you'll make a great mother. I always knew you would," said her father.

By the time her parents left, they were appeased and looked forward to visiting their daughter once she was ensconced in her new home. After all, it wasn't every day your daughter married a billionaire — a relation of JFK, no less.

***

A few days before Christmas, Cate was back at Luna's to say her fond farewells to the ladies at the naked knitting club.

Luna had gone to town for the festive season, decorating the room with swags of spruce tied up with white ribbon and embellished with pine cones, all to tie in with the Wiccan Yuletide festival. She was in good spirits handing out mugs of a special spiced mulled wine, and vegan biscuits in the shape of stars; or 'pentagrams', as Cate thought.

It had been fun sitting and enjoying the company each of the ladies knitting a snowman decoration, complete with an orange carrot-shaped nose, scarf and hat. Alice was, as usual, on hand to help Cate with any difficult bits. She wasn't doing much knitting herself as she had baby Carlos with her.

At one point, while Alice was sorting out a part that Cate had messed up, she handed the baby over to her. For the first time in a very long time, Cate was happy to cradle the cooing baby in her arms. He was a sweet baby, gurgling and laughing as he played with her finger and her ring.

Hey, little Carlos, you are one amazing wee man. If you are half the man of your namesake, you will be incredible, and the world had better watch out.

Just as the evening drew to a close, Luna stood up and retrieved a large gift bag from behind the sofa.

"Cate, we wanted to get you a little something to remember us by. We know that you're moving on and heading off to your new life, but we wanted you to know that we are your family now and we care about you. You have brought so much love into our little group, and we have watched you face some huge challenges and come through to change into the beautiful butterfly you are today. We will miss you. Here, this is a little something from us all." Luna handed over the bag, and surreptitiously wiped away a few tears.

Cate handed baby Carlos back to Alice, and took the bag.

She looked around at the faces willing her to open it. Inside, she found a few individually wrapped gifts. The first one she pulled out and opened was a pair of rainbow-coloured knitting needles with unicorn heads on top.

"I chose those," said Alice. "Every time you use them, they will make you smile and think of us."

Next was a knitting book crammed with patterns for easy projects, along with simple-to-follow instructions and lots of coloured images from Luna.

"I thought you would like to keep making things," said Luna, sniffling into a hankie.

Next was a squidgy parcel, which contained soft fluffy rainbow-coloured wool.

"Oh, that's from Jo and me," piped up Xena. "We thought it would be great to knit a cosy scarf, as Jo said it can get quite cold and snowy in that part of the States."

Finally, there was a smaller package, and as Cate pulled it out, it again felt like a book. When she opened it and realised what it was, she started to cry. It was a photo book of them all together having fun at Carlos' hen weekend.

"I had one made up for Carlos, and thought you might like to have one too — a little keepsake, so you don't forget us," said Lady.

"Oh, they're all wonderful. How could I ever forget you lot? You have been there for me when I needed you most; you picked me up and kept me going. What would I have done without you? You are my dearest friends and always will be. Thank you. I love you all!"

The tears flowed — partly for Cate leaving; for Carlos already gone; for friendship; and for the future.

As Cate left, she promised to join them via Skype when she moved. It felt like the end of an era; one that had introduced her to some wonderful new friends for life.

***

The morning of her departure, Cate received an influx of texts wishing her well and telling her to stay in touch. Carlos called her too, giving her a quick update on married life in Malibu, and reminding her that there was always room for her to visit. He also said he couldn't wait to visit her and hit the Big Apple.

Cate made one last trip down to the mailbox and was surprised to see two envelopes with her new married name. As she made her way back up to the apartment, she opened the first one. It was an ostentatious Christmas card with a scene of a partridge in a pear tree, embellished with golden pears and crystals. Without having to look inside, Cate knew who had sent it. She opened it and printed inside was the text, 'Wishing you a Fabulous Season — Pete & Gill Hamilton'. At the bottom, there was a short note from Gill, "Darling Cate, I hope that we can put the past behind us. Congratulations on your recent nuptials. I do hope that we will have the opportunity to make it up to you, and to meet your new husband. Love, Gill x."

Cate couldn't believe Gill's audacity. She shook her head in utter disbelief, as she ripped up the card and envelope, and threw it into the nearby bin.

In the next envelope was a large embossed invitation, inviting her to the opening of 'Les Femmes' exhibition by Sir Percival Davenport at the Tate Modern, the following March. She smiled to herself as her mind filled with the wonderful memories of her day as a muse. On the back of the invitation, Sir Percy had handwritten a short note that read "I need my Circe at my side to make this my most spectacular exhibition ever. Please say you will be there. Love always, Percy x."

Absolutely, I'll be there. I can't wait to see the painting and find out what the world thinks of it.

She tucked the invitation into her travel bag, where she had packed away the kind gifts from the ladies.

Cate walked out of the apartment for last time, knowing deep in her heart it was time to move on. A new life awaited her on the other side of the Atlantic; one that she was sure was going to be a tremendous learning experience — as Warren's wife and Loren's stepmother.

Watch out America! Cate Kennedy is on her way, and she means business.

I can and I will.

ACKNOWLEDGEMENTS

This book idea has been a dream of mine for well over a decade, and for the story of Cate and her Naked Knitting friends to finally come to life, it took more than just my desire to write it — it needed the support and encouragement of a team of wonderful individuals to assistant in its 'birth'. Therefore, I would like to take this opportunity to thank everyone involved, in particular, the following people:

Mark, my dear husband — who helped me to believe that it was possible to reach for my dream, and who incessantly kept telling me to 'write the damn book' for the past fifteen years!

Sean Patrick, my Publisher at *That Guy's House* — if we had not been introduced, this book would still be just an idea in my head.

Susan Ellis-Saller, my Editor — who worked diligently to polish the rough diamond of a story, shaping it to become a more fluid and all-around more enjoyable reading experience.

Ellen Mullen, my Editing Assistant — who worked with me to finalise the manuscript by reading it aloud for me, and patiently helping me to try to eliminate rogue typos and errors.

To my wonderful Proofreaders – Felicity Griffin Clark, Kathryn Haratine, and Judith Quin; thank you for your dedication to read and re-read the book.

To my team of Beta Readers — who were the first to read the draft book and provided much valuable feedback, so the storyline and characters could be refined and enhanced.

Anastasia, Graphic Designer/Illustrator — who created the caricature image, which is seen on the front cover, to loosely portray 'Cate'.

Peter Watkins, Digital Content Consultant at *Naked Broccoli* — for the cover design and interior layout.

***

Additionally, I would like to say a huge thank to my family and friends who believe in me and have supported me wholeheartedly on this journey.

Last, but by no means least, to you, my precious reader — a massive thank you, from the bottom of my heart for choosing to read this book. Enjoy!

The Naked Knitting Club

Find out more about the author,
get to know the characters and download
some FREE knitting patterns
at

www.thenakedknittingclub.com

Also, sign up to receive updates
regarding the release of
upcoming books in the series, events,
book readings/signings, and more.

Join the Facebook Group
TNKC_Readers

Where you can join in the fun and share photos
of you reading your copy of the book.

Lightning Source UK Ltd.
Milton Keynes UK
UKHW011818301118
333254UK00011B/871/P

9 781912 779376